D0325236

BAD BOYS DO IT *Better* 2

In Love With an Outlaw

A NOVEL BY

PORSCHA STERLING

© 2017 Porscha Sterling
Published by Leo Sullivan Presents
www.leolsullivan.com

ALL RIGHTS RESERVED

Any unauthorized reprint or use of the material is prohibited. No part of this book may be reproduced or transmitted in any form or by any means, electronic, or mechanical, including photocopying, recording, or by any information storage without express permission by the publisher.

This is an original work of fiction. Names, characters, places and incidents are either products of the author's imagination or are used fictitiously and any resemblance to actual persons, living or dead is entirely coincidental.

Contains explicit language & adult themes suitable for ages 16+

The Hit.

Outlaw

"Aye, bruh. You gon' be ready for tomorrow?"

"Hell yeah, nigga. I stay ready so ain't nuthin' to prep for. You just make sure you got my ride straight," I told Yolo as I walked into the basement of Kane's spot, ready for our regular poker game.

As tradition right before a big job, we hung out and played cards and just chilled. No business was discussed, no alcohol was drunk, and no weed was smoked. We simply talked shit and had fun. We needed to keep our mind clear for the next day but also, we didn't know how things would turn out and we wanted to make sure our last memories together were good. We planned everything we did to a T and we were good as hell with it too. That said, there was always a chance that something could go wrong.

"Yeah, I got the rides. They came in today. Custom made and fly as hell, just like you asked for," Yolo said, nodding his head as Cree began to shuffle and deal the cards.

"Only Luke would ask for that flashy shit," Tank said, laughing as he grabbed up his cards. "You couldn't just go for a regular ole getaway truck, huh? You better be glad we good with this shit. Cocky ass nigga."

Sitting down, I grabbed my cards up and took a deep breath, thinking a lot but not saying a word. The last couple weeks I'd been at Janelle's so much it was like I'd practically moved into her shit. Her sister was gone and she was alone after kicking her roommate out. She told me she didn't like to sleep in the apartment alone and that was all she had to say. I made it my business to be with her every night.

That was some new shit to me. I'd never been the type of nigga to come home to a woman every night. Definitely not the *same* woman. Shit… I just didn't come home to women period. And no woman had ever been at the spot where I laid my head. That wasn't my rule though, it was Kane's. Kane made us all promise not to bring a woman to our cribs unless she was wifey. Main reason for that was, if a bitch got mad about some shit, the first thing she'd do was set a nigga up on some bullshit. I fought Kane about a lot of the stuff he made us do but that was not one of them.

"Tank, when that baby due, nigga?" Kane asked, smirking as he looked at Tank.

"Hell, I'on know. Bitch might not even be pregnant. I ain't gon' to the doctor with her ass and her stomach still flat as hell," he replied with a sigh, dropping his head as he rubbed on the back of his head.

"Well, if her ass wasn't pregnant she is now," I piped in, cheesing because I knew I was about to piss him off. "I been seein' you swervin' by her spot, nigga. Don't act like you ain't still climbin' up in that."

Cree and Yolo laughed as Tank raised his hand and shot me a bird, frowning hard when he did it. He was trying to play it off like Faviola had trapped his ass up but I knew better.

"How the hell you been seein' me, anyways? What, you spyin' on a nigga?" he asked, I shook my head.

"Naw, never that, bruh. Chick I been dealin' with lives next door."

"That lawyer chick?" Yolo asked as he played the first card and I nodded my head.

"Yeah, she's sisters with Cree's girl."

Cree's head shot up and he frowned at me, shaking his head. "That ain't my bitch, bruh. She bogus, yo. Her mouth reckless as fuck… I can't deal with that shit. Shit bad for a nigga's nerves."

"Oh, that's why I saw you lookin' at her Instagram page when I walked in, huh nigga?" I teased him, playfully reaching out to grab his phone but he batted my hand away.

"Man, fuck you, Luke. How you know I was on her page anyways?" he asked. Smirking, I slapped my cards down on the table and reached in my pocket to grab my phone.

"Because I follow her ass, too! She got a fat ass, shawty fine as fuck!" I said, laughing, trying to get a rise out of Cree. Going through my phone, I went to Instagram and pulled up the page, showing the screen to Kane, Yolo and Tank as Cree pouted to himself like a lil' bitch. I knew he was feeling her or else he wouldn't be all in his feelings.

"Damn, she is sexy as hell. Got dat donkey booty," Kane said, laughing. "Why you ain't messin' with her no more, Cree?"

Head bent down as he played with his cards and his face balled up in a tight frown, Cree shrugged his shoulders and played his hand.

"I told you already. Her mouth reckless as hell. I can't deal with that shit."

"Shit, her body reckless, too!" Yolo said, grabbing my phone so he could scroll through the pictures.

"Man, put that shit up, Yolo! Ain't you got a woman? You been hangin' round with Sid every damn night at the club. Her ass put a little ass dress on and got you seeing stars and shit," Kane laughed and I joined in.

When Kane wasn't all on my ass about something, he was the jokester of the group. I feel like he did it purposely so that we all stayed close. Kane was tough to deal with but, more than anything else, he loved all of us. He fought hard to keep the bond between us tight. To him, nothing came before family. The poker games, meeting up at my granny's house on the weekend… all that was his idea. Whenever any of us fought, we could bet on getting a call from Kane before we went to bed that night telling us to gon' head and fight that shit out so someone could get their ass beat and we could squash whatever it was we were mad about. He was hard on us but always the peacemaker at the same time.

"She lookin' good and shit. But y'all know I always been feelin' Sid. She just…" Yolo paused and shrugged like he didn't know how to finish his sentence.

"She just wasn't pretty enough for you, nigga," I finished for him, laughing my ass off as I played my card. "Yo' pretty ass always on top of yo' shit so you be damned if you with a chick who ain't in heels and shit. Hell, you ain't wrong. I like my bitches bad, too."

"Oh, this lawyer chick look like that?" Yolo asked with his brows raised, and I stopped to think about my response.

"Hell no, she ain't like that! But my baby got exactly what a nigga need so I ain't trippin'," I said, finally. Then I saw the way that every one of my brothers were gawking at me like they had never seen me before.

"You know… she cool."

"She cool now?" Cree asked with a smirk, and I knew he was about to say some bullshit. "Before you said she was basic."

"Still is."

"What? Don't tell me Luke's flashy ass done fell in love with a regular ole chick," Kane said, grinning hard as hell right into my face. "You with the basic sister and Cree with the model? Fuck goin' on with y'all niggas?"

"I ain't with nobody, bruh!" Cree shot out. "I done told y'all that shit already!"

"And I ain't in love with nobody," I replied, coolly. "We just chillin' and havin' fun. That's it."

"She a D.A., right? Didn't you say she worked with Pelmington?" Tank asked, giving me a pointed look, and I nodded my head, careful to avoid Kane's eyes because I already knew he was looking straight at a nigga.

"Well, just be careful," Tank said. One of the rare moments that he decided to act like my older brother. "If it's fun, let it be that and watch your back. But if you gon' make it serious, make sure she ready to watch your back for you."

Nodding my head, I didn't say anything and we all sat in silence as the card game continued going. My thoughts were now on Tank's warning, which I know was exactly what Kane wanted to say, based on the way that I caught him staring at me throughout the night. Could I trust Janelle enough to make shit with her official? Better question, did I want to make it official?

I couldn't lie and say that every day I spent with her I wasn't starting to feel her more and more because I was. Sure, I still swung by to see other chicks when I wasn't with her but it wasn't the same with them as it was with her. They were just for sex and that's it. I wasn't trying to hear them talk and I didn't want to sit around and chill once we were done. But Janelle had me on some married couple shit. On some 'you wash the dishes and I rinse and dry 'em when you finished' kinda shit. I was walking around her house in loafers, white tees and boxers, comfy as hell with her cooking, cleaning and taking care of a nigga like I was hers. Was that what I really wanted? Hell, it seemed like it.

"Your turn, Luke," Cree said and I focused back on the game, clearing my throat.

All that shit about Janelle had to wait. I had a job to do the next day and I needed to get my head in the game.

***

After the game of poker, my brothers and I hugged, dapped each other and parted ways so that we could each go to our cribs and get a good night's sleep to prep for the next day. I was always chill as hell the day before a hit but then the day of, I got too hype. It was something about the dangerousness of it that got to me. Like, I knew I could be killed or end up in jail but my mind stayed on that end goal. I was driven when I had a goal in mind and nothing could stop me. I guess that's why I pursued Janelle the way I did. But she was a goal I didn't even know I had in mind.

Standing in front of her spot, I took a deep breath as I walked up the stairs, feeling crazy as hell that I was about to do some soft shit. She was used to me coming over every night and staying with her but I wouldn't be able to do that tonight. Still, I didn't want to tell her that through text, knowing that she had cooked and everything thinking I was coming over. So I decided to stop by, spend a few minutes with her and leave. Which was going to be hard as hell.

Kane had another rule the night before each job. No sex. We had to be on point mentally, physically and emotionally. Every part of us had to be invested in the job so that meant that we couldn't do anything that would sway our focus. If you ask me, didn't nothing get me focused more than sliding up in something wet but those were big bruh's rules and I went with them.

"Hey… you know the key is still under the mat, right?" Janelle asked as soon as she opened the door and saw me standing there.

It took me a minute to answer because I was caught off guard by what she had on. Her hair was wet, like she was fresh out the shower and she was standing in front of me with some skintight yoga pants on and a half shirt that stopped right under her breasts. Her flat stomach was on display, showing off her thin waist.

But that ass…

When I first started messing with her, she didn't have much to work with but it was plumping up nicely. I had to give myself credit for a job well done. Crazy thing was, Janelle didn't even seem to understand the effect this shit she had on had on me. She was just wearing it because it was her. She was effortlessly sexy. Other chicks had all kinds of tricks in store to make my ass feel this way but she had none. She was herself. Basic and beautiful as hell.

"Yeah, but I ain't wanna just walk up in yo' shit," I told her as I stepped in, nose in the air taking a deep sniff of whatever it was she had cooking. I caught a whiff of something and it had me feeling all good inside, like when you know someone was expecting you and had made something special just for you.

"Since when?" she asked giggling. "You never have no issues walking up in here any other day."

By the time she closed the door, I was already in the kitchen searching for food. Didn't even know I was hungry until I walked in but now I was ready to eat. Except… there wasn't anything there but a small microwaveable meal.

"Damn, you don't cook for a nigga no more? What's this shit 'bout?" I asked, pointing at the small package of food on the counter.

Janelle placed her hand on her hip and gave me a look, twisting up the corner of her lips like she smelled something that stunk. Attitude on fleek. I guess that extra attitude was what came with all the extra ass.

"I wasn't expecting you to come over here. You told me that you was hanging out with your brothers tonight," she said, waving me off as she walked in the kitchen. Stepping around me, she grabbed the small dinner on the counter, pulled a spoon out of one of the drawers and started eating while I just looked at her, feeling all kinds of disrespect coming from her way.

"So what that mean that I can't come over? You can't leave some food in the fridge for a nigga? Shit, I'm hungry as fuck!" I fumed, peeking at the food as she took large bites while rolling her eyes to the back of her head like it was so good. Doing the most.

I grabbed the plate right from out of her fingers and snatched the spoon, walking into the living room as I started to eat, shoveling it all into my mouth. She had me fucked up if she thought I was about to just sit around and watch her eat.

"LUKE! You not even supposed to be here," she said, walking behind me. "You told me you had plans so how the hell am I supposed to know that you were coming back?"

Not paying her any real attention, I sat down and continued to eat, grabbing the remote as I propped my feet up on the ottoman in front of the couch.

"It's cool. I'mma leave you in a minute, ma. I'm stayin' at my place tonight. I just came over to let you know."

"Good because I have plans. Chris asked me to go see a movie with him and I said I would."

She said the words with ease, like it was nothing, as she walked back into the kitchen, pulling the refrigerator door open like she was looking for something to eat. No need. She could have her shit back because she'd officially ruined my appetite by bringing up that light-skinned, thick-necked nigga at her job. What the fuck was he taking her to the movies for? Wasn't shit out worth seeing. And at this time of night… naw, that nigga wanted to fuck. Not on my watch.

When I looked up at Janelle, she was standing in the kitchen with an apple in her hand and her eyes on me. Waiting to see how I would react. I saw a twinkle in her eyes at the same moment that the edge of her lips began to twitch… like she wanted to laugh or something. I could tell she was trying to get a reaction out of me but I didn't play those types of games so it wasn't happening. Janelle must have forgotten that I could read her like a book. I wasn't the average street nigga. I was on an I.Q. level that backed up my cockiness. When I said that I knew it all, it was because *I really knew it all*. And that applied to her and her bullshit games too.

"A'ight, let me know when I need to be out to make room for that nigga to come on in," I told her, shrugging a little as I turned back to the TV If she wanted to play games, I had one for her ass.

"Oh," was all she said but I ignored her, keeping my eyes on the TV.

Checking my watch, I knew it was about time for me to get out of there and go home to prep for the next day. I needed to go over the plans and run them over and over through my mind to make sure I had everything together. This job was a little different from the others because this time we were letting my lil cousin in on it. His ass had been trying to hang with my brothers and I for a minute but we always told him no. However, this time Kane said that he was ready so, even though his role was small, we let him in on the job.

It was almost midnight when I saw Janelle go into the room, saying something about taking a shower to prepare for her date. That raised both of my eyebrows. Grabbing my phone, I checked to see what theaters had movies running that late and where they were. Of course, being that we lived in the city that never sleeps, there were some running that late. I didn't give a fuck though. Her ass wasn't going.

"Aye, cancel that date wit' pretty boy," I told Janelle as soon as she walked out of the bathroom, wrapped up in a towel with her hair pulled up on the top of her head. Snatching her neck in my direction, she looked at me with confusion before her eyes dimmed and she caught the meaning of my words.

"What? Why? And shouldn't you be gone by now if you're not staying the night?" she asked me, pressing her perfect lips together in a way that had me thinking about all the things I wanted to do with them. Tonight and every other night after that. Shit… I couldn't have sex though.

"Naw, I'm not going nowhere and neither are you," I told her, looking at the TV so I didn't have to meet her eyes.

I didn't want her to see how much the thought of her going out with someone else really was bothering me. Mainly because it was bullshit. She wasn't my chick and I wasn't her man… I still fucked other women. I hadn't gotten rid of any of my hoes for her so why did I care if she was seeing other niggas? Especially niggas I knew were only temporary anyways. Janelle wasn't ever going to be with that pretty boy nigga in no serious way. Not ever. Period. And it wasn't because I wanted it that way either, even though I did. It was because he wasn't her type. She thought he was but she had no idea what was good for her.

"Luke, you can't tell me what to—"

"I said what I said and I ain't sayin' nothin' else."

There was nothing else I needed to say. She understood. Had an attitude about it but she got it anyways and dropped the topic. That's why I loved her ass. Shit, I mean that's why I liked her. I *liked* her.

"I got an early morning so let's go to bed. No sex though," I told her as I cut off the TV and tossed the remote on the table in front of the sofa. Grabbing her hand, I didn't wait for her to object but simply pulled her to the room.

Being with her was against the rules but I wasn't leaving so that was the end of it. But I wasn't going to have sex with her. That was one rule I wasn't willing to break. Unfortunately, me telling Janelle that we wouldn't have sex made that the only thing on her mind.

Laying in the bed, I took my shirt off but kept on my sweats. I was trying hard as hell to fight the urge to be inside of her so I wasn't taking no chances. I didn't watch her while she put on her night clothes and I laid down all the way at the edge of the damn bed so that I wouldn't brush up against her skin. But as soon as Janelle got under the covers, she came right over on my side, wrapping her arms around me from the back before pushing her fingers down towards the one place I didn't need her to be.

"Stop," I mumbled, swatting her hand away but she persisted on. I swatted her again but it did not a damn thing because she responded by grinding against me, tossing her hot pussy at me, teasing me by practically daring me to dick her down.

"Stop fuckin' playin', Nell. You gon' get some shit started that you won't be able to handle," I warned her, feeling the blood in my body run directly to the one muscle I wanted to push up into Janelle the most. She giggled and my dick twitched. I swear it curved like it was about to find its way to her it's damn self if I didn't do something quick. Sighing, I pushed my erection down between my thighs and squeezed my eyes shut, trying my hardest to ignore the heat coming from off of Janelle's body.

"But how you know I can't handle it? I'm an animal in the bed, you ain't know?" Only Janelle would say some lame shit like that.

Chuckling in spite of her dorky statement, I replied back, "Oh? What kind of animal?"

She had no response and for some reason I found that funny too. "See, you sayin' shit you can't even back up. Now go to sleep."

"If I were an animal, what kind do you think I'd be?" she asked, laying her chin on my arm as she looked down into my face. Frowning, I nudged her off and groaned loudly.

"Nell, what kinda stupid shit is that to say? Turn around and count sheep or some shit. You obviously bored as hell."

Huffing, she lay back on the bed and didn't say another word. But the silly shit she'd said kept running through my mind. I couldn't let it go and then eventually I found myself actually thinking about it.

"I think you'd be an owl."

"WHAT?!" she barked and I laughed a little before deciding to explain myself.

"You're mysterious, elegant… wise. You sleep during the day, not literally but figuratively. You do everything that is expected of you, goin' through the motions of your regular ass life." She jabbed me with her elbow and I chuckled before continuing. "But when I'm here at night, you wake up and become a different person… And when I stick my dick up in you, you hoot and moan just as loud as a damn owl, too."

"LUKE!" she yelled and nudged me against the arm. Then she pushed her body close to mine and leaned over into my ear. "I'm not that loud… am I?"

I didn't even dignify that with a response because if she kept up that grinding shit she'd been doing, she was about to find out exactly how loud she could get. Exhaling heavily, I pushed her away from me one final time. But it was the last time. If she tried something again, I was just going to take it as a sign from God that it was what He wanted because I wasn't going to turn her down.

There was nothing for a few seconds and then, all of a sudden, I felt Janelle's bare breasts on my back. She'd removed her shirt and was pushing them up against me, rubbing her skin on mine, awakening all kinds of emotions within me. That was it. I was done saying no.

I turned around so fast that Janelle barely had time to react. A small squeak of surprise rushed past her lips but I didn't give a shit, it was much too late to be having second thoughts now. I tried to warn her.

Grabbing her by the arm, I pulled her so that she was under me and dove headfirst right in between her legs, sucking hard while holding her clit between my lips, spitting and slurping, keeping it nasty, just like I knew she liked it. I wasn't holding back and I wasn't worried about anything Kane had to say about what I was about to do either. Janelle had awakened the beast in me and I was about to get what I wanted by any means necessary, fuck what anybody else thought.

She gasped when I finished getting my fill of her. She hadn't cooked shit but a nigga still ate. And I was greedy with it. She tasted so good to me that it was to the point that I didn't want to give her the dick unless I could suck on her first. Imagine that shit! Outlaw actually eating pussy for the pleasure of it… damn, she had my mind all kinds of fucked up but I really didn't give a shit.

"Damn…" she panted, arching her back when I stuck my fingers inside of her.

Bending my finger, I made the 'come here' motion and she went crazy when I pressed right into her g-spot. She was about to cum but I stopped, quickly replacing my finger with my dick and not missing a single beat. She came in seconds and, seeing that she was satisfied, it was time for me to get mine.

Grabbing her wet hair, I held it tight and fucked her hard, thumping the headboard against the wall. Pictures and shit began to fall off the wall but I didn't give a shit and neither did she. The only thing we saw was each other. The only thing we cared about was each other.

I was about to cum when I realized that I wasn't wearing a rubber. Now the ordinary nigga would've said 'fuck that' and gon' head and bust right up inside of her but I wasn't the ordinary nigga and I wasn't trying to be caught up with no kids. Clenching my jaw, I pulled out quick and started jacking my dick. But then Janelle did some shit that had me about to drop some bands on an engagement ring. Without missing a second, she flipped over on her stomach and arched her back, pushing her fat ass high up in the air.

"Cum for me, daddy," she whispered and I lost my whole damn mind.

With a heavy exhale, I let go, busting all over her ass as she winded it round and round for me. I've never seen something sexier in my entire fuckin' life. Once I was done, I just looked at her, totally caught up in everything that she was. She was amazing and everything about her blew my mind. She was a lady and a freak. Like me, she was nothing like the person she appeared to be. There was a whole 'nother person lying beneath the surface and I knew that whatever game I *thought* I was playing by just fuckin' around with her was starting to get more serious than I'd ever expected.

"Nasty ass freak," I mumbled as she got up to clean herself. I watched her closely, still stroking my meat because I was hungry for more. But I needed to let her be. I'd already broken the rules and I had a huge job tomorrow. Instead of my mind being on it, I was totally consumed by Janelle. I was fuckin' up big time.

When Shit Got Real.

Janelle

I felt the shift of energy as soon as I walked into work this morning. It wasn't like I hadn't been chilling with Luke for some time now, but it wasn't until *this* morning that I actually started to feel the shift even though I hadn't seen him at all over the weekend. Things didn't feel the same for me. The porcelain statutes of Lady Justice, standing in the foyer of my workplace while holding the scales of justice, didn't seem like an inspiration as she had so many mornings before. Today, she felt like a mirror to my shame. Like she was judging me for falling for the bad boy. I was sleeping with the enemy.

Every day I walked in here pretending to be one of the ones fighting for a cause that was somehow lost between here and my trek back home into Luke's arms. In the moments with him, I didn't care that he was the opposite of everything I stood for and everything I'd spent my life wanting. I only cared about him and I only cared about us. There was nothing else.

Until I came *here*.

"You're finally here!" Chris interrupted my thoughts, startling me. "Pelmington's going to make an announcement about that huge armored truck robbery that happened over the weekend!"

The blank stare that I gave him must have triggered something in his mind to inform him that I had no idea what he was talking about so he continued.

"The robbery..." he repeated again before squinting deep into my eyes. "Have you been watching the news?"

Without waiting for an answer, he grabbed me by my forearm and pulled me into the main room of the law office, pointing at the television screens that hung from the ceiling. There was a small crowd already gathered around watching so I joined in, wondering what it was that I'd missed.

"*...the trucks were said to have over a million dollars in cash and an unknown amount of gold bricks which were being transported to J.P. Morgan Chase. The shipment followed all security procedures set so police are looking at any evidence to suggest this was an inside job.*

According to witnesses, the armored truck was stopped after crossing under a bridge in East Manhattan, when five men jumped out of the back of another truck and apprehended the vehicle by use of military militia style firearms and weapons. Miraculously, only two of the security personnel were injured but are currently in critical condition. The five men made off with the money and the gold in unmarked vehicles but were able to elude police after a thirty minute high speed chase..."

The screen began to show video of the chase and my heart began to beat hard in my chest as I watched. There were two Mustangs, tearing through the city at high speed with a slew of police fast on their heels. But what made my mouth go dry was the fact that there was a method to the madness. The assailants knew exactly what they were doing as if they had mapped out the city, expertly taking turns down small alleys that provided little to no visual access to the helicopter flying above, creating a delay before we were able to locate them again. And then eventually, there was a final delay… just enough because by the time the helicopter was able to place the camera on them again, the cars had stopped and there was no one in them. I knew it even before I saw the police jump out of their vehicles and race over with their weapons out to check the cars. They were gone.

My eyes went to the body of water behind where the cars were parked and I knew right then what had happened. They'd dived into the water and somehow made an escape. But how do you swim with over a million dollars in cash and a load of gold bricks? I wasn't sure but I had a feeling I knew who would.

"You know this is the Murray brothers, right?" Chris asked, shaking his head in disgust as he stood next to me watching the screen. "It has their name written all over it. Flashy sons of bitches."

My mouth went dry and I felt dizzy, like I was going to faint. Pressing my hand to my forehead, I closed my eyes and took a deep breath.

"You okay?" Chris asked and I nodded my head.

"Yes… I—I just need to go to the restroom for a second," I mumbled as I took off, without waiting for him to say a word.

He was right. This *did* have the Murray brothers all over it. The precision of the hit, the way they always seemed to be a few minutes ahead of law enforcement. How they'd chosen loud ass red sports cars as getaways instead of anything else that would blend in. They were taunting the police. They were taunting Pelmington. Which meant, they were taunting me. There would be no way to catch them. They were much too good for that. Too smart. Oh God, I felt sick.

After running water over my face, I got up and walked back outside, stopping only to sip some water from the water fountain so I could try to shake off the crazy feeling in my body and get to work. Pelmington had an announcement to make about the robbery so he was on the case and I knew that meant it was about to be a long day.

"As you all may know, there was a robbery this weekend," he hesitated and a few of the other assistant D.A.s around me snickered.

I twisted in my seat and put the cap of my pen between my teeth, biting down hard on it in order to try to keep a straight face. It was cold inside of the building, which was normal, but I could feel a thin layer of sweat form just above my brow. So much for keeping cool.

"Anyways," Pelmington started again, sitting atop the desk behind him as he took a moment to look each of us in our eyes. "Normally, I wouldn't get involved until there is a suspect and that suspect has been charged because, naturally, that's where our job usually begins. However, this case is near and dear to my heart being that I have a very strong feeling that the Murray brothers are responsible."

Everyone around me murmured in agreement and I almost peed in my pants. Months before, I would have been excited to hear this. I would have jumped at the opportunity to be able to work on a case that, if brought to trial, would become one of Pelmington's biggest so far. But I wasn't. I was devastated, fearful and in a state of absolute panic for so many reasons that I couldn't tell to a single soul.

"Therefore, I'm going to give you all access to every bit of evidence that the police currently have concerning the investigation into this robbery. The four of you will work on this together and find anything that can possibly be used to bring charges against any of the Murray brothers so that we can finally get justice against this notorious crew who think the law is above them. The weakest of them all is…"

Pelmington got up and shut the lights off and then turned on a projector. I gasped quietly when I saw Luke's face illuminate on the screen. My heart twinged in my chest when I saw the man I'd been spending the better half of the last week with staring straight into the camera, his jaw taunt and his eyes raw with anger. It was his mugshot and I'd seen it many times before but this time it was stirring up a feeling in me much different than any other time in the past.

"Luke Murray or Outlaw, as he likes to call himself. The reason Luke is the weakest link is because we've already had him in here before. Of all the Murrays, he's the only one who we have been able to get fingerprints, DNA samples and a slew of other things on."

Oh God.

"Janelle, you should know the most about him," Pelmington said and my mouth dropped open in surprise. Like a deer caught in headlights, I looked at him, my mind running with various thoughts and excuses, none of them seeming adequate for helping me now.

"Um… I do?" I managed to squeak out, my tongue feeling like a steel pad in my mouth. A metallic taste settled on my taste buds and I started to get the feeling that I was about to throw up. My nerves were an absolute mess.

"Yes, you should. You are the one who took home the file on my last case on Luke Murray and came up with a wonderful brief on how I could have possibly fought it, even without my primary witness. I'm not positive but, had I had you around at the beginning of the trial, I think I may have had a good chance of winning." He smiled at me and I forced myself to press my lips together and smile back, bowing my head and giving him a gracious nod.

"Good job," Chris whispered, patting me on my back and I gave him the same pressed smile, hoping that everyone took my lack of enthusiasm for humility and couldn't see that, on the inside, I felt like I was dying a slow death.

"I expect you all to work together. Here is a copy of the files for each one of you." He stood up and handed each one of us a manila folder. I grasped mine in my hand and took a deep breath before opening it.

"Because of how high profile this case is, you cannot take these out of the office. I expect you to study everything in these and then discuss amongst yourselves. I'll follow up with you next week to see what you've come up with."

And with that, Pelmington left out, his steps echoing down the hall as we all sat in the room silently, each of us running through our own thoughts. Then, suddenly, chaos erupted as we all dove on our folders, opening them and pulling all of the contents out so that we could learn everything there was to know about the robbery.

I read through the overview from the police quickly, my heart thumping so loudly I could hear it in my ears like a steel drum. I probably read through it without breathing, eager to know everything about what they had, or didn't have, on Luke and his brothers. Then I stumbled on a single sentence that made my blood go cold. I read on, feeling more and more devastated with each word.

Oh God.

"We were able to uncover a partial fingerprint from one of the assailants and it was submitted for processing. One of the guards was able to fire a shot, injuring one of the assailants; however no blood was recovered at the scene. Police have the getaway cars in custody and are looking for any DNA evidence to link a person of interest to the crimes..."

Sitting back, I began to run through the last few days in my mind. I'd seen Luke each day. He'd spent the night with me and nothing seemed off with him at all. He couldn't have possibly been involved in any of this. Or could he?

Glancing down, I checked the time for when the robbery had occurred. According to the documents, everything began around noon on a Saturday. One of the busiest hours in the city, which was insane. There were so many witnesses... why would they do this? Then again, I have to remember who I'm talking about. The Murray brothers were known to do things that seemed so ridiculous and pull them off flawlessly, leaving everyone investigating them looking stupid for even trying to piece it all together.

"So what we gon' do 'bout this shit we startin', Nell?" Luke had asked me on the morning of the robbery. Sitting up in the bed, I turned to him, frowning as I draped my leg across his stomach, pressing my thigh against his chiseled abs. We'd made love all night and then again that morning. I was so sore but I could go for more. A lot more. He was just

that good.

"What do you mean?" I asked, grabbing a lock of his hair in between my fingers. I twirled it around and waited for him to answer.

"I mean… we just gon' keep hidin' and shit or you gon' be mine? Like, I'm ready to make you my woman for real. Take you places and shit. I can't deal wit' dis duckin' and dodgin' shit you got me on," he said with a frown. His tone was combative and I sensed that he was picking a fight. But why? We'd just had the most beautiful night and here he was trying to ruin it.

"What do you expect me to do, Luke? Introduce you to my daddy or something? Parade you around like this shit won't upset my entire life? I could lose my job—"

"Fuck that job!"

"WHAT?!" I yelled, jumping straight out of the bed. Standing beside the bed, I hovered over him with my arms folded in front of my chest.

"How could you say that? You know how much my job means to me!" I told him, frustrated that I was so close to tears.

"And how much do I mean to you?!" he asked, standing up so that he was right in front of me, looking down on me as his words cut me straight to the core. "I don't mean shit to you now? What da fuck can I mean to you if I can't even take ya ass on a single date? Why da fuck do I have to beg you for simple shit?!"

We fought and he left, after I told him to, stating that I couldn't deal with the fighting anymore. Although I tried to diffuse it, he had continued on, pushing me until I started to cry, unable to come up with words to make everything better. There was no way I could have the best of both worlds and Luke knew that. He knew exactly where the argument was going to lead when he started it. And now I knew the reason why he had even started it in the first place.

Thinking back, I saw just how much an expert Luke was. He needed a reason to leave me that wouldn't make me suspicious once I found out about the robbery. He had purposely picked a fight with me so that I could kick him out, leading me to believe that I was the reason behind him storming out that morning. He couldn't tell me that he had to go handle business or meet up with his brothers because that would have been too obvious for me to later figure out what he had been up to. He was a genius.

"It's crazy, isn't it?" Chris asked, assuming the look on my face had something to do with the case. "I mean… If they weren't the bad guys, I'd probably like them. They are bad ass how they do this shit. Makes our job tough."

"It does," I agreed with a sigh. Closing the folder, I started to nibble on the top of my pen cap, thinking to myself about my options. To be with Luke meant to derail my career. To not be with him meant… I wasn't quite sure what it would mean but I knew I didn't want it. Not now.

"You look so cute when you do that," Chris said, cutting into my thoughts. I glanced at him, wondering what he meant until he pointed his eyes at the pen between my lips.

"It's a bad habit," I told him with a sheepish grin on my face. He smiled at me and I couldn't help but notice his perfect teeth. His perfect everything. Chris was model fine. He was the type of guy that you looked at and immediately began to doubt yourself, telling yourself that there was no way you could get him. The fact that he even paid attention to me still played with my mind sometimes.

"You know, you still owe me that date." He shot me a teasing smile and I blushed, looking away as I tried to ignore the stinging sensation in my cheeks.

"I know," I replied, finally able to look back into his eyes. He paused for a second and we watched each other. I didn't remove my eyes from his as I wondered what it was on his mind.

"Well, I'm not going to bug you about it," he finally said. "You just let me know when you're ready to go and I'm there."

Smiling, I nodded my head, loving the way that he tactfully told me that he was feeling me but also managed to give me some space. It was such a huge difference from Luke. He didn't tactfully do *anything* and he damn sure didn't believe in giving me space.

"It's a deal," I told him and he nodded his head before turning back to the case files in front of him.

Sighing, I did the same, trying to force myself to focus. Here, I was an attorney—a prosecuting attorney. Here, I had a duty and I swore that I would dedicate my life towards it. That should be my only concern at the moment. It had to.

It's Not Unbelievable.

Sidney

My feet hurt. My back hurt. Shit… everything fuckin' hurt. I don't know why chicks did this shit to themselves but I was done. Yeah, looking all done up and stuff was nice but it wasn't me and I was tired of it already. Finished. *Finito*. Stick a fork in it and kill that shit.

"Where you goin'?" Yolo asked as I tugged one of his hoodies down over my head. Grabbing a rubber band, I pulled my semi-straightened hair up into a messy ponytail and tugged at it until it felt as right as it was going to get in the crazy half-curly, half-straight state it was in. I'd flatiron it so much the past few days, it was a miracle my shit wasn't fried.

"I'm goin' home. Damn, you ain't tired of my ass already?" I bit the inside of my bottom lip, trying to hide my smile as I stared at him. He looked at me with them sexy gray lookin' eyes, dimples showing in each of his cheeks and I almost got pregnant. Yep, just like that.

"Naw, nigga. I ain't tired of you yet. Take all that shit off," he told me. Leaning up, he reached out and tugged at the bottom of the hoody but I scooted away. I walked over to the edge of the bed and grabbed a pair of his basketball shorts and pulled it over my hips, wiggling much more than necessary because I knew he was watching.

Since Yolo saw the 'new me' at the club the other night, I'd been hanging with him ever since, keeping my hair straight and trying to keep up with the other chicks he hung with, trading in my Jordans for heels. He loved it and I loved the way that he looked at me when I dressed up but, like I said earlier, I was officially done with that shit. Have you ever had to work a damn bar all night at a club in a pair of stilettos? No? Well, then you probably have no idea how bad that shit hurt. My damn toes were permanently folded up under each other like they were screaming out 'Westside!' Being a girl was overrated.

"I'm serious, Sid. Take that shit off and get back in the bed," Yolo mumbled as he finally sat up and leaned against the headboard.

Unable to stop myself, I turned to look at him as I pushed my feet into a pair of his Nike slides. He was so damn sexy that just looking at him gave me butterflies in my stomach. Sitting on the bed, wearing nothing but boxer briefs, I could see his print straight through them and my baby was still on hard, ready for me to jump in his lap and ride him like I was a jockey and he was my prized stallion. And those abs… damn. Wait… why was I leaving again?

"Naw, I gotta go. I ain't kicked it with Favi in a minute and I need to see what my girl is up to," I forced out, making myself pull my eyes away from his body.

Walking around the room while collecting my things, I was aware of that fact that Yolo was staring at me and it had me doing some crazy shit. He had my nerves bad to the point that I walked by my purse four damn times before I actually saw it. I grabbed it, keeping my head down as I stuffed the dress from the night before into it.

"You workin' at the club tonight, too?" he asked and I nodded my head.

"I might swing through. Check up on you."

A wave of excitement shot through me but it was short-lived. Something inside of me was unsettled about the fact that I felt like I was back in the same routine with Yolo as always. How long it would last this time, I didn't know. The only difference this time was that we weren't hiding and doing our shit in private like before. Or were we? Besides popping up on me at the club, it's not like he took me anywhere.

"Why you got that crazy ass look on your face?" Yolo said and I snapped my head up to look at him, not even realizing that I was looking any kind of way.

"What you mean?"

Standing up, he walked over to me and didn't stop until he was right in front of my face, my eyes level to his chest. His closeness to me sent my body in an uproar and I had to take a deep breath to settle my beating heart. No matter how much I hung with the niggas, dressed like a nigga and talked like a nigga, Yolo was always able to remind me how much of a woman I was. Just him being close to me stirred up the juices between my thighs.

"I mean, how you twisted yo' face up and shit when I mentioned checkin' up on you at the club. What's that about?" he asked and I shrugged, taking a few steps back to distance myself from the effect that he had on me.

"It's just that… how you gon' do all this checkin' up like you my man or some shit?" I asked him, feeling a little surer of myself the

29

more I thought about it. "I mean, what if I want another nigga to swing through tonight?"

The humored glitter in Yolo's eyes told me that he knew my ass was on some bullshit. That was the problem with being with someone who knew you so well… anytime you tried to play some games, they could always call you on it.

"Don't fuck around with me, Sid," Yolo said, dismissing me with a slight nod of the head. Turning around, he started getting dressed like I wasn't still standing in the same spot, staring at him with my hand on my hips. This nigga had me fucked up if he thought that he was the only one wanting to be the only one. I mean… he was, but that was only because I hadn't tried anything with anyone else.

"Oh so it's unbelievable to you that I would have some other nigga checkin' for me at the club?" I countered as I watched him put his clothes on. With every stitch of clothing he pulled on, I thanked God because I knew it would be easier for me to pick an argument if I wasn't looking at his sexy ass body.

"No, it's not *unbelievable*," was all he said.

Rolling my eyes, I decided to drop the argument altogether because it was pointless. I didn't have anyone else looking for me at the club except for Yolo so he had a point and I didn't. Shit!

"Let me get my keys and I'mma drive you home," he told me and I simply nodded my head, sitting down as he walked to the bathroom to do his morning hygiene, which I knew would take a minute. He was a pretty boy through and through and he wasn't going any damn where unless he looked perfectly put together.

I started twirling around in the desk chair he had in his room as I waited, enjoying the smell of his cologne from his hoody. It was the same one he'd worn the night before and it still smelled just like he did, bringing back memories of the night before. Pushing my hands in the pockets, I leaned back, my mind thinking on how he'd grabbed me into his arms, stealing me away from the bar and a gang of customers so I could dance with him during a slow song. Our song… the one I'd lost my virginity to him on, 'So Beautiful' by Musiq Soulchild. I was the envy of every chick in the club last night but I couldn't even focus on that because I was so happy just sharing that moment with Yolo.

Midway into my daydream, I realized that my hand was hitting on something hard in the hoody and I pulled it out, discovering that it was Yolo's phone. Now listen… I've never been the type of bitch to run through a nigga's shit, mainly because I've never had a real boyfriend *but even if I did*, I wasn't the type to go snooping for shit. In all the time I dealt with Yolo, I never was the type to be following him all over town or sneaking around on his Facebook page to see what he was up to or anything like that. In my mind, if I had to put all that energy into doing that shit, then we didn't need to be together. But, in addition to that, Yolo never lied to me about what he was up to so I never needed to ask.

That said… Yes, I was about to go through this nigga's phone. I know, it's not something I'm proud about but, right then, I needed to know if this nigga was still on some bullshit. The past week, I'd been fuckin' up my feet and burning all my damn hair to keep his attention and I wanted to at least know if it was for a good damn reason.

The phone had a passcode but, remember what I said about

knowing somebody so long that you knew everything about them? That shit goes both ways and I knew that Yolo's passcode to every damn thing was his birthday. In seconds, I was in and I went straight to the messages, eager to see if he'd been texting other chicks while we were together.

The first few messages were from his brothers and I scrolled right by, not even the least bit curious to see what them fools texted each other about. Then under the message chain from Outlaw, I saw exactly what I was looking for: LaTrese. Clicking on her name, I leaned back in the chair and began reading.

LaTrese: I saw you with Sidney. That you now?

Something about her even texting him about me made me catch an attitude quick. Damn, was this bitch keeping tabs on his ass? Last I heard they weren't even together!

Yolo: Why you care? Where ya nigga at?

LaTrese: Why you always on that bullshit, Yolo! I did not cheat on you!

Yolo: Me give no fucks.

Latrese: Oh you don't care bout me cuz now you got you a nigga too. Explain this shit to me. How you go from me to that dyking ass bitch—

Closing out of the messages, I locked the phone back and set it on his desk. I couldn't read anymore because if I went any further, I would be knocking on that bitch's door. I couldn't stand LaTrese, even though it hadn't always been that way. We'd never been the best of friends or anything like that but when we were in school, I always thought she was cool. We had mutual friends and hung out a little bit—she was the first girl to try to give me a makeover one time. But after she got with Yolo, that killed all that shit. And once she found out from him what I really meant to him, she turned into the evilest bitch I'd ever met.

"You ready to go?" Yolo asked as he walked out the bathroom, looking like he was ready to make an appearance somewhere rather than simply drive me home. He was dressed simply, for him anyways, but was still fresh to death.

"Yeah," I told him and stood up, watching him as he walked to the desk to grab his phone. He looked at it and paused before turning to me. I cut my eyes away from his, feeling guilty about going through his phone all of a sudden.

"You went through it, didn't you?" he asked and I looked up, my eyes instantly falling right into his face. He was smirking and staring directly at me with a knowing look. There was nothing left for me to do but admit it.

"Yeaaaah," I said slowly, pushing the words out before I had a chance to think of a lie. I stuffed my hands into the pockets of his hoody and dropped my head, feeling like shit. See, this is why I never went through his stuff!

"Don't act like that," Yolo said and then walked over to me, wrapping his arms around my body. He pulled me close and then put his hand under my chin, lifting up my face so that I could look right into his eyes.

"You know I've never lied to you, Sid. Don't you?" he asked and I nodded my head. "You don't have to go through my shit. That's not for me and you. If you wanna know something. Just ask. A'ight?"

"A'ight," I told him right before he kissed me on my lips and pulled away. He sighed and turned around to grab his keys as I fell even deeper for him, loving the way that he reminded me that things with him and I were different. Certain things he vowed never to do to me when we were younger. One of them was lie… and he never did.

"Let's go," he said. "And make sure you send me the time that you'll be at the club so I can roll through."

"Okay," I replied. I walked to him and he turned around, placing his arm around my shoulder as we left the house. Everything about this moment felt perfect. I didn't want anything to come and ruin it.

Cali Wasn't the Same.

Carmella

Cali just wasn't the same.

Putting on a brand new bikini that I'd just purchased, I took a few shots for Instagram, loving the way that my body looked, which meant my followers would too. As I sat and watched my notifications blow up, I still didn't get the satisfaction that I usually did after posting a picture.

Today made a whole week and some since I'd been gone and I hadn't heard one word from Cree. I wasn't surprised either. He was stubborn and so was I. Neither one of us wanted to be the first to call the other. But to be real about it, I was about to break down and hit him up first. He'd pretty much broken down at the airport and begged me to stay. For someone like Cree, that was a big thing and I knew it. Even though I hadn't known him that long, I knew he wasn't the type of nigga to beg. He wasn't the type to wear his emotions on his sleeve but, that day, he had. For me. Thinking about it made me feel like I should do the same and hit him up, letting him know that I missed him and that I wanted to come back.

But still, I hesitated.

I mean… what would I be going back for? My life was in Cali. I went to school here, lived here, and had friends here. Was I really ready to uproot my entire life for a man I'd just met? My answer? YES!

But that wasn't the logical me talking. And although I ran off of my emotions most of the time, I was still a Pickney at heart. And being the daughter of George Pickney meant that I thought logically *most* of the time.

"Carm, over a thousand likes in a few minutes. That's what's up, chick," Sasha, one of my closest friends, said as she sat next to me on the beach. I shrugged, not even really feeling what she was saying because my mind was on Cree.

"Why you actin' all distant and shit? We're at the beach!" Sasha said, holding out her hands like I didn't already know. The beach was one of my favorite places to be but I just wasn't into it at the moment.

"This about that guy you met?" Sasha asked, rolling her eyes as she sipped from out of a glass she was holding in her hands. I didn't answer her.

Sasha was one of those friends who was so use to men using and taking advantage of her that she didn't see anything else. She couldn't be happy about me when it came to any man because she was too busy trying to find proof that he was the liar and cheater that she already thought he was. Initially, I didn't want to tell her about Cree but she was my best friend so I did. Boy, did I regret that shit. She spent the next half hour listening to my stories about him, rolling her eyes and telling me that I was stupid for being so hung up on a man who was so rude and ignorant all the damn time.

"I know you don't get it but you don't have to," was all I said before pulling out my phone to check my responses on Instagram.

It was the same old shit. A bunch of people liking the pic and a whole bunch of thirsty ass niggas commenting underneath about how fine I was. Some even said some shit that would have had me smacking the shit out of them had I seen them in person. I was just about to put my phone down when I saw a notification come through from someone named Creed0908. It could have been anybody but the fact that the word 'cree' stood out to me, I focused on it. Clicking the notification, I went to the profile of the person who owned the username and saw that the page was private. But one look at the profile pic told me that it was Cree's Instagram page. He wasn't in the picture but his headphones were, along with a few other items he'd taken a photo of to show his love of music.

I clicked the notification screen again to see which pic that he'd liked but the notification was gone, like it had never happened. That's when it dawned on me what he'd done. He was creeping on my page and had clicked like by accident. Well, too late, nigga. Yo' ass was caught.

"Damn, what got you smilin' like that?" Sasha asked, pushing her hair from her face. It was windy outside. Perfect weather for such a sunny day and now my ass was finally in a mood to appreciate it since I'd caught Cree missing me as much as I was missing him.

"Nothing. Just checkin' out some stuff on IG," I told her before putting down the phone. My mood was renewed just like that and I felt good. But then Sasha had to say something to ruin it all for me.

"Have you gotten the school shit worked out yet?"

Sighing, I rolled over on my back, laying down flat on my beach towel. School was the last thing I wanted to think of at the moment. Mainly because I was failing one of my core classes. I was smart...

brilliant even, so it's not that. My problem was that I didn't always apply myself like I should. So although I passed tests with flying colors and little effort, I was rarely in class and I didn't always complete assignments on time.

Being brilliant and beautiful, most teachers didn't give me too much of an issue about that. They knew I knew the material and they were still getting a check so what was the problem? Well, now I had Professor Tingsley, a white man in his mid-forties who had a major stick up his ass and found any and every reason to give me a failing grade.

"No, he still isn't budging on the grade. I've passed every exam with an A but he's docking me for attendance, missing two projects and some essay assignments. It's bullshit. I'm in college… it's not mandatory to attend; I'm paying my money for him to teach me shit. If I can pass the tests, doesn't that mean I've been taught the shit?!" I argued, rolling my eyes before pushing out my bottom lip in a pout.

Sighing, Sasha leaned over me and looked me into my eyes, shaking her head.

"Well, you knew all this when you signed up for the class. I guess you thought your ass was going to help you pass but not everything is that easy, Carm," she told me, giving me a hard shot of truth.

"Yeah but I'm about to lose my scholarship around this shit. And if my daddy finds out… I don't even want to think about what that will mean. The only reason he doesn't get on me for takin' so long to finish school and doing the pics on IG is because I've always kept my grades up," I confided in her although I was speaking more to myself than anyone else.

Sasha stayed silent but I knew she understood. She'd been friends with me long enough to understand how it was being the daughter of George Pickney. I loved my father but he was a hard ass when it came to certain things and grades were one of them. Janelle was his favorite because she always did everything right, Mixie was his next favorite, then Vonia because although she was did the exact opposite of everything he asked, she was his baby.

Me? I was dead last. I knew my daddy loved me but I always felt like I came short of what he expected. Sasha always said that my modeling was a cry for help for him to say something. She said that I knew it wasn't a good look for an attorney running for office to have a daughter posing half-nude on the Gram and that I did it to get a rise out of him. I didn't see it that way. I was just doing my thing.

"Well, if you need money, I have an idea to help you out," Sasha said, grabbing my full attention. "And you'll get to see your lil' rude boo thang from Brooklyn too," she added with a roll of her pretty brown eyes.

Ignoring the fact that I was more excited about the prospect of seeing Cree than making money that I desperately needed, I turned to look at her.

"What is it?"

"My brother is doing films or something in Manhattan. I'm not sure exactly for what but he's always asking me to slide you his info so he can work with you."

Mouth dropping open, I just stared at Sasha as she dished out this new info with a shrug like it wasn't nothing.

"Bitch! And you're just now tellin' me about this?! I could have been in movies and you're holding back?" Reaching out, I playfully pushed her on the shoulder but I was only half-playing. I still couldn't believe she hadn't told me this before. Like when he had *first* asked!

"I knew you were doing your own thing and Zeke is always mixed up in some shit," she gave me a wide-eyed look but I still didn't really know what she meant. "Like, it's nothing illegal, I'm sure, but you just never know with him. I didn't want you to get caught up in whatever he has going on but since you need help, it couldn't hurt giving him a call."

At the moment, I didn't give a shit if what Zeke was doing was illegal. I could use the exposure and I could definitely use the money. Plus, the possibility of seeing Cree again would be an added bonus.

"Here," I said, giving her my phone. "Put his number in there and I'll hit him up tonight."

"Alright, but please make sure you check everything out before you go. Zeke be trippin' sometimes," Sasha warned me but I wasn't trying to hear it. In my mind, it was already a done deal.

I Got Plenty Hoes.

Janelle

"Damn!" I cursed as I tugged the edges of my coat tightly around my body. It was cold as hell outside and I don't know what convinced me that it was a good idea to actually leave my apartment to go to church rather than just watch it online. But the more I looked at my life, the more convicted I felt so I woke up that morning determined to go to *somebody's* church, something I was steadily regretting.

I hadn't seen Luke since the day of the robbery when I told him to leave. He'd texted me and called me but never once said he wanted to come over and I didn't invite him. Part of me hoped that he just would never come back, and then I wouldn't have to make a decision concerning my life with him and my dream for my career.

Looking up, I saw that I was nearly to my corner and I started strutting even faster, determined to make it back before the next gust of wind came and blew me right on my ass. I loved everything about New York but the winters. It was something I would never get used to and anyone looking at me right then knew that I hadn't yet adapted to them because here it was, feeling like -50 degrees outside and my ass was in heels and a somewhat heavy coat, freezing my ass off.

I was almost to my apartment when I stepped on something slippery and one foot went one way while my body went the other. The need to 'look cute' went straight out the window as I struggled, flailing my arms in the air, as I tried to retain my balance. Legs scampering, arms flapping… looking just like I was catching the Holy Ghost right on the sidewalk after hearing a good word on that Sunday morning.

"Oh sheeeeeiiiiiiit!" I screamed as I reached out for anything to help me break my fall. Nothing came and in seconds, I fell down right on my ass, dropping my purse and everything else on the sidewalk.

"Damn… you good?" someone asked me and I looked up into a pair of calm brown eyes, pulled tight with concern. It was a guy I hadn't seen around before but that wasn't saying much. It wasn't like I got out all the time.

Rolling my eyes, I nodded and forced out a bit of embarrassed laughter as I tried to collect my things and get up.

"Yeah, I just missed a step," I told him, thankful when he reached out to help me up.

"You missed a few steps," he laughed and I cringed from shame. Is this what I get for not listening to the devil and instead dragging my ass to church this morning?

"Let me help you get your things," he said and I shot him a gracious smile as he began to help me. It wasn't all the time you met someone so kind in the city.

"Thank you," I replied with a smile and watched as he bent down to pick up my phone that had fallen onto the sidewalk. I prayed it wasn't cracked but, with my luck, I knew it was.

"Aye! AYE!"

Turning around, I looked in the direction of the voice, knowing instantly exactly who it was. With his head out the window as he drove up to where I was standing, Luke's piercing eyes were focused on me and the man who had helped me scrape my ass from off the ground.

"AYE!" he said again, as if he really needed to. He already had both of our attention.

"Yes, Luke?" I asked with attitude, frowning at him. Of course, he didn't answer, he simply slid his car to the side; parallel parking on the side of the road, then cut it off and hopped right out. Frown on his face, ready to act all territorial like his ass had actually been around the past few days.

"Well, I'm going to go ahead and go," the man said, turning to me as Luke walked up on us. Pressing his lips together, he gave me a tight smile before stalking away, careful not to look anywhere but straight ahead. Frowning deeply, Luke stopped and stared him down the whole time until he bent the corner to walk down the other side of the street.

"What the hell is up with you?" I inquired with narrowed eyes. As if just remembering I was there, Luke spun around to look at me, his eyes still pulled tight into a glare.

"I should be askin' you the same damn thing. Nigga, I been callin' you!" he declared, walking up on me. "What, you blocked a nigga again?"

"No, I didn't block you, Luke," I said, rolling my eyes. "I was in church!"

"Church?!" he mimicked, his eyes narrowing even further. He repeated the word like it was something he'd never heard before.

"Church?!"

"Yes, Luke. Church!" Placing my hands on my hips, I stared at him as a blank look covered his face. Then suddenly, his expression broke and his features folded right back up into his signature frown.

"Nigga, you don't go to no church! Lyin' ass!"

Pushing past me, he walked to my front door and reached under my mat, grabbing the spare key that his ass wasn't even supposed to know was there. Then he unlocked the door, placed the key back where he got it from and walked inside like he owned the place, slamming the door shut behind him. Standing there, all I could do was blink and think 'no this nigga didn't!' It never failed. As much time as I spent with Luke, I couldn't understand his ass one bit because he was always doing some off the wall shit that I couldn't explain.

Turning around, I stomped up the stairs, wincing a little in pain from the throbbing coming from my leg. I must've bruised it when I fell down. As soon as I walked in the house, I was greeted by the sight of Luke walking around my living room, lifting up sofa cushions as if he were looking for something. Can you believe his ass didn't even have the audacity to straighten my shit back up after going through it? He just flung the cushions on the floor after he was done. Everyone who knew me knew that I was a clean freak and didn't anything piss me off more than someone messing *with* my things or messing *up* my things.

"What the hell are you doing?" I barked at him, walking over to straighten up my couch.

"What the hell it look like, Nell?" he said, using the pet name he'd given me. "I'm makin' sure you ain't had no nigga in here while I been gone!"

Excuse me?!

The black woman came out of me in an instant as I snapped my head back and gave him a vicious screw face. Listen, no matter how educated you *think* a black woman is, the right situation can pull the hood right out of her ass if the timing was right and that's exactly what I was on, watching Luke run around, searching through my things, tossing shit every damn where as if he was my man.

Yes, I had feelings for him and yes, we had something going on but things were not official between us. But not just that, I'd been through the jealous boyfriend shit before and it was the worst relationship I had in life. The last thing I wanted was to go down that road again. This shit he was up to right now was turning me off.

"No, what you *need* to do is get the fuck out my shit!" I snapped, holding one finger in the air as I glared at him. "You have been gone for days and I haven't once said a thing to you about it. On top of that, you are *not* my man to come up in here rearranging my shit!"

Spinning around, Luke turned to look at me with his eyes wide as hell like he couldn't believe what was coming out of my mouth. I couldn't believe his dramatic ass, honestly. He was always on one. He was always flipping about something when anyone with common sense knew he was dead wrong. And here we go yet again.

"Nigga, what you mean?! When it comes to this shit—" He used his finger to point all around the room we were in. "—You bet not be lettin' another nigga run his monkey ass up in this shit! You won't let me take you nowhere and, bein' the stand-up nigga I am, I dealt with that." He placed his hand on his chest, slapping hard like he was being the bigger man about this situation. His ego was big as hell.

"I may not be able to say shit to you 'bout who you spend ya time with out there but in here, it's me and you, ma! In here, ain't no other niggas allowed because Outlaw don't share space wit' no fuck niggas! Let me catch another nigga in here fartin' all over the fuckin' couch cushions and shit and I'mma fuckin' spazz on his ass! You gon' mess around and I'mma coordinate a meet and greet with that nigga and one of my hot balls. Ya hear me?!" Luke asked, his nostrils flaring as he poked his chest out. Straight testosterone was all I saw and nothing else. He might as well have been beating his chest and loudly declaring that he was a man.

"Yeah whatever," I said with a sigh, ready to just be done with it. He was in his feelings and that was the worst place for a man to be because all they did was end up acting childish. And Luke was childish nearly twenty-four seven so he really didn't need any more help.

"That's what the fuck I thought!" he added, staring at me with a straight face, like he was regulating something. I rolled my eyes and walked by him, heading to the room. Reaching out, he smacked my ass just as I walked by, making sure to squeeze it extra hard.

"Aye, and make me a sandwich while you bein' all submissive and shit," he yelled out just as I got to my room door.

See? Childish.

After changing out of my clothes, I walked out to see Luke sitting on the same couch he'd been rummaging through, laid back with his eyes open, staring at nothing, obviously deep in thought. Everything in my living room was back in place, perfectly situated like he hadn't been tossing everything around only minutes before. As I walked in the room, his head turned slowly until his eyes locked on me, soft and gentle. It was crazy how quickly his moods changed and I think that was part of what I liked about him.

I was so controlled with everything, even my reactions. I was patient and I thought everything out before I did it. Even when it came to me getting mad and going off on someone, it was hard to push my buttons because I forced myself to always be in control. But Luke was the opposite. There was no controlling him. He was wild and irrational, made no damn sense half the time, really. He was just who he was and he didn't apologize about it. You either loved him or hated him but he didn't give two fucks one way or another.

"You know what pisses me off?" he asked but I didn't say anything since it didn't really seem like the type of question he wanted answered. "Remember that day you said that you was goin' to the movies wit' dat nigga, that shit made me so fuckin' mad, yo…" He paused, laughing sarcastically but I could tell from the tight way he held his jaw that he really didn't think a damn thing was funny.

Standing there in front of him, I watched his face intensely knowing that the only reason I said anything about the movies and Chris was to see if he would get jealous. I usually didn't play childish games like that but something about him had me feeling unsure of my status in his life so I did it anyways. He was becoming more important to me… my feelings were definitely involved and I wanted to see if his were too. But once I said it, Luke barely reacted. All he'd told me was to let him know when he had to be out so I could get ready. Then he told me 'not to be wearin' no short shit'. Typical response for him. I don't know why I expected more.

But now… it seemed like he was finally opening up about it.

"I ain't never took a chick to a fuckin' movie. You believe that?" he asked and, once again, I stayed silent. "Reason why? I don't like watchin' all that gay ass shit y'all like to see. But also because when I go, I don't want no chick askin' me to get her no popcorn or no shit just because she think it's cute. I don't want her tryin' to hold a nigga hand and shit. I just wanna sit back and enjoy what the hell playin'. But when you said you was goin' out to see a movie wit' that muthafucka, I swear I ain't never wanted to beat a nigga ass so bad in life."

Blinking, I just stood in place looking at him, wondering if I was supposed to be flattered or not by what he was saying.

"I got hoes…plenty hoes!" he continued, holding his arms out as if to illustrate just how many hoes he had. Sucking my teeth, I wanted to walk away. Did he really think I wanted to hear this?

"And I ain't never been worried 'bout what they doin' or who they with but then here yo' ass come and I'm ready to catch a fuckin' case, wonderin' if you actually would have the guts to fuck another nigga," he said and shook his head somberly. "How you think that shit make me feel, Nell?!"

I was truly at a loss for words listening to Luke's logic, watching him in front of me looking like someone had really hurt his damn feelings. Can you believe this? He actually seemed like he expected me to feel sorry for him or actually understand his backwards ass!

"So you have hoes… plenty hoes," I started, holding my arms out to mock him. "But you want to act crazy because of me going on a date with someone? How are you going to get mad over the same shit you do?!"

"Because I'm a nigga and you a chick!" he argued back, frowning his face up at me. "Shit, it's a lot of shit I can do that you can't! You wanna piss standin' up too?!"

I couldn't with his ass right now. But after having a good time in church, the last thing I wanted to do was argue. On top of that, there was no point in arguing with Luke over anything concerning me having another man in here because Chris and I weren't even like that. Not once had we even talked about anything close to sex. I liked him and he seemed to like me but that was it. If it ever got to the point where it went further than that, I'd tell Luke but the time hadn't come.

"Alright, Luke," I said with a sigh, taking the peaceful route. "I promise not to have no other men in here."

"For real?" he asked, lifting one brow and I nodded.

"For real." I shrugged, not really taking it serious even though it seemed to be so important to him.

"What 'bout this church shit you just started with? They got niggas there too?" he asked, his face pulled tight. His ass was really serious!

"Yes, there are men at church but none of them will be in here!" I told him with a slight chuckle. Luke didn't crack a smile at all, just stared at me, probing my eyes with his as if he were trying to make sure

I was telling the truth.

"I promise," I added, rolling my eyes.

And just like that, Luke was good. Smiling, he stood up and walked over to me with the biggest grin on his face I'd ever seen on a man. There was a sparkle in his eyes and I knew exactly what was coming next. Without a shred of hesitation, he walked up to me, grabbed me around my waist and lifted me up, placing me on the small dining room table behind us. The mischievous look in his eyes set something on fire within me and my stomach began to flip-flop inside of me in anticipation for what was next.

Lord, please forgive me but I'm about to have sex with this man, I thought, begging forgiveness for my pending transgressions.

In seconds, Luke was leaning over me, with one hand gripping my waist to keep me steady as he pounded into me hard. Wrapping my legs around him, I rode the rhythm he created, loving the feel of him inside me.

"Damn," I cooed, letting my head fall back as he picked up the pace, rotating and pumping hard into me.

"You like that?" he asked as he pumped and I nodded my head, squeezing my eyes tightly shut.

"Yeah I know you like this shit!" he replied cockily and I could hear the wide ass smile on his face through his tone. "You know you like all this dick!"

Luke and his ego will *never* part.

I was so into everything that was going on and the way that he was making me feel, that I didn't even notice someone was unlocking my door until it was wide open and the cool breeze from outside was swooping across my ass and tickling my nipples.

"OH SHIT!"

Gasping, I looked over Luke's shoulder right when I heard the voice and my eyes fell right on the sight of Carmella, standing at the door with her eyes and mouth wide open.

"CARMELLA—" I screamed, pushing Luke away but he only gripped my ass harder, steadily pumping. Turning around, he glanced over his shoulder to see what all the commotion was.

"Shit, man! Close the damn door or walk the fuck in! Can't you see we doin' somethin'?" he barked, still humping into me like nothing had even happened.

Still wearing a shocked expression, Carmella backed away from the door and slammed it closed as I sat there frozen in place with my mouth wide open in horror. Luke, happy that the interruption was over, bent down and licked my ear, smiling hard like he hadn't just been caught by my sister with his pants down, ass out, fuckin' the shit out of me on the table that we all had to eat on. His ass was wild.

Groaning, I cowered down and pushed my head into Luke's chest, totally embarrassed about what had happened but a little turned on at the same time, which surprised the hell out of me. I knew I was a freak but damn! I was a little freakier than I thought.

The Snitch.

Carmella

So Janelle was officially getting her freak on! And with Cree's fine ass brother, too! I was shocked as hell when I walked in her apartment to see him digging up in her guts right on the damn dining room table, but just because I was shocked didn't mean I was blind! I had a mental picture of everything he was working with in my mind and it was there to stay.

"You lyin'!" Sidney shrieked after I told her everything that I'd just walked in on. Janelle would probably have attitude once she found out I told somebody about her lil' freaky side but I didn't care. It was about time for her to stop being such a goody-two shoes and I was glad Cree's brother was helping her with that.

"Nope! I walked in on both of they asses! He didn't even stop when he saw me either! Just kept pumping that shit into her like he was digging for gold," I laughed, holding my hands out as I did a dance like I was pumping, playfully gyrating my hips.

"Daaamn," Faviola added, licking her lips. "So Outlaw can fuck somethin', huh? I always knew his stroke game was official. You can tell just by lookin' at him that he got that good dick."

"Bitch! Only stroke game you need to be worryin' 'bout is ya baby daddy who keep givin' out samples of his to every chick he meets!"

Sidney added with a frown. "I'm still tryin' to figure out what brother other than Tank you been with! I guess Outlaw ain't it."

Sucking her teeth, Faviola rolled her eyes and I couldn't help but laugh. Faviola wasn't someone who I would normally be cool with but I liked her. She was real with her shit, if nothing else, and I could identify with that because I was the same way. We loved sex just as much as niggas and we thought of it the same way they did. We weren't ashamed of our bodies and didn't have no issues showing it to the world either. The only difference was that people gave me a pass for the shit I did because my daddy was rich whereas Faviola was from the hood so she had to deal with people always trying to call her a hoe. Shit still didn't bother her none.

"Don't try to roll your eyes, heffa!" Sidney continued, reaching out from where she was laying on the bed to push Faviola hard in her arm. "What other Murray did you fuck with other than Tank?"

Crossing her arms in front of her chest, Faviola pressed her lips together and I watched her, instantly getting curious. For some reason, she actually seemed like she really didn't want to tell, which wasn't characteristic of her. She was always open with everything she did and had no regrets.

"Was it Cree?" I heard myself ask and instantly got pissed when I felt the familiar ache of jealousy go through my chest. Who cares if it was Cree? I was sure he had messed with a lot of women in the past just like I'd messed with a lot of men. Didn't matter.

"No," Faviola mumbled, shaking her head and looking down.

"Well, who the hell was it?" Sidney asked her, her voice wavering almost like she was now scared for Faviola to answer. "Was it Yolo?"

Sighing, Faviola rolled her eyes and shook her head again. "No, bitch. It was not Yolo. The only other Murray I been with outside of Tank was Tone."

Closing my eyes, I let out a deep breath, thankful that she hadn't been with Cree, Yolo or Outlaw because I didn't want any drama coming up between my sister or anyone I was friends with. I'd never heard of Tone, which wasn't something strange because Cree had a few brothers I didn't really know anything about.

"Damn, Tone?" Sidney said, shaking her head sadly. "I really miss that nigga. I ain't kno' y'all messed around."

Looking at Faviola, my eyes widened when I saw her wipe a tear from her eye and sniff sadly. Sitting down on the bed next to where she was, I put my arm around her, rubbing her gently on the back as she took a deep breath and tried to get herself together.

"I was with him when he was killed," she said, and even though I didn't know Tone, I felt the mood in the room shift as I listened, eager for her to continue on.

"I didn't know that!" Sidney exclaimed and jumped up on the bed, sitting Indian style with her eyes transfixed on Faviola as we both waited for her to go on. "What happened?"

Faviola licked her lips and sighed once more before she began again.

"Well… it was a cold and windy night…" she paused and looked at us, both of our eyes wide as we hung off her every word. Then suddenly her face cracked and she began to laugh.

"Bitch, I'm lyin'!"

"HELL NAW!" Sidney yelled and grabbed a pillow, slamming it down hard on her ass. "That wasn't fuckin' funny, yo! You always fuckin' playin'!"

Smiling, I shook my head as Faviola laughed on, getting a kick out of her whack ass sense of humor.

"No, real talk though!" she started, still laughing as she wiped tears of glee from her eyes. "I did fuck around with Tone so it wasn't all a lie. I wasn't with him when he was killed but I did see his ass right before. I was fucked up over that shit, remember?"

There was a beat of silence as Sidney dropped her head, looking at nothing in particular as her memories flowed through her mind. Then she nodded her head, bringing her attention back to Faviola.

"Yeah, I remember that shit. I ain't kno' why you was so broken up 'bout his ass. Damn, why you ain't tell me y'all was messin' around?"

"Because your ass would've told Yolo and he got a big ass mouth! Personally, I didn't care if anyone found out but Tone ain't want it gettin' back to his baby mama," Faviola shot back, sucking her teeth. "Tone was cool as hell. He was like a cross between Outlaw and Cree... laid back but wild when he needed to be. Only other one who knew we messed around was Tank since they was living together. His stupid ass."

She scoffed, tossing her head back before falling down flat on the bed.

"The only reason I even fucked wit' Tank was to see if he could sling the dick like his brother. And that nigga is official wit' his shit but I swear I ain't mean to get pregnant and fall in love."

Hell, I didn't mean to fall in love either, I thought, probably thinking the same damn thing that Sidney was right now.

"So you and Tank knew each other before y'all hooked up at the club that night? Let him tell it, his ass got caught up from a one night stand!" Sidney said as she grabbed her phone that had started to beep. Looking down at it, she frowned before placing the phone face down in her lap.

"Yes, Tank and I started messin' around and been messin' around for some time now. That twerkin' shit I did at the club that one night was to make him jealous. We was already fuckin'. My problem was, he kept tryin' to act like I wasn't shit to him so I came to the club that night ready to show the fuck out and I did. Cree was actin' like he was better than a bitch when I hit that split but Outlaw's eyes was on my ass like he was ready to fuck somethin'! Tank saw that shit and snatched me up quick!"

Faviola laughed, slapping her knees as she recalled the events of the night she claimed her baby was conceived. This was some crazy shit, even in my book but it was her story and who am I to judge? Maybe I needed to go twerk crazy at the club to get Cree to start acting like he actually felt something for me. I mean, not like I really care about his ass or anything. Ah, shit…

"Bitch, I ain't kno' none of this shit. You been holdin' out," Sidney said and gave Faviola a crazy look. Shrugging, Faviola reached over and grabbed the phone from Sidney's lap before looking at the screen.

"Hey!" Sidney yelled, and tried to grab the phone but Faviola moved it away.

"I'm not the only one who has been holdin' out," she said, trying to unlock it. "I saw that ugly ass expression on your face when you looked at this phone. Who was it? Yolo? I kno' y'all back fuckin' around."

"So the clothes worked?!" I asked, perking up as I looked at Sidney who had finally been able to snatch her phone from Faviola's hand. She nodded and a girlish smile came to her lips. I smiled as well, seeing her soften up. Sidney was so rough around the damn edges, it was crazy but it was obvious she was beautiful. One look at her and I knew that if I was able to get my hands on her, she would be drop dead gorgeous, making niggas drool while running behind her and I was right.

"Yeah, but I ain't really gettin' my hopes up 'bout that shit because I kno' he got other bitches in the picture," she said and looked away, her expression saying that her ass was a muthafuckin' lie. It was obvious her hopes were already up and she was praying like hell that Yolo didn't have anyone else in the picture. I couldn't help feeling the same way because I hadn't known Sidney all that long but I liked her. I really didn't want to see her get her heart broken.

Sighing, I stood up and checked my watch to see how much time had passed. It was cool hanging at Sidney's for a little bit but I was hoping that Janelle and her man were done. After my flight, I was ready to take a hot shower, get into some food and lay my ass down somewhere.

"Well, I'm about to go," I announced as I grabbed my purse and the handle of my suitcase. "Hopefully the lovebirds are done by now."

"What 'bout you and Cree?" Sidney asked before I had a chance to walk to the store, stopping me as soon as she said his name. "Y'all still goin' strong?"

Turning around, I saw her and Faviola were both looking at me, waiting for me to dish the details on the Murray I was messing with now that they'd spoke on theirs.

"Cree is Cree and I am me. We ain't together," I told them with a shrug, like he didn't mean shit to me even though he did. He *really* did but I wasn't ready to admit that yet.

"So why you came back? It wasn't for him?" Sidney pressed further and I shook my head.

"No, I came back for a business reason and I'm not staying for long. I'm only on break for a little bit until after Thanksgiving," I told them honestly, and then turned to leave. "I'll get up with y'all later."

"Mmhmm," they both said, watching me as I let myself out.

I knew they didn't believe what I was saying but I didn't care. To be real about it, all of our asses were lying about something. I was lying about Cree not having anything to do with why I was back, Sidney was lying about not getting her hopes up about Yolo and Faviola's ass was just a whole damn lie. I still wasn't fully convinced that she hadn't actually fucked with Yolo, Outlaw or Cree. Leave it to her sneaky ass to claim that the one she slept with was the one who wasn't around anymore to call bullshit on her story.

Walking into Janelle's place, the first thing I noticed was that it smelled just like a Glade air freshener. She was trying hard to get rid of the sex smell but it didn't matter. I had a vivid mental picture that would never let me forget about what had happened in here.

"I'm baaaack!" I yelled out, even though I really didn't need to say anything since they were both sitting in the living room, both of their hair wet like they were fresh out the shower.

"Y'all asses was gettin' it in in the shower too, huh?" I teased as I drug my suitcase in and slammed the door closed behind me. Looking back, I saw Janelle looked mortified but Outlaw had a mischievous grin on his face as he cut his eyes at her, smiling hard like the Cheshire cat.

"No!" Janelle shot out. An obvious lie.

"Don't downplay my sex game like that, lil mama," Outlaw said, jabbing Janelle in the ribs with his elbow. "You kno' I was beatin' the brakes off that shit. Don't fuckin' lie on Sunday, knowin' ya ass done been to church and shit."

Janelle groaned and I giggled as I walked over. This was my first time really meeting Outlaw and I liked him already. I could already tell he was going to drive Janelle crazy, and to be honest, he seemed more my type than hers, but that might have been exactly what she needed. The boring ass types that she normally went for were smart and all, but I was convinced all their asses were secretly crazy.

Take her ex, Josh, for example. He was the picture-perfect type for her, studying to be a doctor, great life and great family with money but he was insanely jealous of Janelle to the point that he wouldn't let her do shit. It's been a minute since she was able to finally shake his ass off but I still felt like her relationship with him was why she always stayed in the house with her nose stuck in a damn book.

"Glad to see you, sis," Janelle said as she stood up and walked over to me, hugging me tight. "Even though I didn't know you were coming. Or I would have been... better prepared."

She gave me a look and I knew she was still embarrassed about earlier, but Outlaw, on the other hand, was chinning and grinning as he looked on from behind her. Pulling my focus from him, I looked at her.

"I called you earlier and texted!"

"I was at church!" Janelle said with her arms out.

"Church?!" I repeated, snapping my neck back as I looked her up and down. I heard Outlaw mention it earlier but I thought 'church' was code for something else.

"Yeah, she told me that stupid ass lie too," Outlaw chimed in, waving one hand at us as he held the remote with the other, looking at the TV and flipping through channels.

"It's *not* a lie!" Janelle countered, rolling her eyes. "I've been going online for quite some time and decided I wanted to actually visit in person today."

"Ohhh," I said, and nodded my head but didn't say anything further. See, my family wasn't religious so the whole idea of Janelle going to church was foreign to me but to each her own. Reaching down, I grabbed the handle of my suitcase and pulled it hard, tugging it down the hall to the room formerly known as Val's so I could settle in.

"Luke, you wanna help Carm with her bags?" Janelle asked, turning to Luke who was focused in on a football game. It looked like the Falcons were playing and I paused for a minute as I looked at the TV, wondering if my ex was on the field.

"Naw," Outlaw answered quickly, not even turning from the game.

"LUKE! That wasn't a question!" Janelle shot back at him, turning to face him with her hands on her hips like she meant business. Outlaw turned around to stare at her, his face blank like he was trying to figure out why she was so mad and then he cocked his head to the side and smirked at her, gold grill shining. Damn, when I say his ass was *sexy*!

"Well, nigga, why you paused like yo' ass was waitin' for an answer?" he retorted smartly, and I saw that the smart ass mouth that Cree had obviously ran through the damn family. Difference was, while Outlaw was joking around with his smart ass comments, Cree was dead ass about his.

Blowing out a heavy breath, Janelle sucked her teeth and walked back to the living room, plopping her ass right back in her seat just as Outlaw stood up. As she pretended to sulk in response to his rude behavior, he leaned down, giving her a sloppy ass kiss right on the lips, tongue and all, leaving a smile on her lips once he pulled away. I grinned as I watched how cute they were, knowing without a shadow of a doubt that my sister's ass was in love. She had been with Josh for years and he never made her look at him in the way that she looked at Outlaw, her eyes fluttering slowly like she was drunk with a silly ass smile on her face that was only reserved for him. Oh yeah... she had it bad.

"So I guess I gotta help you wit' dis shit," Outlaw said, walking over to me and plucking the handle of my suitcase out of my hands before I could say a word. He walked away down the hall and I glanced at Janelle who simply shrugged in response. Wasn't shit she could do with him and she knew it.

Once I got to the room, I thanked Outlaw for helping me with my things and then waited for him to leave so I could close the door. But instead of leaving right away, he paused, just as he got to the door and turned around, his eyes focused on me.

"Aye, my brother know you here?" he asked, his face straight but his eyes twinkling as if he was thinking about something funny.

"Naw," I answered with ease and shrugged, once again trying to pretend that Cree wasn't shit to me. Maybe if I pretended enough, people would stop asking me about his ass because damn, how the hell was I going to get over him if everybody kept throwing him up in my face?!

"You gon' tell him?" Outlaw pressed, a hint of a smile teasing the edge of his lips.

"Naw," I repeated. Another shrug.

"You on some surprise shit? Like, you gon' jump out the bushes on my nigga?" he pushed further.

"Naw." I shrugged again.

"Well, what the fuck does this mean?" Outlaw said and I looked at him, seeing him make his shoulders jump.

"Huh?" I asked, frowning at him.

"This shit," he worked his shoulders a few more times. "You keep doin' this shit. What the fuck is this?" He kept jumping his shoulders and it dawned on me that he was imitating my shrug. "You got a nervous twitch?"

Laughing, I rolled my eyes at him. This nigga was crazy as hell!

"NO! I just don't really wanna answer any questions about Cree, that's all," I replied, honestly. "We aren't on good terms."

"Ohhh…" Outlaw said, smiling as he nodded his head like he knew something I didn't know. I started to ask but decided against it. After the last few minutes of interaction with his ass, who knew what went on in his brain to make him react the way he did.

"You kno' I'mma tell bruh, right?" he said suddenly and I snapped my neck, staring at him as he just smiled at me… that same mischievous, evil ass smile.

"NO! Please, don't do that! I'm just goin' to be here for a little while and then I'm out," I pled, putting my hands up as I talked, hoping that he would listen.

"Naw, mama," Outlaw replied as he shook his head to the side and began to back away from the door. "I don't keep secrets from my niggas. I'm snitchin' on ya ass."

Groaning, I watched as he walked out of the door and then down the hall, already pulling his phone out of his pocket probably to do just what he said he was gonna do.

"Hey!" I yelled out, leaning out the room door. "I thought snitches got stitches!"

Outlaw turned around and looked at me with the cellphone in his hand and then smirked. Janelle turned towards us, her face frowned up as she wondered what was going on.

"Well, pull up on my ass wit' dat .44, lil' nigga, if you 'bout dat life!" he shot back before placing the phone to his ear. "Aye, bruh! Guess what…"

Sucking my teeth, I stepped back into the room and slammed the door closed behind me, placing my back to the door. I took a deep breath and held it, trying to get my mind right to deal with Cree now that he knew I was back in town.

A Hopeless Case.

Teema

"You can do this, Teema. Why can you do it? Because you're a positive person with dreams and goals that surpass your current situation. Stay focused and stay positive."

Those were the words that I had to tell myself every single morning before I walked through the double doors to my job. I hated a lot of the things I had to deal with being a CNA, but nothing came close to always making me lose it like dealing with my bitch of a boss, Danielle.

Danielle and I somewhat grew up together. I lived in the hood but she stayed in the nicer area of the city, however, we both attended the same high school. All throughout high school, she made it her goal in life to tease me about being the little dirty girl of the school. It was true, although my clothes were clean, they always *looked* dirty. I did the best that I could because I practically took care of myself, but fortunately, most people didn't pay me any attention. Except Danielle. It was like she got high off that shit because she never missed an opportunity to tease me. I used to hide in the bathroom when I saw her coming in order to escape her. She made my life a living hell when all I wanted to do was keep to myself and be left alone.

Eventually we grew up and both of us went our separate ways. But after I had my daughter Kenya and moved away, I ended up running into her again. After applying everywhere I could for a job and being turned down, Cyndy finally got me a job where she worked and I felt like I was finally getting my life together. A week later, my manager was fired for letting a patient sit all day in his shit after he called her a bitch and Danielle was hired to take her place.

Not even a day on the job and she was back to her old ways of antagonizing me every day just for the hell of it. To make things worse, I'd heard through the grapevine that she had a fling with my baby daddy at some point after I had Kenya and we broke up. The fact that I had a baby from a man she'd been with who had subsequently tossed her away like yesterday's trash, only added fuel to the fire. And I really don't know why! The nigga treated me like shit too!

"Hey Teema," my friend, Cyndy, said as she walked up to me. I scanned my badge to clock in before turning to her, immediately noting the annoyed look on her face.

"Your girl is on one today. Just wanted to warn you," she told me in a hushed voice as we walked down the hallway.

"Thank you for that," I replied flatly. "I'm going to try and stay out her way because I got cramps. I'm already aggravated after dealing with my mama this morning and Kenya pooped all over herself this morning as soon as I turned into the parking lot of her daycare. I'm running late because I had to clean her up. I couldn't just leave her with them people like that."

"Damn, girl. I'mma pray for you," Cyndy said, giving me a look before she started to walk away.

"Do that," I told her with a sigh. "I'll see you during lunch."

"Okay, Tee!"

Taking a deep breath, I reminded myself that I was going to stay positive because I needed this job and kept walking to the locker room. There, I locked up my belongings and put a smile on my face as I turned to get started with work.

"This is going to be a good day," I mumbled to myself, still trying to convince myself that it was true. But as soon as I walked out of the locker room, I saw Danielle standing right across the hall, her hands on her hips and her eyes on me.

"You're late!" she snapped as soon as she saw me. No good morning, hello or nothing.

"I know, Danielle. I didn't mean to be late but Kenya had an accident on her way to—"

"I did not ask for all them excuses and I really don't want to hear them," Danielle cut in, speaking loud enough for everyone in the hall to hear. It was first thing in the morning and the hospital was crowded, filled with workers, patients and their family but Danielle only saw them all as the perfect audience to watch her embarrass me.

"This is a hospital where we are paid to take care of people who need our help. That means that you need to be on time. In the last month, you have been late a total of three times and each time I step to you on it, your excuse is your daughter." She rolled her eyes when she said 'daughter' and I felt like snatching them straight out of her head. "It's not anyone's fault but yours that you have a child with no daddy to help you with it. That has nothing to do with your responsibilities here. If you couldn't figure out how to be a good mother and still handle your responsibilities, maybe you shouldn't have laid up and gotten pregnant! One more time and I'm writing you up."

Having said her fill, Danielle turned around and stomped away, leaving me clenching my teeth together to avoid cursing her out. I had a lot of patience because had I been anyone else, Danielle would be checking in to the hospital as a patient. The only thing that kept me straight was knowing that if I lost this job, I would have nothing and no way to take care of my daughter.

My entire check went to bills, food and things I needed to buy for Kenya. The check that my mama was getting for her disability went to rent for my small ass apartment because I couldn't cover it along with everything else. I didn't even have a room or a bed of my own to sleep in. The one room in the house went to my mama, who was always complaining about her back, and she shared it with Kenya. I slept on the couch in my own damn apartment just so they could be comfortable. Still, I didn't complain because I knew some way I would be able to change my life and make things better for Kenya, even without her father's help.

After working so hard that my feet were literally swollen from walking around the entire hospital, it was time for lunch. Walking into the locker room, I sat down so I could pull off my shoes and rub my feet before leaving to go to the lunch area. My work shoes were in horrible condition and that's probably why I was so sore now. There were holes and the bottom half was even peeling off. I used superglue to keep it on because I knew if Danielle saw them, she would say she was writing me up for not keeping up with my professional appearance. One day I would replace them but right now I just had too much on me to deal with.

"What are you doing?"

Closing my eyes, I groaned inwardly after hearing the voice behind my back. I was tired and beat down, but even then, Danielle couldn't allow me a few minutes of peace.

"I'm takin' a minute to relax before I go to lunch. I'll be back in thirty minutes to finish up my shift," I told her, keeping my head down so she wouldn't come around and see the look on my face.

Reaching down, I rubbed my foot one last time, wincing from the pain.

"You must either be deaf or dumb," Danielle replied and then walked over in front of where I was sitting. I kept my head down; refusing to look at her because I knew it would make it that much harder to keep my mouth closed.

"You were *late* this morning. That means you don't get a lunch because technically you already took it. Now what you need to do is put them raggedy shoes back on your ugly ass feet and get back to work. I let Brandy go home early so I need you to stay late to cover her shift."

My neck snapped up and I shook my head. There was no way I could stay late because I had to pick up Kenya from daycare. The last time Danielle made me stay late, I asked my mama to get Kenya from daycare and they told me she showed up late and drunk. From that point on, I swore that I wouldn't ask her to do anything for me again. I really wanted to kick her out but I needed her check to help with the rent.

"I can't stay late! I have to pick up my daughter from—"

"Deaf or dumb, once again!" Danielle interrupted with a snap of her neck. "Didn't I tell you that your duties as a mother have nothing to do with your job here? Now if you have life issues affecting your responsibilities, then I'll let you go and hire someone else! You're lazy and sloppy with how you do everything as it is but I keep you on because I'm a good person. Don't make me regret it!"

Dropping my head, I didn't say a word as I started to put back on my shoes while she watched me. It felt like the longest few minutes of my life. I stood up and my stomach growled loudly to which Danielle responded by laughing. She was so fuckin' evil and I didn't really understand why. Most people say that women act that way when they are jealous but that wasn't it. What did I have that Danielle could be jealous about?

"You can start in Mr. Knot's room. He needs changing," Danielle said and I winced.

Mr. Knot was a patient who Cyndy and I referred to as Mr. Nazi, a racist white man who deliberately shitted on himself each day and smiled the entire time one of us had to clean him up. The bigger the mess he could make, the better. He was the one who got my old manager fired after he called her a bitch.

Squeezing my hands into fists, I walked down the hall slowly and recited my mantra, telling myself that I could make it through this day and that I just needed to stay positive.

Instead of getting off at 3 o'clock like I normally did, I left the hospital at 8 o'clock, racing down the road to get to Kenya's daycare. I'd called and let them know I would be late and the daycare owner, Ms. Williams, told me she would stay with Kenya for me. I was grateful and wished I could give her a little something for doing me the favor but I couldn't afford it.

"Thank you, Ms. Williams!" I said, breathing hard after running from the parking lot into the building. My feet were still on fire, making me walk with a limp, but I was happy to finally see my baby.

"No problem, baby, but you're going to have to figure something out because I can't stay this late. Technically, my eyesight is too bad to drive at night so I always leave before the sun goes down."

Ducking my head, I nodded sadly. "I understand, Ms. Williams. I will and I'm sorry. I can follow you home to make sure you get there safely."

Although I'd offered to be nice, I really hoped that she would say no and just go home. But instead, she nodded her head thankfully and began to grab her things. Turning, I reached down and picked Kenya up from where she had been playing with some blocks and other toys and hugged her tight. She smiled at me and that alone made my entire day.

By the time I was pulling into my apartment, it was almost 10 o'clock at night and I had to be back up at 4 in the morning to get ready for work. I drove around and pulled into my parking space, seeing all the lights off in my place even though my mama should have been home. Shrugging, I figured maybe she'd fallen asleep early, and being that I'd had a long ass day, I was happy for that.

Boy, I couldn't have been more wrong.

Just as I was getting Kenya out of her car seat, the front door of my apartment opened up and out popped my mama, her hands on her hips and staring at me with a frown on her face like I'd already pissed her off just by being here.

"The lights off!" she huffed as I started towards her.

"What?" I asked with a frown, walking by her to go through the door. As soon as I was inside the pitch-black living room, I sat Kenya down and flipped a switch to turn on a light. Nothing happened.

"Is there a power outage?" I muttered and then turned around to run out the door and see if the other apartments were dark. I inhaled sharply when I saw that everyone had light shining out of their windows. Every apartment but mine.

"No outage. You didn't pay the damn bill, that's what it is," my mama scowled from behind me. "I missed my stories and Jeopardy because of this shit."

"They told me they were going to give me an extension," I whined, tears stinging my eyes. "I need to call the office."

"No, don't call them!" she said quickly, stunning me.

"Why not?"

"I—I paid the rent but I was a little late," she stammered, eyes darting around as she spoke. "You know it's due on the first but my check don't come in until the first and I gotta cash it… so they just been complaining. If they call, that's why so don't answer. I'll handle it."

Something was off about her statement but I was too tired and overwhelmed to care.

Turning around, I drug my feet as I walked back inside and grabbed Kenya into my arms. Holding her tight as if she were my lifeline. Technically, she was because these days, she was the only reason I even wanted to live. I walked into the kitchen and found some candles, lighting them so that I could see well enough to undress her and wipe her down using some warm water from the faucet in the bathroom. Once I laid her down, I gave myself a cold bath and walked out of the bathroom with my head down and my shoulders slumped. I felt defeated, frustrated and hopeless. Was this the reward I got for just trying to make it in life?

"When are you gonna have the lights back on?" my mama asked, leaning over to look down at me as I tried to get comfortable in my place on the couch. "All that workin' you do at that damn job and you ain't got nothin' to show for it. I think you got some money hidin' somewhere, you just stingy."

"Stingy?!" I snapped, unable to hold my anger back any longer. I'd been biting my tongue all day and my patience had finally ran out. "You think I wanted this to happen? You think I want my baby to come home to a dark ass house?"

"Apparently," was all she said, rolling her eyes as she walked away.

She slammed the door behind her and I turned around, pushed my face into the couch cushions and quietly cried myself to sleep.

I'm Not a Nigga.

Sidney

"I'm goin' out," I told Faviola as I pulled my black skully down on my head, swooping my loose hair into a loose ponytail at the back of my head before sitting down in her room to put on my shoes. Brand new black and white Jordans, clean as hell and yes, I stood in line all damn day to buy these shits as soon as they came out and yes, my ass would do it again. I paired the shoes with some black skinny jeans that sagged a little bit because I ain't like shit gripping my ass, boxer briefs because I didn't do panties, a white tee with a white long-sleeve shirt underneath it and a black and white Nets jacket to finish my look.

Yolo had hit me up asking if I wanted to come chill with him and I was finally ready to go. He had asked me to wear something sexy and that's why I hit my phone with the screw face as soon as I saw the message. I was tired of the dresses and heels shit so this time, I was doing me and fuck everybody who didn't like it. I loved Yolo so much that it hurt but I'd be damned if I let a nigga change me. Well… not for long anyways.

"Yeah, whatever. Go hang wit' yo' boo," Faviola said, with a flick of the wrist without even looking my way. Standing up with her eyes planted down on the screen of her phone, she was about to walk right by me when she stopped, looking me up and down just as I rose up from the chair.

"You wearin' *that*?" she asked, a skeptical frown on her face and I nodded, looking down at my clothes.

"Yeah, what the hell you expect me to wear?" I inquired back, feeling a little offended from how she looked at me. Hell, I was matching and I was killing the game with my unique style so I didn't know what the problem was.

"I thought you was goin' to hang with Yolo and his brothers." Watching her look me up and down again with her nose slightly turned up started messing with me and I got an attitude. In all the years that I've known Faviola, this was how I dressed. I go a few nights looking like a chick and all of a sudden she was here looking at me like I wasn't shit.

"I am!" I snapped back at her, cocking my head to the side.

Pressing her lips together into a vicious duck face, she looked me up and down again, moving her head so that her platinum blond weave shifted right along with it.

"A'ight! Have fun, nigga," she said before turning around and prancing away.

I knew the fact that she added 'nigga' was supposed to be a dig at me but I didn't care. That was the problem with switching the style up on folks. They started to always expect that shit and that's why I was popping up on Yolo looking like the same ole Sidney I'd always been.

Yolo was at his grandmother's house along with his other brothers so I decided to just walk over, even though it was cold as hell outside. She was only a few blocks down and the closer I got, the more excited

I became. Ms. Gloria's house was like a second home to me when I was younger because I used to always go over there to hang out with Yolo. But with age came bullshit and I hadn't been there in a while. I was happy to finally be heading back.

"SID! What it do, nigga!" Tank yelled out as soon as he saw me walking up the sidewalk. Looking up at him, I smiled as I opened up the small gate in front of Ms. Gloria's house.

"What's up, Tank?!" I greeted him, slapping his hand as he held it out to greet me. "I came to hang out wit' y'all crazy asses."

"Aye, as long as you comin' in peace and not wit' that crazy ass broad you be fuckin' wit', I'm good."

"You mean the crazy ass broad *you* be fuckin' wit', fam!" I shot back with a chuckle.

Laughing, he sat back down in his seat and grabbed up the magazine he was using to roll up a blunt. Everyone was there except Outlaw, so I took turns greeting them all, Kane and Cree before settling my eyes on Yolo who was sitting behind them all, his eyes planted on me.

"Wassup, nigga?" I greeted him the same as I did his other brothers and then took a seat right next to him, smiling hard.

"Sup," was all he said. Nothing else. No smile, no nothing. What the fuck?

"Aye, where da fuck is Outlaw's dumb ass at?" Kane piped up and I laughed. He was always fuckin' with Outlaw and I still found it to be hilarious.

"Probably somewhere hidin'. You know his Dolphins lost. His ass owe me some money for that shit," Cree laughed as he sipped from something in a red cup. I looked at it curiously, wanting to try it. I knew it was something Yolo had cooked up.

Turning to Yolo, I looked at him and saw that he was holding a red cup too. I leaned over and looked inside as he stared at me. Pink liquid and it smelled good.

"Aye, can I try?" I asked him and he pushed the cup at me, forcing it into my hands.

"Do ya thing, bruh," he told me.

Bruh?

Totally not feeling his attitude, I turned away and focused on the others as they talked shit, laughing and smoking weed like there was no better place to be. It was like old times when I was a kid and used to hang out with them over the summer. To be honest, I couldn't wait for the summer half the time just so that I could run and fuck up some shit with the Murrays.

"Kane, how my sis-in-law doing, man?" Tank asked and my ears tuned in immediately. Kane had a woman? Hell, I didn't know it! But it wasn't really a surprise that I didn't because Kane kept his personal life private and it had been a minute since I really been around the whole crew.

"Nigga, why you stay tryin' to wife my ass wit' somebody?" Kane replied, laughing as he puffed on a blunt. "I don't kno' how ole girl doin' because I ain't checkin' for her ass and she ain't worried 'bout me either. Just let shit be."

"But what 'bout my niece?" Cree piped up, finally pulling his lips away from his cup long enough to speak. "It would be nice to see my fuckin' niece from time to time. Like, shit, nigga… last time I saw her ass was on Facebook before her fuck ass mama blocked me."

"Yeah, I get my shorties next weekend, all of them," Tank added. "Maybe you can figure somethin' out so they can meet they lil' cuz—"

"Ain't shit I can do, fam. I send her money for my daughter and she send that shit right back to me. She don't want me involved and that's all there is to it. Ain't shit left to be said," Kane said with a hint of finality in his tone, letting everyone know he meant for them not to bring up the subject again.

Damn, I thought as I sipped from Yolo's cup. *Kane's ass got drama too.*

The liquid burned as soon as it touch my lips, like Yolo had mixed some cinnamon shit in it and I gagged, sputtering out coughs before leaning over to spit it right out in the grass in front of us. When I was able to stop coughing, I looked up and saw Cree's eyes were on me, shining as if he was laughing his ass off on the inside.

"You good, fam?" he asked and I started to chuckle, nodding my head.

"Yeah nigga, it's all good. This some strong shit!"

"That's Yolo for ya ass… nigga, stay mixin' up the good shit," Cree added, glancing over at Yolo who didn't say a word in response. This wasn't like him at all. Yolo and Outlaw stayed being the life of the party. It was Cree and Kane who was usually on the silent chill shit.

Suddenly, Cree's phone started to ring and I turned to Yolo, ready to deal with whatever was up with him. He acted like such a damn female sometimes that it was probably good I didn't half the time. Couldn't have both of us acting like we were PMSing over some bullshit. But when I looked at him, my eyes pinned directly in his face, he just kept his focus straight ahead, a deadpan expression; even though I knew his ass could feel me staring.

"Aye, this Outlaw's ass right now," Cree said as he looked at the screen of his phone.

"Tell that nigga to bring his ass," Kane instructed. "I got business to discuss and I want him here."

"A'ight," Cree replied before putting the phone on speaker. "Yo, bruh!"

Aye, bruh! Guess what..." Outlaw started and I turned back to Yolo, ready to get in his ass to see what was up with him while everyone listened to Cree's conversation with Outlaw.

"What is ya problem?!" I asked him, nudging him in the side. "You asked me to come out here and chill just so you could act like this?"

I watched as Yolo clenched his jaw before turning to me, locking his eyes into mine. He wasn't saying a word but I knew him enough to know he was pissed off at me about something. I also knew him well enough to know what it was and that he was about to play it off until later.

"Naw, you good, son," he replied, keeping his eyes on mine. "I just wanted to see if you wanted to chill."

"Son?" I repeated, narrowing my gaze into his. "Is this 'bout the fact that I'm not wearin' a dress? You mad because I came over here expectin' you to be cool wit' me just bein' me?" I pressed my palm to my chest, clearly mad as hell and definitely offended, even though I had suspected this was his issue from jump. There was something about hearing him say it aloud while looking into his eyes that made the pain of realization that much more intense.

"This not 'bout you bein' yaself, Sid!" Yolo said in a low tone, his voice still coarse as he spoke to me. "I don't give a shit 'bout no fuckin' dress and no heels! That shit was nice but it ain't never been you so I kno' you ain't gon' do it all the damn time. But you come out here sittin' wit' ya legs wide open, dappin' niggas up, spittin' and shit, and ya fuckin' boxers showin' like you a damn dude! If I wanna hang out wit' my niggas, I will. But if I wanna hang out wit' my bitch, I wanna hang out with my bitch! And I don't want no bitch who lookin' and actin' like my niggas!"

My mouth fell open as I looked at him, getting increasingly agitated the more he talked. I couldn't believe this shit!

"You didn't have a problem with the way I fuckin' acted back in the day when I used to hang wit' y'all! Back when you was tryin' to hit it!" I barked back, my voice a little more elevated which I would worry about later because at the moment, I didn't give a shit about his brothers hearing me.

Eyes so tight and delivering a glare right into my face that was piercing enough to make the dead shudder, Yolo jumped up, grabbing at his pants that were so baggy, they almost fell off his waist. He was in Brooklyn and still on that baggy southern shit like he was still in

Miami... but did I say anything about it? Nope!

"I wasn't worried 'bout that shit because I was a fuckin' kid! I grew the fuck up, Sid, and it's some shit I don't do no fuckin' more! Yo' ass need to grow the fuck up too!" he shot at me, delivering one final hard stare before walking over to his brothers who were sitting in dead silence, smoking and sipping even though I knew they'd heard all that shit.

"Aye yo, I'm out," Yolo announced, slapping hands with Cree, Kane and then Tank before turning to leave just as Outlaw ran up to the gate. Yolo stopped for a second to greet his youngest brother, then hopped in his ride, cranked it up and drove off, without saying a single word at me. God, why did I deal with this shit?!

"SID!" Outlaw yelled as he walked out, his hands out with a big ass grin on his face. "Yo' nigga, wassup!"

"I ain't no nigga!" I snapped back at him, grabbing my things, which wasn't much else beyond a small backpack I kept a few things in.

Looking up, I saw Outlaw's face drop along with his arms as he looked at his brothers for some clarity at what was wrong with me. None of them said a thing so he shrugged and came up with his own reason for my attitude.

"Yolo must ain't hittin' it right," he smirked and shrugged before walking up the stairs and plopping down in the seat Yolo had been in. "I saw yo' ass in that dress you had on the other day at the club. If you need a nigga to knock that attitude out ya ass the *right* way, give me a call. Most times, I'm right next door. I just be over there chillin' and shit."

Neglecting the fact that he was usually next door 'chillin' and shit' with another damn woman, he leaned over and grabbed the blunt from Cree and stuck it between his lips, puffing nonchalantly as I stared at him. Niggas ain't shit. No wonder Yolo acted the way he did with me. Look at who his brother was!

"Naw, I'm good on that shit, yo," I told him as I walked down the steps. "And I like Janelle." I gave him a look, letting him know that I wasn't about to fall game to his shit.

"Word?" he piped up, his brows shooting straight up in the air. "Then she should be able to vouch for a nigga because I got her ass straight too! That's what's up!"

Grumbling, I rolled my eyes and walked away, feeling defeated as hell as they all poked fun at Outlaw. I could hear them speaking but my mind was on Yolo and I was still fuming. Why I let him affect me in this way, I had no idea but I couldn't help it. He made me feel weak and I hated that shit. But no matter how much I felt about it, I knew that as long as I was around him, he'd always have a power over me until I was strong enough to officially be sick of his shit. I just needed to do what I was doing before and stay the fuck out of his way.

Reckless.

Outlaw

"*D*amn, Sid done changed. Her ass 'bout as moody and shit as my chick. She used to be fun back in the day," I grumbled before taking another hit of the blunt. Shit was raggedy as hell and I could tell Tank rolled it. Baby makin' ass couldn't roll a decent blunt for shit.

"Yo' chick?" Cree piped up, cutting his eyes to me. "So you done made it official wit' the D.A. chick?"

"D.A.?" Kane asked, but I ignored him, already picking up his mood when I walked up and saw his ass eyeballing a nigga like he wanted to start busting on me for being late. I was a grown ass man!

"Naw, but I been fuckin' wit' her mind because the shit is hilarious to me seeing her get mad," I laughed, thinking about how Janelle had gone off on me after Carmella walked in on us fuckin'. Why she tried to blame me, I really didn't know because she was the one who had missed the call saying her sister was on the way. But I still let her go off for a minute before I flipped it right on her ass, pissing her off further before pushing up on her while she was in the shower. She was weird as hell but that was my baby though.

"You need to end that shit," Kane said with his authoritative tone, like he could really tell me what to fuckin' do. I hated that shit.

"End what, nigga?" I asked, giving him a hard look as he stayed focused on nothing in particular, looking ahead as he tapped his fingers on the armrest of his seat.

"End that fake ass shit you got goin' on with the D.A. bitch," he clarified before turning to me. "She already causin' problems. You stayed with her before the last hit and your mind wasn't in it. Real shit, we all know you the reason why Benny got shot. Our lil' cuz coulda been killed behind that shit. Ya fuckin' problem is that you don't fuckin' think, Luke! You already got us wrapped up in enough shit as it is! We got enough eyes on us as it is! This why I'm always on yo' ass because you stay doin' some reckless shit!"

Gritting my teeth, I turned away from him, looking straight ahead and noting that my grandmother's car wasn't in the driveway. Good thing because I already knew it was going to be some shit. Kane was the oldest of us all but that didn't make his ass my fuckin' daddy no matter how much he tried to act like he was. He could pull that shit on Cree, Yolo and Tank with no problem, but me and Tone never listened to his ass like that. Times like these, I missed the shit out of Tone because he would always stand up for me when Kane started trying to shine on a nigga.

"Listen, yo," I began, voice tight but low, because believe it or not, I didn't really want to get shit started. "You can't tell me what to fuckin' do, bruh. I done told you that shit. I respect what you feel but I'm a grown ass man and I stick my dick where I please *when* I please."

"Why can't y'all just chill wit' this shit, yo?" Cree started, trying to be the peacemaker between us as usual. "Not today, man. We got business to discuss and y'all on some bullshit."

"Fuck naw," Kane started, shaking his head. "We ain't got no business to discuss. I ain't discussin' shit wit' that nigga around. When he get rid of that bitch then we can get back to business but I ain't gettin' locked up behind that stupid ass nigga."

Cree and Tank both groaned but I only got even more heated. Here he was again, trying to make it seem like I was the weak one of the crew, like I was the constant fuck up. Yolo's ass wasn't even here but Kane ain't say shit when he walked out because he was so focused on the fact that I was late. Now he wanted to go and say some fucked up shit to make it seem like I didn't know how to conduct myself when it came to business. This was some bullshit.

"I'm out," I said, putting out the blunt before stuffing it in my pocket. Cree stood up and held his hands out like he wanted to stop me but I moved out the way, shaking my head.

"Naw, let his pussy ass go, Dent," Kane said and that was all I needed. I fuckin' snapped. Eyes tight, face screwed up and hands balled up into fists, I turned to Kane, ready to fuck some shit up if he said the wrong damn thing

"Ya know what? *Fuck* you, you bitch ass nigga. Always got some shit to say!" I gritted on him, standing my ground in front of him. Kane jumped up, nearly bumping my chest, standing with his fists to his side, staring me dead in my eyes. I looked right back at him, begging him to do some shit I ain't like.

"Get da fuck out of here before I beat yo' muthafuckin' ass, Luke!" he yelled, bumping against my chest but I ain't move one bit as I glared back at him.

"What you waitin' on nigga?" I questioned through my teeth, my tone dripping with venom as we glared into each other's eyes. "I ain't takin' no mo' ass whoopings, bruh. I put that on God. Try that shit though, dawg!"

Kane held my eyes, for a beat. We weren't saying anything, but in that moment, I knew he understood me and I understood him. I wasn't the same nigga that was gonna let him knock me on my shit and take it for the sake of not causing nothing between my brothers. Those days were now gone.

"Cree, get his ass up outta here," Kane said finally, backing up with his glare still holding mine. "'Fore I fuck his lil' ass up."

Kane wasn't gon' do shit and he knew it, but I'd let him have the last word this time because I knew the truth.

"Naw, let me walk wit'cha, bruh," Tank said and stood up to leave with me. I dapped Cree up and turned around to leave with Tank right behind me. I was close with all my brothers, even Kane although we fought most of the time, but Cree and I were closest so I knew that Tank had a reason for wanting to take his place.

"You gotta kill that attitude, nigga," Tank started as soon as we were a little down the street from my grandma's house. "Kane don't mean no harm and you kno' that shit."

"Fuck dat nigga," I shot back, still pissed off. "He always on my ass 'bout some shit. Yolo wasn't even fuckin' there and Kane ain't say shit to him when he left. But he wanna fuck wit' me over some silly shit."

"He got a reason for this shit. Believe that. Kane ain't fuckin' wit' you for no reason. You kno' when you get in trouble, he the main one tryin' to get your ass out. He just don't want you to get caught up in any mess. You know you our baby bro," Tank said with a teasing smile. I cut my eyes at him because he knew I hated that shit. I wasn't a baby nothing.

"Yeah, I feel ya. He still can cool off wit' dat shit though. Real talk."

We walked in silence, both of us in our own thoughts until we got to the corner where Janelle lived. I thought for a minute about walking up to see what she was getting into for the day but then decided against it.

"What's goin' on wit'chu and this lawyer chick, nigga?" Tank asked me and I shrugged.

"Ain't shit really. She cool peoples but that's it," I told him nonchalantly.

"She must be more than that for you to go off on Kane when he said to leave her alone," Tank replied, and gave me a knowing look like he could tell there was more to the story. He was right but I wasn't ready to admit it just so he could side with Kane.

"Naw, it ain't that. That was 'bout respectin' me as a man. He can't tell me shit 'bout who I choose to chill with. That's all."

"That's true shit," Tank said with a nod of his head before dapping me up and turning around. "I'll get up wit' you later on. 'Bout to go check on my baby mama hoe ass."

Smirking, I looked at him as he walked up the stairs to the apartment across from Janelle's where Faviola stayed. He was trying to play it off and act like he couldn't stand her but I could see through the shit. Tank may not have been happy about the fact that she was pregnant but he was definitely still messin' around with her and everybody knew it.

"Make sure you strap up, nigga," I told him, smiling hard because I knew I was about to fuck with his head.

"Ain't no point in doin' that shit now! She already pregnant," Tank replied, saying exactly what I knew he would.

"Yeah but you said she a hoe. Don't wanna catch no shit."

Whipping around, Tank frowned hard and I could see him getting pissed off just at the idea of Faviola possibly being with another nigga.

"Fuck that shit. She holdin' my seed in her so her ass is off limits until further notice, fam," Tank retorted and I tried to hold in a laugh. "But on some real shit though… you heard somethin'? She been fuckin' with another nigga?"

Chuckling, I shook my head as I looked at him about to snap over a chick he swore he couldn't stand. I wasn't the only one putting on to save face.

"Naw man, I ain't heard nothin' 'bout ya girl. I'll catch up wit' you later, bruh," I told him and he relaxed instantly.

Before I jumped in my whip, I looked over at Janelle's house, wondering if I should stop by before leaving. Then I shook my head and got in the car, deciding to leave her be for now. I was feeling her and it was getting to a point where I didn't want it to be because neither one of us were ready to face the consequences of being together. She wanted to be a criminal attorney and I was shoulders deep into the street life. The two didn't match and no matter how much fun we had together, it never would.

Kane was right. With chicks like Janelle, things would always be dangerous because she wasn't the 'I'll die for my nigga' type. No matter how much she might love my ass, if it ever came down to her turning on me or getting locked up, her ass would sing like a canary. And I didn't even want to put her in that position where she'd have to choose.

Still…

While sitting in my car with the engine off, looking at Janelle's window, my phone rang. Grabbing it, I answered immediately, seeing it was her calling.

"Why are you sittin' outside?" she asked me as soon as I answered the call, and I couldn't help missing her as soon as I heard her voice. See, this is the shit that I didn't like. This is why I needed to stop spending so much time over here with her ass. She had me thinking and feeling crazy shit. Just the sound of her voice did something to me. She made me want to just say fuck it all and forget about all the reasons why we couldn't work. And that's why she was so dangerous.

"'Bout to leave. Just walked back over," I told her as I ran my hand over my face and sighed.

"I saw you when you came back over with your brother," she replied, her voice soft and quiet on the other line. "I was just wondering if you were coming back in because I—I was thinking of leaving out."

"To go where?" I asked, feeling a tight feeling in my chest for some reason. She sighed and I knew already what that meant.

"I don't know… I just didn't want to be alone. May see what

Carmella is up to. I thought you were going to be with your brothers all night. But… if you want to come up, I'll stay in with you."

The way she said it, with her tone dropping as she added the little part at the end, let me know that what she really wanted was to stay with me. She was basically letting me know that all I had to do was say the word and she would be mine for the night. I couldn't think of anything better that I wanted to do at the moment.

"Yeah… I'm comin' up."

When she didn't respond immediately, I felt my body go tense.

"Door's unlocked," she finally said and I could hear her smiling through the phone before I pulled it away and hung up. Sitting in the car, I almost wanted to curse my damn self out for allowing her to step in and change the course of my actions so suddenly. I had just said I needed more distance between Janelle and myself and here I was again, agreeing to lie up under her ass for the rest of the night.

Shit.

Going in Janelle's house, I halfway expected her to be standing on the other side of the door in some sexy lingerie that my manhood was already approving of just from the image that ran through my mind. But when I walked in, I saw her in the kitchen popping popcorn in some sweatpants and a tank top, looking effortlessly sexy with her hair in a messy bun at the top of her head. Her ass was sitting up nice in the sweats and I knew it was because I have been hitting her from behind every night. She was filling out nicely, hips spreading and some more shit that made me lose it whenever I looked at her. Damn, she was so fuckin' fine to me, which was crazy because that's not what I'd been thinking when I'd first seen her. I was intrigued by her, and yeah, she looked good but that wasn't what had initially drawn me to her. What I'd been attracted to was deeper than the physical.

"What we doin'?" I asked as I walked up in the kitchen behind her, wrapping my arms around her stomach.

"Watchin' a movie. I'm getting the popcorn ready," she said and turned her head a little, trying to hide her smile but I caught it anyways.

"Oh so this yo' way of makin' it up to me that you wanted to bail on me to see a movie wit' that goofy lookin' nigga?"

Bashful, she dropped her head and her smile spread as she nodded her head. I knew she was really feeling a nigga and this right here proved it.

The movie was straight, even though it was too girly for me. Wasn't no real shootin' or nothing but it was funny as hell... some movie with Kevin Hart and Ice Cube in it. Cube used to be a straight goon and now he was doin' family movies and shit, jokin' and actin' a fool with Kevin Hart. That shit cracked me up.

"Movie over," I announced with a grin as I walked over and turned off the TV "Time to go to the room."

Janelle rolled her eyes and held her hand up to stop me. "Not tonight, Luke. I just wanna relax. I gotta get up early to go to work in the morning!"

"Ain't tryin' to hear it," I told her and then scooped her straight up from the couch, tossing her over my shoulders. She screamed and started squirming around but it was half-assed because she knew she didn't really want to go anywhere.

As soon as we got into the room, clothes came off. We were all over that bed, enjoying each other's bodies. Janelle wasn't the thickest girl I ever been with, she wasn't the freakiest and it wasn't like she was introducing me to some new shit that I ain't never tried. But the difference with her was that shit just *felt* different. I've gotten bomb head so many times I can't even fuckin' count it, but it was something about seeing Janelle's lips wrapped around my shit that made a nigga... Damn, she drove me fuckin' insane.

"Aye, I'mma go outside for a minute," I told her once we were finished. She moaned out a response and rolled over in the bed, pulling the covers over her head as I got dressed. I kept my eyes on her as I put my shoes on, loving the outline of her body under the sheet. Shit... did I really say 'loving'? I mean... she looked a'ight.

"Hey nigga, what you doin' out here?"

Sitting on Janelle's front stoop, smoking an L, I turned around and saw my brother Tank walking out of the apartment next door. I wasn't even surprised to see him there. He talked shit all the time about Faviola but look where his ass was at. The whole thing seemed crazy to me too because Tank talked all that shit bout her but was forever spending the night with her. Whether he admitted it or not, there was something about her ass that had him stuck.

"Needed to smoke one and Nell get an attitude 'bout a nigga lightin' up in her spot," I told him as he took a seat right next to me. "Figured I'd chill outside for a minute."

"Favi don't even give a shit if I light up right next to her ass," he said, scoffing as he took the blunt. "Bitch pregnant and still think it's a'ight for her to smoke weed and shit. I'mma end up fuckin' her ass up one day."

Shaking my head, I didn't reply as I reached in my pocket and pulled out my phone. When I was with Janelle, the shit stayed on silent because I didn't want no other bitch blowing me up and messing up our vibe. Scrolling through my missed calls, I saw that Kane had hit me up a few times before leaving a message for me to call him when I got a chance. I knew he wanted to talk about shit from earlier but I wasn't feeling it.

"Kane call you?" Tank said and I nodded my head. That was Kane's M.O. As the big brother, he never liked for something to happen between us and we slept on that shit. He always wanted to clear everything up before we started a new day.

"Yeah but I ain't feelin' callin' that nigga back for another lecture. I'm good on that, bruh."

Tank blew out a breath and then adjusted on the seat, clearing his throat. I glanced at him out the side of my eye and I knew that he was about to start up, defending his brother. Tank and Kane were close and he always had his back.

"Man, listen… there is some shit that Kane won't tell you but I will because I'm tired of y'all niggas fightin' all the damn time," he started. "The reason Kane is so hard on you because out of all of us, you and Tone are the most alike and neither one of y'all niggas listen. Only difference was that Tone was smooth with his shit. He was stubborn as hell but he was chill wit' it. Yo' ass on the other hand, got a fucked up temper and a big ass mouth." He cut his eyes at me and I shrugged. No point in denying the obvious.

"Just like how Kane rides your ass, he used to do the same to Tone which is why that nigga was always takin' up for your ass. On the night that Tone was murdered, him and Kane had a fight 'bout these new niggas Tone started hangin' with. Kane didn't trust them cats but you know that ain't sayin' much because Kane don't trust no damn body. Anyways, Kane told him to stop hangin' wit' them niggas and they startin' fightin'. You remember that shit?"

Pressing my lips together, I nodded my head. I remembered that shit vividly and just thinking about it had my chest burning. It was the last time I saw my nigga alive.

"I remember that shit. Them niggas almost came to blows over that shit."

"Right," Tank said and then sucked his teeth as he shook his head. "Them niggas found out where Tone kept his stash at, robbed his ass and left him with a bullet in the fuckin' chest. Nobody even called Kane to tell him Tone was gone. He woke up in the middle of the night, knowin' somethin' was wrong. By the time he got to Tone's spot, he was gone."

Bowing my head, my throat went tight as I listened to Tank speak about the night my brother was murdered. Yeah, I'm hard and shit but if it had to do with my family, it fucked with me and I couldn't hold that shit back. Tone was my blood and every time I think on the fact that he died alone without none of us there to help him, it messed me up inside.

"Bruh, the only reason Kane so hard on you is because you and

Tone the same," Tank continued as I got myself together. "He takes the shit that happened to Tone personally because he felt like he didn't do enough to stop him and make him see that them niggas he was wit' was foul. Kane takes the blame for his death and every time he sees you doin' that typical crazy shit you on, it scares the shit out of that nigga, thinkin' that you either gon' get locked up or worst and he won't be able to help you. He's just tryin' to keep your mind right."

Shaking my head, I understood but I still wasn't feeling it. "Yeah. But I'm not Tone. And I'm not a dumb nigga... I know who to fuck wit' and who not to fuck wit' without Kane dictatin' that shit to me."

"Yet, you the one fuckin' wit' the same damn chick that was just tryin' to get you locked up for life not too long ago," Tank countered, staring at the side of my head. I glanced at him, catching his eyes but then looked away, not really wanting to hear no shit about Janelle.

"She ain't like that, bruh," I told him, swallowing hard.

"But how you kno' what she like? You think you can trust her enough to let her know what we do? She ever even been to yo' spot? Seen where you lay yo' head when you not here? She ever met Grandma? She live right around the damn corner... you told Janelle where she lives? You ain't even really told her 'bout us, huh?"

I stayed silent, knowing exactly where Tank was going with all his questions.

"The reason you don't tell her nothing worth tellin' is because you don't trust her. You got feelings for her, but deep down, you know your ass is dead wrong 'bout what you doin'. You know that you puttin' the rest of us at risk by fuckin' around with her. You know Kane is right."

Licking my lips, I didn't say shit because Tank had pulled my damn card. As much as I felt for Janelle and as much as I liked being around her, I couldn't put all of my trust in her. What we had didn't leave her apartment, meaning the only thing she knew about me was whatever she found out while I was there. I didn't tell her shit about anything that went on with me outside of her apartment, she didn't know where I went when I left, who I hung with, nothin' 'bout my family outside of knowin' that I had a lot of brothers. And only reason she really knew that was because we all rode up on her at her spot when her roommate had that party over there. She didn't know shit because I knew better than to tell her shit.

"I'm just havin' a little fun," I told Tank, sighing as I prepared to stand up and head back inside. The cold wind was whipping furiously like it had beef with my ass, chilling me straight to the bone, but that wasn't the real reason I was going back in. Tank was spitting some real shit that I had been thinking about but just wasn't ready to deal with.

"Well, have yo' fun, bruh, and end that shit. You know Pelmington on our ass 'bout that last hit and we got another job comin' up. Wise up, nigga."

After dapping up my brother, I walked back inside of Janelle's spot, my mind fucked up in a way that it had never been before. Not when it came to a female. In the past, whenever I needed to get rid of a bitch, I got rid of her ass… no questions asked. I kept my feelings out of everything mainly because I had never come across anyone who made me want to do anything different. I guess you could chuck that up to the type of chicks I usually went for. My normal type were more like

Carmella, Janelle's sister. Banging bodies, not much to the personality, loved when a nigga threw a lil' money at them, low-key wild as hell and freaky as shit. But for some reason, I actually liked hangin' with Janelle's weird ass.

When I walked into the room, Janelle was snoring loud as hell, her mouth wide open, wrapped up in the covers and leaving none for me with her unsharing ass. Chuckling, I snatched the sheets off her body and watched her face twist up in annoyance right before she groaned.

"Damn, Luke, why you always doin' that shit? You know I don't like it," she mumbled as she reached out for the edge of the sheet near her and pulled it over her body. Smirking, I snatched it off again and this time her eyes shot wide open.

"LUKE!" she yelled, sitting up in the bed as she frowned at me, her eyes narrowed. She looked so damn cute when she was pissed off.

"Get that ass in the air, nigga. I'm ready for round two," I joked right before diving into the bed, kicking my sweats off. She rolled her eyes as I pulled my shirt off my head but I knew she wanted it because she just sat there and watched me, lust in her eyes when she licked her lips. My eyes went to them and I no longer had the energy to hide my need for her from showing through in my face.

"Take that shit off."

My tone was low, thick and filled with my urgent need to feel her as I pulled at the waistband of her panties. Cocking her head to the side, she smiled and shook her head softly. She was on some games but I had one for her ass.

Pushing her down flat on the bed, I situated myself right between her legs and pushed her thighs open. Flicking my tongue out of my mouth, I started tickling her clit through the thin lace fabric, my dick getting hard when I heard the way that she moaned in response. Her thighs spread wider and I snatched at the lace material that was blocking me from getting to my prize, pulling hard until I snatched them right off.

"Luke!" she whined but I didn't hesitate, diving right in tongue-first, licking and sucking everything in sight. She arched her back deep, pushing her pussy into my face and I responded by sucking even more, sticking my fingers inside. Shit, she was wet as fuck.

Leaning up, I slipped on a condom and then wasted no time, pushing right inside of her with one thrust. She gasped, moving her hips to adjust to my size right before I started rocking her body, gently at first and then harder and harder. Janelle wrapped her legs around my waist, pulling me closer into her as I looked down, watching her many fuck faces. That shit turned me on, watching her bite her lips and moan for more.

"Cum for me, baby," I ordered, jabbing her harder, just the way I knew she liked it. As expected, her face twisted up and her body began to shudder as she grabbed onto my shoulders, tightening her legs around my waist. She gritted her teeth, trying to hold in a scream but I thrust even harder into her, wanting her to let that shit out.

"FUCK, Luke!" she shrieked, gripping me hard just as her body started to shake, pussy muscles contracting and gripping my dick, making it hard as hell for me to hold out.

"Shit!" I gritted and pushed my face into her neck, holding her tight as I felt the nut building up inside of me. My grip hard on her body, I fucked her even harder as she raised her hips and fucked me back, both of us on the verge of an orgasm. She came first, biting me hard on my shoulder as she moaned into my skin. I came right behind her, holding her so tight, I wondered afterwards if I'd hurt her.

Collapsing on the bed, I pulled the condom off, swiped my hair from out of my face and tried to catch my breath while wondering if she had it in her to go again. My dick was still hard and I couldn't think of anybody else I'd rather give it to than her.

But then something happened to end that shit quick.

I Love You Not.

Janelle

Once again, I was choosing Luke over my job but I didn't care at all. I had to be to work in hours but here I was messing with his ass.

Rolling over, I put my back to him as I yawned, ready to fall back to sleep until my alarm clock said otherwise. But then he grabbed me from behind, pushing his hips into me so that his dick was sliding down the crack of my ass. I giggled pushing back slightly. I was teasing him but I needed to stop. Luke didn't take teasing too well and if I kept it up, he would really try to slide right on up in there.

"Stop, Luke!" I giggled when he reached down and positioned himself right at the entrance of my ass. I pushed him away and then turned around, nudging him even harder.

A'ight, nigga," he told me and lay down. "I'll save that for another day."

Watching him lay next to me with his eyes closed, I felt an overwhelming feeling come over me. I couldn't believe that I was here… lying next to this man who I had hated the second I laid eyes on him for the first time. He was so different from anything or anyone I'd ever been with but every second I realized I was falling deeper and deeper for him. Turning around, I put my back to him and took a deep breath, finally realizing that my feelings for him were stronger than I really cared to admit. Still, I knew the truth.

"I love you," I said before I even realized the words had come from my lips. I actually regretted them as soon as they were said; wishing I could go back in time and snatch each word from my mind as soon as I'd thought them. But it was out there… may as well deal with it.

"Huh?" Luke replied, and I felt his body shift next to mine. Maybe he didn't hear me… maybe I actually don't have to deal with it. I closed my eyes and went completely still, my first instinct to pretend that I'd fallen asleep just that quickly. I don't know why I thought he'd go for it. This was Luke 'Outlaw' Murray, and though he was a lot of things, he definitely wasn't stupid.

"You love me? You meant to say that shit?"

I mused. Did I? Did I mean to say it? I really had to stop and think about it for a minute because I truly didn't know. No, that's a lie. I did know. I wanted to say it. I wanted to scream it from the mountain tops, tell the world that I'd finally found love. True love made you feel that way but the problem was that I wasn't sure I wanted him to know it just yet. Exhaling, I bit down hard on my bottom lip and then decided to just own up to it.

"Luke… I think I love you," I said finally, forming a slight frown as I tried to push the words out. The room went completely silent around me. Both of us lay in the bed, looking into each other's eyes unmoving and not speaking, almost like we weren't breathing. Then Luke closed his eyes and sighed heavily, running his hand over his face. My heart dropped as I watched him. This was not the reaction I expected.

"You can't love me, ma," he said, crushing my heart and soul. "That's not what this can be about."

I pulled away from him, my movement sharp just like the pain in my chest. Fighting, I tried to keep my face straight, keep my emotions at bay. It shouldn't have been this hard. That was my M.O. I was Janelle Pickney and I was *always* in control, *always* thought ahead and planned out everything that I did so I *always* knew how to react. But this... this was not anything close to what I expected when I decided to tell Luke I loved him.

"What do you mean?" I heard myself ask, although I didn't need him to repeat it. I didn't even want him to repeat it but it was like I couldn't help asking, even though I knew that as soon as he said it again, it would be like delivering another round of stabs to my heart.

"I mean that you can't love me, Nell," he told me, standing up. Watching him, I saw as he walked around the room and grabbed his clothes, putting them on while trying to avoid my stare. His jaw was clenched tight like he was angry about something but I didn't understand. What about love was there to be angry about? Feeling panicked, I tried another angle, eager to make sense of this situation that I was struggling to understand.

"But I thought that we—"

"The only thing we got is what's in this room," he said, shaking his head before finally placing his eyes in mine. "We fuck, we chill and that's it. But beyond that it's nothing, love. We both knew when we started this shit that it couldn't go anywhere beyond this apartment. You've said that yourself. Don't mess up a good thing. Let's just have fun while it lasts and keep our feelings out of it."

Luke put on the rest of his clothes and then grabbed his keys off his dresser before walking slowly over to me. I was still on the bed, in the same spot, same position, trying to get my heart to understand what my brain was already beginning to comprehend. Leaning down, Luke kissed me softly on the top of my head, right on my hairline, and then turned around and walked away. Leaving me alone without saying a word.

***

The next morning, the first thing I did was check the news to see if there was anything about a bank robbery or a large sum of money stolen. I was looking for anything to explain why Luke had left so abruptly after I told him how I felt about him. I was hoping that maybe he'd deliberately picked a fight with me again because he had a reason. Any reason other than the fact that he really didn't love me.

But there was nothing.

After searching through channel after channel, I was left realizing that everything was exactly what it seemed it was. I'd confessed my feelings to a man who didn't care about me and he left me alone. Being the type of person I was, I tried to get myself to understand that and accept it for what it was. I had to shrug that shit off and move on. But how?

"Hello?"

"Hey Mixie." I smiled into the phone once I heard the voice of my younger sister. Of all of us, Mixie was the therapist. She was the one who you could actually talk to and know she was going to give out good advice. Carmella was the one you spoke to if you wanted a friend who was going to tell you what you probably shouldn't do but support you while you did it. She was the type of friend who would hand you the box-cutter to flatten tires or pick out the sharpest keys on the keyring to go scratch up somebody's shit.

"Dang, I thought you forgot about me," Mixie said, and I could hear her smiling through her tone. Just her voice was relaxing. She reminded me so much of our mother in so many ways… not just looks but even her overall presence.

"Never that. I've just been busy," I told her and paused as thoughts of Luke immediately came to my mind. Tears came to my eyes and I sighed, trying to blink them away. I was failing miserably at not thinking about that man.

"What's wrong?" Mixie asked, even though I hadn't even told her that anything was going on. That was just how she was.

I swore she was clairvoyant because she knew things without anyone telling her half the time. When we were little, Mixie would just walk up to people and hug them, even people she never met. For my parents, it drove them crazy. But after a while of hearing people tell her how much they needed her hug, we all realized that was just Mixie. She was caring and she knew when people needed her.

"I was dating this guy and…" I paused, wondering how much I should really tell her about Luke. "…and he's different. Not my normal type at all and he's wrong for me in every way. But I fell for him anyways. Then yesterday I told him I loved him and…"

It was too painful to continue. Just thinking about it hurt but saying it seemed nearly impossible.

"He didn't say it back," Mixie finished for me.

"He said that all we have is sex and everything else is what it is. He doesn't want more than what we have." I sniffed and wiped a tear from my cheeks, hating that I was getting so emotional.

"I'm so sorry, Jani," Mixie said, using the nickname that my mother had given me and my sisters also used sometimes. "But… think about the first thing you said to me. He's not your normal type and he's wrong for you in every way. Maybe him saying that is a good thing, because deep down, you know that the relationship isn't right. It's fun but that's all it needs to be. Just loosen up, have a fling, keep your emotions out of it and then eventually move on with a guy that actually deserves you. Let him be your fun thing."

My fun thing? Was it possible to back track and make someone who meant so much be reduced to a meaningless fling? I was doubtful.

Still, I knew that every word that Mixie said was exactly what I needed to hear. It was the same thing that I'd told myself before, but it just seemed different coming from another person. It was almost like confirmation of what I already knew. I wasn't supposed to be with Luke, *never* should have even entertained the idea. I couldn't bring him home to my father or to meet my sisters. He was and should have always been just a fling.

"Thank you, Mixie. I—"

I stopped short when I heard a man's voice in the background telling Mixie something that I couldn't understand but it made her giggle. Like a girlish giggle that is reserved for the man you're messing with.

"Mixie… who is that?!" I paused and frowned into the phone. I talked to my sisters regularly and not once had Mixie ever mentioned that she was dating someone. Not ever in life. I'd had a couple serious relationships but Mixie hadn't had any as far as we knew. I wasn't even positive that she wasn't still a virgin.

"That's my fun thing," she said with another giggle and my jaw dropped, leaving my mouth wide open. "I'll call you later, sis. But remember what I said!"

And with that, she hung up the phone, leaving me shocked and speechless. Seconds later, Carmella came waltzing into the living room, wearing a bra and short silk pajama shorts, humming a tune to herself. When she saw the stricken look on my face, she paused, bunching her eyes together before walking over.

"What's up with you?" she asked, a half-smile on her face before she plopped down on the sofa next to me. I pulled myself out of my trance and placed my cellphone down on my lap.

"I was just talking to Mixie. She had a man over there." Carmella just stared at me, no expression at all on her face. "Like a real man who she's…" Like a child, I made the symbol for sex with my hands, forming an 'o' with one hand and sticking my pointer finger through it.

Laughing, Carmella rolled her eyes and shook her head.

"She's fucking," Carmella brashly said for me. "You can say the word, Janelle. I saw Outlaw creep out of here last night. You're gettin' your share of dick too."

Running my hand over the top of my head, I pushed my hair

away from my face and sighed.

"I just didn't know she wasn't still a virgin."

Carmella rolled her eyes once again and gave me a look that made me feel like I was the most clueless person on the planet.

"Mixie lost her virginity a long time ago. Like you, she's a closet freak. She's probably worse than you because she flips men faster than me." She laughed, seeing the look on my face. I was totally surprised at everything that she was saying. So my little sister was hoeing around all this time and I had no idea.

"When Outlaw comes back can you ask him if he really told Cree I'm here?" Carmella asked, her voice tinged with longing. "I haven't heard from him and—"

Her face balled up into a frown that formed worry lines in the middle of her forehead as she looked away. I could tell she was really feeling Cree even though everything she told me about him seemed to be reasons why she shouldn't like him. Whatever they had seemed to be just as crazy as whatever Luke and I had going on.

"I don't know if Luke will be over here anymore," I told her, trying to keep my face neutral. She lifted her head and gave me a funny look, staring deep into my eyes as if she was trying to read my thoughts.

"He was just here… y'all broke up?"

Shaking my head, I sighed and looked away, begging for the tears to not come.

"We were never together," I confided. "And that's how he wants it to stay."

Silence passed between us and I knew that Carmella was processing what I was saying, understanding even the words that I was not saying.

"Well, the best way to get over one nigga is to get on top of another one!" she said with a shrug before standing up to walk into the kitchen. "That guy from your job is the perfect pick too. Call him up and tell him to come over tonight. Once you let him get all up in that thing, you will be asking me 'Luke who?'"

She laughed and I pressed my lips together in disapproval. The last thing I wanted to do was hop right into the bed with another man. Especially not one I worked with. But, like I said, Carmella was the one who always told you what you shouldn't do.

Then again… she was partially right. The best way for me to stop thinking about Luke would be to start spending some time with Chris. I didn't have to move all that quickly but I could at least take him up on his offer for a date, right?

With my phone in my hand, I pressed on the message icon so I could send him a message. In the process of scrolling, I paused, staring at Luke's name. Against my better judgement, I clicked it and began to read over the last message he'd sent to me.

Luke: Send me the name of this 'church' you goin' to.

Me: Why? You wanna come and catch the Holy Ghost?

Luke: Idk what that is but somebody gon' catch a fade, a bullet and a shallow grave if I see you smilin' in some goofy ass nigga's face.

Me: LMAOOOOOOO!

I found myself smiling after reading those messages, thinking about how jealous Luke had acted when he drove up and saw me talking outside to another guy. That wasn't how someone acted if they didn't care, right? Oh God, I was doing the typical woman thing and searching for answers I wanted, instead of seeing things as they were. The ego will tell you that there is no way someone couldn't love you even after they've said it and proved it, making you focus on trying to find evidence of love in that one person while ignoring another who only has his eyes on you. Luke had thrown me away and Chris was begging for a chance, but I couldn't even pay attention to Chris because I was so consumed by a man who didn't want me. Sometimes the heart was a piece of shit.

Even still, I couldn't help feeling like I needed to wait. I couldn't message Chris just yet. Somewhere deep inside, I felt like things between Luke and I weren't exactly finished and I wasn't ready to spend time with anyone else until I knew for sure he'd let me go.

Bad Habits.

Carmella

I was sitting at the bar of one of the hottest clubs in the city, enjoying a drink and looking fine as hell, not worrying about a damn thing. Definitely wasn't worried about Cree, even though I was feeling some type of way about the fact that Outlaw had told him that I was in town, and I still hadn't heard a single thing from his ass.

See, that's the shit I don't like. I was sexy as fuck. No man in the history of the world had ever told me no when it came to anything. I'd even been known to pull a few gay guys in the past and make them reconsider being with a woman because I was just that fine! But beyond that, I was smart as hell. Fuck what they thought, this body came with brains, I came from a good family and a bitch had my *own* money. What man could resist that? Obviously, Cree's dumb ass.

Maybe he was gay. Yeah, that had to be it. Naaaawwwww, let me stop right there. The way that his ass handled all my juiciness in the bed told me that nigga *definitely* was not gay. He was just stupid. Obviously.

"Bitch, you probably the finest thang in this damn place. Well, next to me anyways," Bryan said as he pursed his lips and sat in the seat next to me, looking fly as hell.

Bryan was the guy who had asked for Cree to take our pictures at the club a few months back before Cree went the fuck off and showed his ass. Since I'd been in Cali, I'd hit him up a few times, and we built a good friendship with him telling me all of his relationship problems and me sharing a few of mine.

He was cool as hell and the perfect person to go to the club with. Every girl needed a gay friend; he was the best of both worlds: man enough to tell me exactly how a nigga thinks but very much in touch with his feminine side so that he could give me some good ass advice. Plus, I didn't have to worry about him getting jealous when we hung out because of all the attention I got. If anything, I got jealous of his ass because Bryan definitely pulled more than his share of niggas.

"Can't nobody outshine yo' ass, Bry," I told him, laughing as I eyed his ensemble. He was wearing all black, with a white vest and white fedora hat with a black sash tied around it. His long sleeved shirt was pulled up, showing off his muscular arms, which were covered with tattoos. Bryan was sexy, and had he not been gay, I would have been the first in line ready to pounce on his ass.

"I know it," he replied cockily, ducking his head a lil' bit with his lips poked out as he took the compliment. His ass was crazy!

"Now what is goin' on with you and Cree? He know you here?" Bryan asked, sipping from his drink. I exhaled and grabbed my glass, shaking the liquid a little while, I thought about my reply.

"His brother told him I was here but he hasn't hit me up yet. I really don't know what to do about him. It's like I feel something for him but he gives me nothing. He's the first man I've ever met who has done that. I just—"

Looking up, I noticed that Bryan wasn't paying me the least bit of attention. His eyes were locked on a man who was sitting across from us on the other side of the bar, looking directly at him. He was attractive, and from the way he kept his eyes on Bryan, sending strong signals from all the way on the other side, he was trying to get into something tonight.

"You know what, you go ahead and go on over there," I told Bryan, laughing a little as I shook my head. "I'm about to stop thinking about this nigga and follow your lead. Might find me a little something to have fun with tonight."

"Girl, the best way to forget about a nigga is to get under a new one and we both know that."

I rolled my eyes and giggled. I'd just gave this same advice to Janelle.

"Find you somebody who knows how to act, rock that nigga's world and don't give a fuck about Cree!" Bryan said, smacking his lips before getting up to join the man on the other side of the bar. I watched them for a few minutes, finding myself smiling at the way that Bryan appeared to be all bashful and shy once he sat next to the man who was obviously happy that he'd come over.

The bartender set a drink down in front of me and I frowned, looking up at him. I hadn't even finished the drink I was working on and he was placing another one in my face like he was trying to get me drunk.

"Who you workin' for?" I asked him, sexily, flirting with my eyes as I looked at him. He blushed and shook his head softly. He was a white boy, not my normal type, but he was fine and in charge of the liquor so I knew he could give my ass a good time.

"I'm not even done with this drink yet. You trying to get me drunk?"

He laughed a little as he started making someone else's drink. "No, this one is courtesy of the man over there," he told me, cutting his eyes to somewhere off to my side.

Looking over, I felt all the breath leave my body when I saw that it was Cree, sitting by himself sipping on some brown liquid in a glass. He looked like the epitome of what it was to be a sexy thug, his hair low-cut, rocking a long-sleeved cream shirt, his neck adorned with multiple gold chains, ears iced out to the max, black jeans and black Tims. His eyes were on me, watching me without expression, like he didn't even know about the eruption of emotions stirring up in my body just from seeing him.

Eyes not leaving mine, he took a final sip from his glass as he stood up, expression scrawled as he walked over me. I couldn't read a single thing through his face, couldn't tell if he was happy to see me or not.

"You bought me a drink?" I said, once he came over, mainly because I didn't know what else to say and he had my nerves bad.

All kinds of sensations were fluttering around in the pit of my stomach but I tried to keep it cool. It was crazy how his ass had an effect on me like no other. For one, I knew I looked good as hell. In fact, I'd told myself that plenty of times before I left and when I walked in the club, there wasn't a nigga inside whose eyes hadn't told me the same thing as I came in. Wearing a cream and gold sequined dress that fit every curve on my body with gold red bottom heels, gold jewelry—all real, I might add—and my long, curly brown hair flowing down my back, wasn't a bitch who could touch me tonight. But still, Cree's stare had me wondering if all this was enough. Did he like how I looked? Did he miss me?

"Thought you was lookin' thirsty," he replied, sitting down next to me and I rolled my eyes. Here he was with this bullshit. I was just about to light into his ass when I saw his face break, a smile forming on his lips. Oh… that was his try at joking around.

"Don't choke on them stale ass jokes, nigga."

"I'm just kiddin', mama," he continued, his southern accent heavy. "I know you hate for a nigga to call yo' ass thirsty."

"Because I'm *not*," I sniffed, flipping my hair over my shoulder. Grabbing the drink, I sipped it, noting that it was not what I'd already been drinking but it was delicious. I took a breath, feeling the liquid flow through me, warming my insides before I glanced in Cree's direction, seeing that his eyes were still on me.

"You gon' sit there and act like you ain't miss a nigga, Mel?" he asked and I cocked my head at him, wondering if he was trying to pick a fight or be romantic. It was so fuckin' hard to read Cree and I hated it. Men were supposed to be simple and that's how they'd always been for me but he wasn't.

"And if I did?" I snapped, not wanting to admit shit to him first. Of course I missed him, but I'd be damned if I stated my feelings before he did so it could go right to his big ass head.

"If you did, then I'd have to tell you that I missed yo' ass too."

He caught me off guard and my thoughts hemorrhaged. I looked at him, trying to see if he was playing around again, but his eyes were serious and his expression was blank, not a single smile on his face as he just stared at me.

Ducking my head, I focused on my drink and didn't say a word. Mainly, because I didn't know what to say. Can you believe that? Carmella Ann Pickney, the sister who was always slick at the mouth with it, was rendered speechless by Cree's ass. Mouth on stupid, I decided to stick with facial expressions and just cut my eyes at him, rolling them a little before going back to my drink.

He laughed, moving closer to me and I swear I felt my heart nearly stop the closer he got. The fine hairs on my skin rose up on my arm and then he touched me, running his thumb from my shoulder down to my wrist before grabbing my hand and lacing my fingers through his. Suddenly shocked into action by the warmth of his touch on my skin, my heart started slamming in my chest, beating so hard that I had to take a deep breath before turning to Cree.

"Yeah, you missed a nigga. I can tell even tho' you wanna act like you can't say shit. Plus… you came back to me. Just like I asked." He brought my fingers to his lips and kissed every one of them while I just stared, lips parted as I panted quietly, watching Cree do all the right things for once in his life. And it was about damn time he did!

Releasing my fingers, he swiveled around in his seat and placed his elbows on the bar, signaling for the bartender to bring him a drink. I was grateful for the pause because my senses were on fire and my brain had gone numb. Looking across the bar, I saw that Bryan was looking dead in my face. He winked at me, making me smile, before turning back to his man of the hour.

"So when you leave?" Cree asked me, bringing my attention back on him. I could tell by the look in his eyes that he was a little low-key irritated about my answer even before I said it.

"In a few days, unless something happens with this business opportunity that I'm checking out. I'm only staying until after Thanksgiving. Janelle and I probably won't be going home for the holiday."

Nodding his head, he turned around just as the bartender placed his drink in front of him. He grabbed it, drinking thoughtfully as I took the opportunity to look at him once more. He was like his brother Outlaw in a few ways but so different from him in others. For one, while every time I'd seen Outlaw, he was dressed flawlessly, he never looked as put together as Cree always did. Cree dressed nice to the point that you could tell his ass was also a little anal about how he looked when he stepped outside. Shirts perfectly ironed, no wrinkles, shoes without a single blemish, jeans pressed, and line-up always on fleek. He looked good and smelled even better... with his sexy ass.

Turning to me with his drink in hand, Cree kept his eyes on me and swallowed it down in one gulp, not even flinching even though I knew that brown liquid had to burn on its way down.

"Well, I guess I got a few days to convince you to stay then," he said, and then stood up just as my jaw dropped, grabbing my hand and lifting me from my seat at the bar.

I walked slowly behind Cree, my hand in his as every nigga we passed by turned and caught a glimpse of me as we came through. I was used to the attention, I loved it, but I tried to act like I didn't notice it because of Cree. Taking me into the middle of the dance floor, he turned to look at me and I gave him a wide-eyed look. I knew for a fact this nigga was not about to ask me to dance!

"You dance?" I asked him, cocking my head to the side. He hesitated, giving me a pensive look, and then shook his head slowly.

"Naw."

"So what we doin'?" I giggled, when he grabbed me around my waist and pulled me close to him. I laid my head on his chest and relaxed into him as he held me in his arms. God, he smelled so good.

"I just wanna hold you for a lil' bit," was all he said and it was the perfect response.

The D.J. had slowed the music down a little, playing something nice and slow that set the mood just right. Body pressed against his, I let out a long breath as Cree held me close, rocking a little from side-to-side. He wasn't doing much, but he didn't have to because just being close to him had all of my senses fulfilled. I knew this moment wouldn't last with us. It never did. Cree had a way of making me feel like the only woman in the world but then in the next moment, he would make me feel like he didn't give a shit. He was such a complex being, but I loved being around him more than I ever had any other man.

The song ended and I pulled away from him, reluctantly, because I really wanted to stay but I'd had four drinks since I'd been there and a bitch had to pee like a racehorse.

"I'll be back," I told him and he gave me a look, his body tensing like he didn't want me to go. "I'll be right back, Cree! I gotta go pee."

"Well, go then," he said, backing up a little to let me leave and I rolled my eyes at him.

The bathroom wasn't all that packed when I stepped inside and I was grateful because a second longer and I would have been doing the pee-pee dance in my stiletto heels. Walking into the stall, I lifted my dress and popped a squat, exhaling slowly as I relieved myself. Once I was done, I flushed, stepped out, and washed my hands; checking myself out in the mirror to make sure I was on point. Then, grabbing my clutch, I looked around to make sure the coast was clear before opening my bag and stepping back into the stall. Pulling out a credit card, an envelope and some white powder, I made two lines with stunning precision and then snorted them both up, one by one.

Now, I know what you're thinking: Oh hell naw, this bitch is addicted to coke. No ma'am, hell naw, I ain't gon' ever be an addict. I wasn't addicted to a damn thing. I was simply a California girl who knew what it meant to have a good time. I stayed in the club because perks came from being this sexy. Being something of a local celebrity in my area, I got paid to make appearances almost every weekend. Not enough to pay the bills but it was something I still enjoyed. I partied with all kinds of people, black, white, gay or straight, it didn't matter. But the one thing that was always present? Some good nose candy to get your mood straight. And if you've never fucked while high, biittttch, you didn't know what you were missing!

"Shit," I exhaled as I felt the feeling come over me. Closing my eyes, I swallowed hard as the orgasmic shocks went through my body, making me shudder as I adjusted to the surge of energy that shot through me.

If you've never tried coke in your life then I can't even really explain to you how good it feels to be high. Just imagine being in a place where no one can fuck with your mood and every good feeling you felt was magnified by a thousand. It was like the ultimate turn up. The first time I got high, I wasn't able to control it and it had me doing some crazy shit. But the more I did it, the more I was able to handle myself and just enjoy the feeling. There was nothing like it.

Stepping out of the stall, the door opened and three females walked in laughing and talking loud. As soon as their eyes fell on me, all conversation stopped. I turned to look at one and she gave me a stank ass look as if she was sizing me up, instantly pissing me off. Why couldn't women just let another woman know when she looked cute and had it together. Why the attitude?

"Bitch," I grumbled under my breath as I walked by them, taking one last look at myself before I walked out.

"Her nasty ass ain't even gon' wash her damn hands," one of them said just as I got to the door.

Now, had I not been high, I might have just rolled my eyes and walked out without saying anything because it wasn't worth it. I didn't know her ass from anyone, and on top of all that, I knew I'd washed my damn hands. But I had a nose full of blow and I was on one.

Walking over to the girl just as she got to the stall, I reached out and mushed her hard right against the side of her ebony brown face. Caught by surprise, she lost her footing and fell forward, banging her head on the toilet right before falling down on the ground, spilling over a little into the stall one of her friends were in. There was a small gash on her head that started to bleed as soon as she hit the ground. Laying there and not moving, she was breathing but she was out cold. Shit!

"Teema!" one of her friends yelled who was in the stall beside her. "Oh my God, Teema!"

Shit!

"What's wrong, Yani?" the other one yelled from out of the stall on the other side.

I didn't wait for an answer. Turning around, I snatched the door open and ran out, laughing my ass off. See, that's what happened when you went out of your way to fuck with someone and wasn't ready for the consequences.

"Can we go?" I asked Cree as soon as I ran back up to him. He gave me one look straight in the eyes and then narrowed his. I looked away, hoping that he couldn't tell I'd been using.

"Yeah." His eyes lingered and he ran his tongue over his teeth. "You a'ight?"

He asked it in a way that made me feel like he didn't really need an answer because he'd made his own assumptions but I simply nodded my head.

"I'm good. Just wanna go somewhere where we can talk… Somewhere where we can be alone."

Never in the world has there been a man who didn't take the

opportunity to have sex with a woman he was feeling so I didn't have to say anything further. Cree led the way to the front of the club where we could collect our coats and I followed behind him, happy he didn't see the big ass smile on my face.

Grabbing my coat, I started to put it on and took one look over to the restrooms just in time to see the girl who I had pushed walk out holding her hand to her head as her two friends stood on either side of her, helping her walk. I didn't feel the least bit sorry about knocking her on her ass either. Bitch might think twice about talking out the side of her mouth on the next bitch.

"You ready?" Cree asked me, and I nodded my head, latching my arm under his.

He gave me a funny look and pressed his lips together in a straight line but didn't say anything else as we turned to leave. For less than a second, I wondered what that look was about but in the next second, I realized I didn't care. I was back in New York, I felt good as hell and I was about to have some bomb ass sex with the only nigga I was feeling at the moment. Life really couldn't get any better.

Hood-Bougie-Cute

Sidney

"This is probably the slowest night ever," I said to Mike as I placed my elbows on the countertop of the bar and stared at the sparse crowd.

It was like senior night in the club because the only people in the building were washed up hustlers and the women who still remembered who they used to be. They were walking around in pleated jeans and shirts pressed to perfection, paired with loafers and a little ass gold chain around their neck. The music was just as bad. I swear the DJ had played 'Cha Cha Slide' and 'Wobble' about three times each.

"It's a weeknight and the Murrays are playin' in that basketball game everybody has been talkin' about. That's where the crowd is," Mike told me, and I groaned, face on full pout.

"Don't remind me. I wanted to go to that shit and I'm mad as hell Bean didn't let me off tonight. Ain't no reason to have both of us in here! Ain't shit happening!" I grumbled, rolling my eyes as I thought about my manager who was also the owner of the club.

Every now and then in our hood, we would have a basketball game that everybody, young or old, was there to watch. Yolo and his brothers always made up a team and played against other niggas in the hood. When Tone died, they let that prized spot as back-up on their team, go to whoever was the best street baller in the hood and they would match up against other teams of niggas who thought they were bout it.

Everybody put money on the game and you could come up good if you won. Kane had changed the rules around a little while back, making it like a tournament. Each team had to put up a thousand or more to compete and the money went to some kid in the hood who had gotten accepted into college or needed money to attend prom. It was a positive thing and it was one of the reasons that people in the area was so loyal to the Murrays. They did crazy shit but they took care of their people and their people took care of them in return.

Being that I loved basketball, I had my heart set on going to the game, especially now that Yolo and I were back messing around. The past few years, I'd been avoiding it and avoiding him, which was hard because nothing got me hype like basketball. But then Bean's ugly ass had to tell me I needed to come in to help Mike because he wanted to see the game.

"Why don't you go ahead and go?" Mike said, making me jump up from the counter. Turning around, I looked at him, my eyes wide while praying in my mind that I'd heard him correctly.

"For real?"

Laughing, Mike nodded his head and I almost wanted to kiss him right on the lips, but I settled on a hug instead, grabbing him tight around his neck.

"Yeah, I can handle this crowd. Plus, I ain't got shit to do tonight."

Looking at him, I lifted one brow. "Oh? No cute lil' girl been able to catch your interest?" I asked him, teasing.

Mike was fine, and at one point I almost let myself start crushing on him, but I'd never seen him with a woman before. I knew he was getting some on the regular because it had come up in conversation but he just never told me who he was getting it from. Typical nigga. He was flipping bitches left and right but none of them were worthy enough in his mind for him to actually be serious with.

"Naw," he replied with a light laugh as he wiped up the top of the bar. "I'm still ridin' solo."

"So am I."

"Bullshit."

Winking at him, I grabbed my small backpack and walked out of the club, instantly loving the fact that the weather was perfect even though it should have been freezing being that we were coming up on winter. The tournament had started hours ago but after checking my watch, I figured I should be able to catch some of it before the final game ended.

Walking up, I saw that the crowd had definitely come out from everywhere this time. There were people everywhere with bottles or plastic cups in their hand and the smell of loud was permeating through the air, even though quite a few cops had stopped by to witness the game. When the hood basketball tournament was going on, nobody was a cop and nobody was a criminal. Everybody was a fan! And every damn body had money on the game.

"Aye, let me get a hundred on the Murrays," I said, walking up to a guy I knew that took bets on the game. We weren't cool but we'd grown up together and he was a legit hustler, always finding a way to capitalize on something. Hearing me, he nodded his head and waited, looking at me hard before I realized what he wanted.

"I'm good for it, damn!" I said, narrowing my eyes at him.

"I don't give a shit, Sid. You know the rules!" he shot back, and I rolled my eyes before reaching in my pocket for my wallet so I could flash him my cash. Nodding his head at the bill, he wrote down my bet and then walked on as I searched around for Faviola. I knew her ass had to be here watching Tank play and making sure that no other bitch was around rooting for him too.

I found her right where I thought she'd be, sitting up front looking hood-bougie-cute with her eyes planted on Tank. I started to walk over to her, watching the game at the same time. I didn't know the score but the Murrays were on the court playing against a team that definitely looked legit. Every nigga on the opposing team was tall as hell and built like a real deal NBA player. This was about to be a good ass game.

Kane, Cree and Tank were dressed in regular old basketball gear; clean ass shoes, sweats and t-shirts. But Yolo and Outlaw took the shit to a whole 'nother level. Yolo was fly, just as I expected. Dressed like he was going to be leaving the court and then sitting in for a photoshoot with *Sports Illustrated*. He was in red and white and matched from his socks to his headband. He was playing hard but you couldn't tell from looking at him. I swear his fine ass wasn't even sweating.

Outlaw, on the other hand, was dressed similar to his other brothers except his sweats hung low, showing off his Gucci boxers, and he was iced out with jewelry that nobody else but his crazy ass would wear while playing in a basketball game. Big ass diamond studded earrings in his ear, thick long chain around his neck, gold bracelets, and rings… just as flashy as he wanted to be. He was the opposite of Janelle and I really didn't see what they saw in each other. They couldn't be more different.

"Ugh, just look at this ugly bitch," a familiar voice said, and I stopped right in my tracks, picking up on the speaker immediately.

Turning around, I saw LaTrese standing with her face all twisted up in disgust as she and her friends stared at me. Groaning inwardly, I shook my head and turned away to continue on to where Faviola was sitting. I swear I didn't want no drama, I just wanted to enjoy the game, collect my money and go home in peace.

I felt LaTrese's heated stare on me the entire time as I walked over to where Faviola was sitting but I tried my best to ignore her. I wasn't afraid to fight because I've been in plenty of fights in the past. But like I said, none of them had been mine. I just never been in a situation where I felt like I needed to be fighting a bitch unless it was to back up my homegirl.

"Damn, you made it," Faviola said, cutting her eyes at me when I walked up. She scooted over on the bench so I could sit next to her. Sitting down, I eyed the cup in her hand and leaned over to sniff the liquid.

"What's that?"

"Juice, what it look like?" she snapped, rolling her eyes. "Girl, you know I'm pregnant so it ain't no drank!"

She raised the cup to her mouth and swallowed it down like it was nothing before tossing it in the can ahead of her. I looked down at her belly, still flat as ever, and thought about what Tank had said about her not really being pregnant.

"How far along are you again?" I asked, getting suspicious. She cut her eyes at me and frowned.

"Damn bitch, you act like you wasn't there when I peed on the muthafuckin' stick! You sounding just like Tank right now but I'm gon' tell you like I tell him too: I'm pregnant so deal with it!"

And with that she flipped her hair over her shoulder, crossed her legs and turned back to the game. I kept my eyes on her and she ignored me, staring straight ahead and tight-lipped, which made me feel bad for letting Tank's stupid ass get into my head.

"I'm not doubting you, Favi. I'm just saying for you to be so far along, you look the exact same. You need to go to the doctor to get checked on—"

"I'm not goin' anywhere until Tank goes with me. I've been takin' my prenatal vitamins so I'm good, but I'll be damned if I walk up in there by myself like I made this baby alone!" she huffed and I shrugged it off, putting my attention on the game.

Faviola was a grown ass woman who made her own decisions. Plus, I could see her point. If Yolo got me pregnant, I would be mad as hell if his ass refused to show up to my appointments, telling everyone he wanted a DNA test first.

Yolo sunk a three and the crowd roared. Never the one to sit around and be outdone, Outlaw stole the ball from one of the tallest niggas on the other team and dribbled it back, dunking that shit with ease. He hung from the basket and swung back and forth, sticking out his tongue and flashing his gold teeth at some females sitting near him, practically drooling all over themselves while looking at him. He definitely wasn't going home alone tonight if he didn't want to.

I felt eyes on me and I turned around just in time to connect with Yolo. His eyes were wide, sparkling with delight then he smiled deeply, poking his chest out slightly which made my heart skip a beat. He was happy to see me and it showed. Pulling his eyes from me, he ran back to join the game but had an extra pep in his step after seeing me there. That was my nigga, fuck what anybody said.

"Yolo ass lookin' all goofy and shit now that he done see yo' ugly ass," Faviola scoffed, from beside me. From the smirk on her face, I could tell she was playing around so I elbowed her in the arm. She cried out all dramatically like I'd killed her and hit me back.

The game ended with the Murrays winning, just like I thought. There were plenty of pissed people cussing after the game because they'd bet on the other team. Like I said, they looked NBA official and everyone thought this was finally the day the Murrays would lose a game. But it was hard as hell to beat a group of niggas who had been balling together their whole life. And that went for on the court as well as off.

"Well, I'll see you at the house. Or maybe not if you plannin' on gettin' nasty," Faviola said, giving me a mischievous smile as she walked away, heading right for Tank.

I chuckled at her comment and watched Tank's reaction when he saw her standing in front of him. He'd been talking with one of the guys from the other team but as soon as Faviola walked up, all eyes were on her. I didn't understand Tank at all because it was clear he was feeling her on some level. But something had him treating her like shit when it came to this pregnancy. I didn't know what it was but I was positive that Faviola was holding back on something.

My eyes went to Yolo who had his on me. With the ball tucked under his arm, he didn't stop walking until he was standing right in front of my face, making me feel like I was the only girl in the world.

"Glad you could make it," Yolo told me, licking his lips, turning me on instantly. He was the spark I needed to set my entire body aflame. I was burning with passion, love, and lust all at the same damn time.

"I am too. It's been a while since I've seen you really play," I replied and he nodded his head. He didn't say a word but his eyes said it all. He was thinking about the reason for that… I had been avoiding him.

"But now you're back and I'm not lettin' you go."

He confirmed his declaration with an appropriate action and possessively grabbed my hand. Turning to his brothers, he yelled out to them that he was leaving. All of them told him bye except for Outlaw who was all up in some chick's face, charming the clothes off her ass right in front of everyone. Frowning, I looked at him for a minute, confused because I thought he'd made it serious with Janelle. Being next door, I saw him at her house almost every damn day but apparently they weren't as serious as I'd thought. She wasn't even at the game.

Yolo began to walk, pulling me behind him with a tug of my hand and I fell in step behind him. Until my eyes fell on LaTrese, who was glaring at us like she could melt cement with her stare.

"Looks like yo' old chick ain't too happy about you bein' with me," I mumbled to Yolo, and watched as he looked around before finding LaTrese. She gave him a pointed look, talking with her eyes and he sucked his teeth, fanning her off with his other hand.

"Fuck her," was all he said and it was enough for me. Without giving her a second glance, I walked hand in hand with Yolo to his car.

"I'm staying in Brooklyn tonight at my spot here. You comin'?" he didn't have to ask me twice. I nodded my head quickly and waited for him to find his keys and unlock the car.

"Shit… I forgot I asked Luke to hold my keys. I'll be right back," he told me and then jogged back onto the court.

Leaning on the car, I watched him, admiring the way he looked from behind. On the outside, I was chill, but on the inside I was jumping for joy. I didn't care who you were, when you knew you was about to get some good sex, it was a celebratory event.

"He's only dealing with your ugly ass to make me mad."

Exhaling heavily, I turned slowly and was met with LaTrese's messy ass who was standing a few feet away from me. Her entourage of two was with her and I could see why she kept them around. They were ugly as sin. LaTrese was the type of female who didn't like hanging with other bad bitches because she thought it would steal her shine. So instead, she chose to hang with two chicks that looked like they were wearing her hand-me-downs, couldn't do their hair and couldn't form opinions unless she gave it to them. One of them looked like she had never seen a lotion bottle in her life; a skinny black female who needed a weave job bad. She had no edges and was sporting braids so raggedy and old, that it looked like she'd borrowed that shit from LaTrese too.

The other looked like she weighed about 400 pounds. Now let me say this, I've seen some thick, curvy women who were fly, dressed to the nines and was sexy with it. But she wasn't it. She had on shoes so tight they looked like they were begging to be free and her toes poured out the front, fat and stubby like Vienna sausages. Her short jean dress was so tight that the buttons were pulling the material. If she sneezed, she would be butt ass naked. Worst of all, she breathed through her mouth, making a wheezing sound like it was painful just to take a breath.

"Trese, I don't have shit to do with you and Yolo."

She sucked her teeth.

"Bitch, I know you don't. But what you are is in the fuckin' way," she explained as her sidekicks laughed at her side. "Whether you think so or not, he's going to come back to me. I won't let you have him."

"And you think that choice is yours?"

Her face spread into a sinister grin, reminding me of the Grinch. But instead of stealing Christmas, she was trying to steal niggas. She stepped forward, closing in on the space between us and I instinctively balled my hands into fists.

"Oh, I'm not gonna fight you," she announced with a haughty sniff, looking down at me from over the bridge of her nose. "No need, because I know in the end you'll be gone and I'll be with him. We have something deeper than you'll ever have."

I didn't say a word as she and her mini-entourage walked away, because I didn't think I had to. At the end of the day, who was going home with him? Oh yeah… that would be me! Bitch, bye.

"You ready?" Yolo asked once he'd jogged back to the car with the keys in hand.

I nodded my head, wondering if I should bring up my little altercation with his ex. Deciding against it, I just opened the door and sat down inside. I'd mentioned her more times to him today than I ever wanted to. This was about us and not about her being jealous of what we had.

With my hand in his, we pulled away and drove right by her. Yolo didn't even bat an eye in her direction, and I smiled, noticing how invisible she really was to him. She was delusional… there was no way in hell she would *ever* be a threat to me again.

Silence.

Janelle

An entire week had passed and still nothing from Luke. Actually, to be precise, a whole week, sixteen hours and forty-seven minutes had passed and I heard nothing from him. Until I did. Finally.

I was sitting in the living room listening to Carmella tell me all about her date with Cree and how wonderful and sweet he was when it happened. I was only half-listening. It wasn't like I wasn't happy that my sister seemed to be caught up with someone who had her to the point where she couldn't wait to share every detail with me. But... the emotion in her voice, the look in her eyes... all of that reminded me of how I'd been when I was with Luke. It was hard to listen to.

"I just don't know how I can like someone like him," she ended with a heavy breath, falling back against the sofa with her arms out as if her energy was spent now that her story had ended.

"What's not to like about him?" I asked with a lifted brow. "You just got done telling me everything that is great about him and how wonderful a time you had. I don't understand why you would think you wouldn't like him."

She sat up and looked down, frowning as her eyes ran back and forth, cycling like her thoughts.

"Because he's rude all the damn time. Like in the meanest ways!"

she sighed. "I always thought I would be with someone romantic and thoughtful… someone who adored everything about me…"

I chuckled and she gave me a perplexed squint.

"You mean like Rachaud?" I asked, referring to her ex-boyfriend, a football player she dated somewhat seriously in her freshmen year of college.

He was a senior at the time and later went pro for the Miami Dolphins. He adored everything about Carmella and treated her like the princess she acted like she was. The problem was that Carmella got bored with him easily, complaining that he had no backbone and was a complete pushover. She would roll her eyes when he brought her flowers before dates and scoff at his compliments. He did all the things that she claimed Cree didn't… the *exact* things she claimed she wanted him to do but she hated it. It got to the point where she broke it off with him over something silly, claimed that she wanted to focus on her studies and be single for a while. Rachaud went with it, which left me questioning him because anyone who knew Carmella, knew that she did not let her studies get in the way of anything she wanted to do. Especially not men.

"Yeah… like Rachaud," Carmella replied, squinting one eye as she thought about it. "Just not as sappy."

I didn't say anything as I watched her face scrunch up while she thought further on that statement.

"Actually, no not like Rachaud. But damn, would it be so hard for him to be nice sometimes?!"

Laughing, I shook my head at her.

"No, it wouldn't be that hard for him to be nice sometimes but that's not him. He's not the type who is just going to allow himself to be wrapped around your pinky finger. He's his own man and he's not going to kiss your ass. At the same time, it's obvious that he wants you to be part of his life so you should be happy about that."

"Well, shouldn't you have been happy that Outlaw wanted you in his?" Carmella shot out smartly, with a haughty flip of her hair.

"I wouldn't know if he wanted me in his or not because I haven't heard from him," was all I said but even those few words stung my lips on their way out.

Why hadn't I heard from him? Was it offensive that I'd shared my feelings with him? Did he really see it as a slight against him that I actually had the *audacity* to fall for him and think that maybe, just maybe, we could have more than a casual fling?

And then he called me.

My phone rang and I startled, not realizing that I even had it with me. Truth was, it rang rarely, and I had stopped carrying it around from room-to-room for the most part. I grabbed it quickly, silencing the blaring before I even took a minute to see who it was calling. Once I saw that it was Luke, all dignity left me. All of the rules of how you should 'never answer on the first ring' and 'never make yourself too accessible' I snubbed as frivolous advice from someone who probably didn't even have a man and answered immediately, pushing the phone to my ear.

"Hello?"

"Aye, I'm—Hol' up… Janelle?!"

Blinking hard, I frowned.

"Yes?"

"Ah shit… my bad, I ain't mean to call you."

My heart dropped. Not to my feet but completely out of my chest. It just flew out of me and shattered across the floor. I swallowed hard and forced myself to breathe air into my deflated lungs so I could speak.

"Oh. Well—"

"How you been doin' tho'?" he asked, warmth coming to his voice.

My stomach began to flip flop.

"Fine."

"Yeah?" he pressed further, and I could almost hear the doubt in his voice. For some reason, it annoyed me, like he figured I was all broken up and distraught about not hearing from him. Yes, I wasn't the happiest I'd ever been in my life but I was far from the saddest. As far as I was concerned, I was doing pretty good without him.

"Yes, I'm fine. As in great, actually. My job is going exactly how I want it and my personal life is better than it's ever been. I'm the happiest I've been in a long time and I just enjoy… doing me. I've been great," I replied back, rushing through my words so he couldn't detect the lies that lay beneath them.

I wasn't great. My job was fine but somehow it had lost some of its radiance now that we were investigating Luke and his brothers. I felt like I was betraying my duty as an attorney but also like I was betraying my heart. It was exhausting and many days I wished that I could just go back to before I met Luke when I was only an assistant district attorney eager to get on a case, any case, so I could prove just how good I was. Now, I barely wanted wake up in the morning when I had to go to work. I couldn't wait until we started on something else.

"Damn," Luke said, sounding genuinely surprised and a little bit disappointed at the same time. "That's good, Nell. It really is. I'm glad that everything is goin'…" He paused and I realized I had stopped breathing. "…great. I'm glad that everything is just how you want it. That's all I could really ask for."

He didn't say anything for a minute and I didn't either. The silence between us was loud, filling up with words that both of us were deciding to leave unsaid. My mouth went dry and my head felt heavy. I rubbed the top of it, pulling the phone slightly away from my ear at the exact moment that Luke started to speak. By the time I placed it back firmly against my ear, I'd missed what he'd said.

"Huh?"

"Nothing."

My throat went salty and I pressed my fingers against my throbbing temples.

"No, what was it?"

"I was sayin' that… we need to meet up again. I wanna see you."

I swallowed hard, trying to dislodge the lump in my throat. I wanted to see him too but I needed more than a simple booty call. I couldn't be the girl he met up with only when he wanted something that anyone could give him. I wasn't one of the ones blessed enough to separate my feelings from my vagina. When Luke entered me, he entered *all* of me. My heart, my soul, my body—all of it belonged to him and long after he'd removed himself physically from me, the most stubborn but beautiful parts of his soul still remained. I couldn't rid myself of him now and I never could since the day I met him. Even before it became love, I didn't want him around me, but Luke always seemed to show up until he became more to me than I'd ever imagined. I couldn't go back to having just his body. I needed everything I was giving to him to be reciprocated to me.

"No."

My words came out like a gentle breeze, barely noticeable, nonthreatening and lacking. I wasn't even convinced that I meant it.

"No?" Luke repeated with a surprised chuckle.

"NO!" I repeated with tenacity. "I'm not doing that with you, Luke. It was fun while it lasted and now it's over. It's not me and it's not what I want."

He countered quickly. Always a few paces ahead of me.

"Well, what do you want?"

I thought about it for only a second. The answer was clear.

"I want to be happy."

More silence between us, but this time I took even breaths through it all, waiting with open ears and an open heart for Luke to declare that he was the one, the only, who could really make me happy. After taking the step to tell him that I loved him, I wasn't willing to put my heart on the line again.

"I guess it's lookin' good for you then. Work's good, your personal life is… good. Oh my bad, you said 'great'. Everything is great. All that shit makin' you happy?"

"It is. I mean… Well, I—I am but…"

I stopped suddenly, feeling that I was just on the precipice of begging.

If a man wants you he'll let you know. Don't throw yourself at anyone.

Those were words my mother had taught my sisters and me. It came directly from her personal story of how she met our father. She knew right when she met him that she wanted him, but he was so wrapped up in starting a career that he didn't really pay her any attention above a friend level. So she lived her life and eventually he came around when the time was right for them both. And that's exactly what I was going to do.

"What, Nell?" Luke asked with urgency and a hint of frustration.

"Nothing. You're right, I'm great."

"Good," was all he said and the next second I was listening to dead air. He had hung up the phone. He was gone.

"Y'all are pathetic."

I didn't even realize that Carmella was standing behind me until I heard her speak. Seconds later, she'd moved in front of me with her hands placed firmly on her hips.

"It's so damn obvious you both want each other!"

My gut twisted.

"But how do you know that?"

"UGH!" Without answering my question, Carmella frowned her agitation, rolled her eyes and stalked away. "I don't see how you can be so brilliant and so damn dumb at the same time, Janelle. If you can't see that he is still all caught up in you, then I don't know what to say. And I wasn't even *on* the call but even I heard that from all the way over here."

She slammed her door, leaving me alone in my feelings and my thoughts, wondering why I couldn't see what she saw. Maybe I was being dense, but I just didn't see things her way. If Luke wanted me, he'd let me know and I wouldn't have to guess. He had always been so open and blunt with everything so I didn't see it being any different when it came to this. He was the type of man who went after everything he wanted and if he wanted me, he would let me know. Until then, I had to move on.

Not Your Average Baby Mama.

Teema

"UGH!" I grunted as I placed a bag of ice to my forehead and plopped my ass down on the couch in my living room.

I had already been having the week from hell after having to borrow money from Cyndy to get my lights turned back on. But then, on top of that, I got my ass knocked out by a Barbie lookin' bitch less than five minutes after being in there. I knew I shouldn't have said shit about her not washing her hands, but I'd heard her call me a bitch under her breath, and on top of that, the bitch *didn't* wash her damn hands! Am I wrong for pointing out the truth? Yeah I was looking at her stank but that was because one look in her eyes told me her ass had been in there getting high. Shit, she still had a little bit of the white powder on her damn nose when she walked out and—had she washed her damn hands—I might have helped a sista out!

Now, here I was, a whole damn day later and still nursing this big ass knot on my head. This was the reason why I didn't go out! Not only was I not the type of chick to hit the club every single time the shit opened, or ever for that matter, but I also had a one-year-old daughter who I took care of by my damn self with absolutely no help from her punk ass daddy.

Well, that was a lie. Kenya's daddy did send me money for her regularly but I refused to take shit from his ass. My friends called me all kinds of names for refusing his money but I didn't care. I wanted to send a strong signal to him that me and Kenya didn't need him for nothing, not even cash. When I got pregnant, I was head over heels in love with Kenya's father. Kane was the first man I'd ever loved and I gave myself to him quickly and completely.

I met Kane when I was thirteen years old. My mama was the neighborhood junkie and I was her dirty ass child. She would leave me home alone for days at a time with no food to eat, so by the time I turned seven, I was already cooking and practically taking care of myself. I didn't have any issues with my life because it was all I knew. For me, that was how life was.

By the time I turned thirteen, my mama's addiction had taken an even stronger hold on her and she was staying away longer. But the difference was that before, even though she was an addict, she always made sure there was food in the house to eat and that I had most of the things I needed. Now? Hell naw… all her funds was going to feeding her demons which left me eating whatever scraps I could find. She stopped caring for me altogether. I wore the same clothes to school each week, even when the thread started to pull out from all the constant hand washing. Eventually, I taught myself how to sew and would try to stitch up my clothes but they still were raggedy at best.

In the winters, I didn't even have a jacket to wear so I stayed home from school a lot. It was too cold to leave out in the snow. One time, my teacher came to my house to ask why I hadn't been in school and I covered for my mama, telling her that I'd been sick and she didn't want me to go out without a jacket. The next day, my teacher came back with an Adidas jacket that she had found in the lost and found at school. I was so damn happy about that jacket that a week later when my mama came home, I showed it to her, modeling it around the house and laughing as she watched me and clapped her hands, telling me how fly I looked. The next day, she was gone and my jacket was too.

I loved the summer because it was easier for me to take care of myself when it wasn't so damn cold outside. Plus, I didn't have school so that meant less people in my business. One summer, I met Kane. He was older than me by about four years, but I loved him as soon as I saw him. I was sitting on a bench waiting for the ice cream truck to come by. I didn't have any money for shit that was for sale in it but at the end of the day, Mr. Wilson, the man who drove it, would let me get a few things that he was going to throw out because of their expiration date. Sometimes it was my only meal for the whole day.

The ice cream truck came and as soon as it stopped, a gang of kids ran up to it, each of them waving money in the air and shouting out all of the things they wanted. I would have given anything to get a pickle or sausage but those were always the first things to go so there was never any left for me. While sitting there, I spotted five boys roll up to the truck on fly ass scooters, sliding right to the front of the line like they were hood royalty.

After ordering so much stuff that they could barely hold it all, they turned around and walked towards where I was. I watched as they sat down on some benches not far from me, enjoying their food as they talked and smacked loudly, not even noticing that I was there. I was used to not being seen so it didn't make a difference to me.

But then Kane looked at me.

I was staring at him with hunger in my eyes, watching him eat every bite that went into his mouth. I was starving, but I was mesmerized by him too. I couldn't pull my eyes away. After his brothers finished, they all ran off to do whatever it was that they did but Kane walked over to me. He said a few words and then held his hand out, giving me the rest of the food and ice cream he'd purchased, along with the change he had left over.

It was curtains from there. I loved him. From a distance anyways, because it took a while before he really paid me any attention. But when he *did*, it was the best thing to ever happen in my life. Until I got pregnant.

Kane has never wanted to have children and I knew that. When I got pregnant he blamed it on me being irresponsible and told me to get an abortion. I refused. About a year before finding out I was pregnant, my mama had disappeared. I wasn't worried until she'd been gone a whole month and I couldn't find her. Even though she hadn't really been there for me, it broke my heart that she wasn't around any longer. She was the only family I had. And then a little while after that, I found out I was pregnant. There was no way I was aborting my child.

So I had Kenya and I thought seeing her beautiful face would change the way that Kane felt about kids. But it didn't. We stayed together but he moved out right after I delivered her. He didn't even show up to the hospital. Not *once* has he even laid a single eye on our child. He didn't seem to want anything to do with her and I couldn't understand it. He used money to cover up the fact that he obviously didn't want her, buying her all the things a baby could possibly need when all she really needed was her father to hold her or tell her he loved her.

Eventually, I got sick and tired of it and left his ass. I'd finally found my mama and she convinced me she was clean, getting a disability check and would be able to help me do things on my own if I let her move in. I agreed and we moved on the opposite side of the city.

Kane still tried to take care of us but I didn't want shit from him ever again. What kind of man doesn't love his child? Maybe I was wrong for not telling him that I wasn't taking my birth control pills like I should have been. Maybe I was wrong for deciding not to get an abortion when I knew that he always said he didn't want kids. But who cares? She was here now!

Since I left him, I haven't seen him or his dumb ass brothers. To their credit, they adored Kenya but I didn't want to have anything to do with any of their asses. Except for Outlaw. He was the only one that I let come around and scoop Kenya up from time-to-time, and the only reason I allowed him to see her was because he was the only one who stood up to Kane for how he was treating her. Outlaw didn't come often but when he did, Kenya loved it. He also called and FaceTimed a lot—until my phone was cut off. It made me feel bad because Kenya's little pretty eyes lit up whenever she saw him. That girl loved her uncle. Sometimes I even wished Outlaw was her daddy.

"Hey ugly, what you doin'?" Cyndy asked me. Miyani and I teased her all the time about how she was a hood chick with a white girl's name.

"Nursing this knot on my head so that I won't look a hot ass mess at work tomorrow," I informed her with a hard roll of my eyes. Kenya started to giggle as she watched me, completely humored by my eyeroll. I did it again and she laughed even harder. I loved my baby.

She looked every bit of me but had Kane's cinnamon complexion and serious, focused stare whenever she wasn't laughing. Which wasn't often. She was a happy baby. Her eyes were light brown, just like mine and she had dimples in each cheek, which I guess she got from Kane's side since Yolo had them too. She was chunky thick and I loved every single thing about her. I couldn't understand why her father couldn't see what I saw.

"That lil' bump wasn't even that bad. But that's what you get for talkin' about that bitch. She was high and looked like she was low-key hood. Them stuck up types will fool yo' ass every time!"

"Well, she don't have to worry about foolin' me ever again because I be damned if I take my ass down to the club again. I thought since we were going to some classy spot I wouldn't have to worry 'bout shit like that," I huffed as I grabbed the remote and turned on the TV to some cartoons so that Kenya could watch.

"Nasty ass bitches don't know no area code. You'll find them wherever you go. Now, what time they put you on the schedule for tomorrow?"

Sighing, I relaxed into the couch as I held the phone in my hand. I hated my job. Initially, I thought being a CNA would be a come up.

146

And it was because the pay was decent. Much more than I got flipping burgers. But the trade-off was that I was wiping asses and bathing people's funky bodies instead. Damn, that sounds bad of me to say since the people I help can't do it for themselves. Either way, it wasn't the *best* job. Plus, I had to deal with Danielle.

She still had me assigned to Mr. Knot's room just to spite me. A few days back, I was wiping the old man's ass when he decided he had more to let loose and let it out all over my hands. I was wearing gloves but no matter how much I scrubbed, I still felt like I couldn't get the stink off. That was the reason why Cyndy and Miyani had made me go to the club in the first place.

"I gotta be in around 6 am. Working a double shift to get Christmas money together since mama promised me she could watch Kenya. I'm so sick of this shit," I told her, shaking my head. But I was determined to give my daughter the world so I had to do what I had to do.

"You must not be too sick of it because you keep sending that nigga's money back—"

"Cyn…" I cut in, trying to stop her before she got started.

"—Kane gives you enough money for Kenya to get her a jumbo pack of pampers, formula or whatever the hell else she needs *and* pay all yo' damn bills with a couple stacks left over! I don't know why you don't just—"

"I told you why! Stop bringin' this shit up anyways," I told her, cutting my eyes to Kenya as if she could understand what we were talking about. "I don't want her hearing 'bout her fucked up daddy."

"You came home the other day in the dark and you didn't have to!

I know you feel some kinda way about that nigga but your pride ain't payin' for shit. You know you wrong, Teema, and that's all I'mma say."

"Yeah because yo' ass done said enough! If Kane wants to be a real father, he'll come here and see his daughter. Until then, I don't want shit from his ass and that's that!"

My voice cracked at the end of my sentence, and before I knew it, tears were in my eyes and my bottom lip was trembling. Not a day went by that I didn't feel that I was wrong for refusing Kane's money, knowing that it could help me give Kenya a better life. But right now she had everything she could want and more and that was without him. I didn't want to feel like I needed the help of someone who didn't want to be in my child's life so my pride wouldn't let me do anything differently.

"Fine, I'm leaving that one alone. I'll see you at work tomorrow, okay?"

"Okay," I said softly, still trying to get my emotions in check.

"And Tee… I don't mean no harm with the shit I'm sayin'. I just care 'bout you and hate to see you workin' all day doin' shit that you hate. I know you really want to do something else with your life and I'm only trying to help you any way I can."

Sighing, I closed my eyes and nodded my head. I knew she was trying to help me but I was good. This wasn't the hardest thing I'd ever had to do in life. I'd had it hard the entire time growing up.

"I understand, Cyn. I love you," I told her.

"I love you, too."

We hung up the phone and I looked down at Kenya who had turned from the TV and now was looking directly at me.

"I love you too, mama!" she said happily, showing off her two little teeth. I laughed, pulling her up into my arms to hug her tight.

"I love you too, Kenya baby. No matter what, your mama always has and always will love you."

Even if your daddy don't.

The Revelation.

Carmella

*L*ooking in the mirror, I made sure that my makeup was still on point, smoothed down the material on my dress and then turned around to check out my ass. Yep, still there and still fat. I checked my nose to make sure there was no evidence of my magic powder, the little bit of nose candy I needed to provide just the right pick-me-up to accompany my game face. I was meeting up with Sasha's brother, Zeke, for the first time, so that he could tell me what I could do to help him so he could help me. When I tell you that I was more than ready for him to give me the details so that I could get to work, that was an understatement.

My money was steadily getting low and I was ignoring my daddy's calls so it wasn't like I could ask him for shit. If I hit rock bottom, I knew I could ask Janelle but I didn't really want to do that either. Especially with how she'd been dragging around the apartment the past few days. For someone who swore she wasn't missing Outlaw, she was doing a terrible job proving it.

The address Zeke had given me led to the biggest house in a residential area that I'd never been to. It still had the swag of the city but there was just enough green around to make it look cozy and at home, with small but expertly manicured lawns and beautiful landscaping. Once I knocked on the door, I was greeted by Zeke's assistant who showed me to a room where I could wait. There was food and drink in there, including alcohol, but I was too nervous to indulge.

Walking out of the bathroom, I was heading back to the room that I'd been escorted into when I saw a handsome man standing near the food, grabbing a donut from the table. I recognized him instantly as Zeke because he was the spitting image of his sister. Sasha had beautiful brown skin that had a reddish hue to it, stemming from her Native American ancestry. Zeke had the same complexion, paired with wavy hair, dark eyes and thick brooding eyebrows. He had a chiseled jawline and a muscular build to his body that I knew took work to maintain.

"So I finally get to meet the sexiest woman alive, huh?" Zeke said with a smile while chewing on a bite of his donut. "I've only been trying to get Sasha to link me up with you for about a million years now."

Laughing, I reached my hand out towards him and he shook it, keeping his eyes on mine.

"I know, I told her that had she already let me know you wanted to work with me, I would have made the connection a while ago."

"Word?" he asked, his brows shooting in the air. I nodded my head, smiling at his boyish but cute expression.

"Did she tell you anything about what I do?" he asked as he turned around to walk away. He didn't ask me to, but I assumed I was supposed to follow and took off in step behind him.

"No, she didn't… she said she didn't really know what you were into," I told him. He stopped abruptly, turned around and cocked his head to the side.

"Really?"

Frowning, I nodded my head. He paused, scrunching up his nose for a minute and then shrugged before turning to continue walking down the hall. A door opened and a woman walked out gulping down a bottle of water and once I saw her, I had to do a double take. She was butt ass naked, walking nonchalantly down the hall like she wasn't standing right in front of us in her birthday suit.

"Hey Zeke, what's poppin'?" she greeted him as soon as she lifted her head and saw us walking towards her. Her eyes ran from his to mine but she didn't even blink… didn't bat a single eye at the fact that I was staring at her like she had six eyes in her head. I made an effort to not look at anything below her neckline but it was hard as hell.

"Ain't shit, Dreeka. You out for the day?"

She shook her head and I couldn't resist glancing at her breasts that were shaking right along with it.

"Naw, just takin' a break. I'll be back at it in a minute."

Zeke nodded his head and continued walking and Dreeka did the same, but I couldn't go any further. I didn't know what it was that he was into, but the fact that Dreeka was doing it in the nude, let me know I wanted no parts of it.

"What's wrong?" Zeke asked when he saw I wasn't following behind him. I didn't say anything right away but he was able to guess just from looking at me.

"I run many businesses here. What Dreeka does isn't what I need you for. You just need to take a few pics for some promotions that I want done. I want to make you the face of a new branding campaign I have going on… your image will be everywhere on billboards all around the country. I'm going big with this shit and I know you're the perfect person to help me get where I'm trying to go. You game?"

He didn't have to ask me twice. Just knowing that I'd have my face on billboards was enough for me. I wanted to get noticed and I wanted to push my career to new levels. It was my dream to get into the entertainment world… maybe even do a reality television show or something. I didn't mind being a housewife or slapping bitches for the camera. I had the attitude, the body and the drive for it. I wanted fame and if Zeke could help me with that, then I was ready for it.

"I'm game as long as I'll have my clothes on. Doesn't have to be a lot of them but I can't be walkin' around showing off my goods," I explained and he nodded his head.

"You definitely won't have to do that. Step into this room so we can go over your contract."

Stopping in front of an open door, he stood to the side to allow me to walk in first. I stepped in slowly, looking around at how nice everything inside was. It was a corner office and since we were on the twentieth floor of the building, he had an incredible view of the city. His décor was very nice as well, very modern and clean with a few pieces that showed off his personal style. It was obvious he loved sports and that his favorite teams all hailed from Chicago, no surprise since that's where he and Sasha were from. He had some photos of his family and even a picture of him and Sasha when they were little. I smiled as I took my seat in front of his desk.

"Here is the contract," he said, pushing a stack of papers at me. "You're due a bonus at the time of signing and you will have a company car."

My eyes shot up from the papers to his and he laughed.

"Don't be so surprised. You're becoming a brand... part of my brand. I'll need you to attend some events and some parties on my behalf and I can't have you showing up without looking the part. Some events we will provide car service, but when that's not available, I can't have you using public transportation. So while you're in the city working, you'll have use of the car and you can stay in one of the condos in this building. Your pick."

"Okay," I started, sitting back in the seat and pushing the papers away. "This all sounds great and all but it also sounds too good to be true. What exactly am I going to be doing?"

Zeke smiled and shrugged cutely, dimples that I hadn't noticed before pushing their way out of the sides of his cheeks.

"I already told you. I just need you to take some pics for our promotions. The catch is that you'll be wearing little to nothing, you'll have to attend events and parties from time-to-time, sometimes on short notice... but that's pretty much it."

Nodding my head, I bent my head down and read over the contract quickly. I felt like I could trust Zeke since he was my best friend's brother but even she had said to make sure I checked him out so I wasn't taking any chances. Everything seemed standard for the most part. Except for when it came to the signing bonus. Zeke was giving me $10,000 just to sign on the dotted line! And with the car and condo being covered by his company, that could go a long way.

The only thing that made me pause was the term. According to the contract, I would have to stay in New York for at least the next three months. Which meant that I'd have to take off some time from school. However, the break would give me time to save money so I could cover my own tuition without help so it really wasn't that much to think about. My father would just have to understand.

"Everything checks out for me. Just let me borrow a pen and I'm ready to sign."

Smiling, Zeke passed me his pen and I scribbled my signature down on the dotted line, smiling hard because my financial woes were over and I was about to become a star.

**

I was ten grand richer, with a car and a key to a beautiful condo in the middle of Manhattan, but I wasn't making any preparations to move just yet. I couldn't use the car yet since I never learned to drive but I had already asked Cree to teach me so I could enjoy my new whip. Leaving Janelle alone in Brooklyn wasn't something I wanted to do so I'd worked it out with Zeke to get a two-bedroom condo so she could come with me. That was the easy part… convincing her to uproot her life and move with me would be the hard part.

With a sigh, I opened up my suitcase to look for something comfortable to put on so I could get out of the tight ass dress I was wearing and relax before meeting up with Cree later on that night. My hand stumbled upon the folder that Janelle had given me a while ago about Cree and his brothers that I hadn't gotten around to reading. It wasn't that I'd been too busy to look because I hadn't. The main reason I hadn't looked because I wasn't scared about what I'd find inside. Everything was going good between us and I didn't want to see anything that would mess that up.

After getting dressed, I grabbed the folder and set it down on the dresser without opening it, stared at it for a few minutes and then sighed. Whatever was inside, I couldn't run away from it forever. So I opened it.

It took only a few minutes for me to go through the first set of papers and read everything about Cree and his brothers. Most of the information was about Outlaw since it was his case but I skimmed through the details surrounding him too. By the time that I finished reading through it all, my mouth was wide open but I knew what I felt afterwards was far different from what Janelle had when she read it.

I was *amazed*. Every single thing I read impressed the shit out of me. A group of bad ass brothers, *educated* thugs, who were on their shit. I didn't care if what they did was illegal; the thrill of it was what got to me. Cree was a *boss*. Up until that moment, I still had my doubts that the car he'd purchased to take me out a few weeks back was actually his. Now I knew for sure it was and that his ass could afford anything he wanted because he was on his Black Mafia ish. Hell, just thinking about it got me hot.

I heard the front door open and I jumped up from where I was sitting on the bed and ran out with the folder in hand.

"JANELLE!" I shrieked as soon as I saw her. She walked in with her head down, looking as if she was texting someone on her phone. When she heard me run in the living room, she looked up and crooked her head to the side.

"What's wrong?"

I held the folder up in the air, high over my head.

"I just read this! I… I can't believe it. This is some crazy shit!" I told her and she nodded her head with a sigh.

"I know. It's scary, isn't it?"

"Scary?!" I barked back with a frown. "Hell no, these niggas are the shit! I can't believe this… they are too dope!"

Janelle looked at me with a blank face, blinking her eyes without saying a word. Then she rolled her eyes and groaned.

"I should've known that you would say something like that. Give me back my folder." She tried to snatch it out of my hand and I dodged her.

"Nope, I'm keeping this. I haven't finished reading it all. And when I finish, I'm going to read it again. They on some shit like that movie with Chris Brown, Idris Elba and T.I…. you know the one with that group of fine ass men who took stuff? What's it called?"

Janelle rolled her eyes.

"*Takers.*"

I nodded excitedly as I began to remember scenes from the movie.

"YASSSSS, that's the one. And I'm datin' the finest of them all. Damn, I can't wait until Cree get his fine ass over here, I'm gonna jump right on top of daddy and put it on him like he never had it done before!"

With my tongue out, I started twerking while waving the folder around over my head. Janelle rolled her eyes and walked on by me but even she couldn't hold back a laugh.

"You have fun with that," she mumbled.

"You and Outlaw still on the outs? I saw you texting somebody… was it him?"

She shook her head, and although she was trying to keep her face straight, I could see beyond that. It was obvious that her separation from Outlaw was making her feel a certain kind of way. Still, in the next second, true to Janelle's style, she adjusted her face quickly and covered up her anguish with a smile.

"No actually that was Chris. We've been talking a lot lately."

I eyed her doubtfully.

"About work?"

"No… not about work. He wants me to go out with him and I've been pushing it off because I'm still…" She paused but I already knew what she wanted to say. "… I'm still hung up on Luke. Believe it or not."

"I believe it. You don't just tell someone you love him and move on the next day. Here is some advice," I started, ready to shed some real knowledge. Janelle crinkled up her nose and looked up at me. I knew why… she was convinced that I didn't have it in me to give advice that she would ever be able to use but I did and I could.

"Why don't you go out with Chris and see how it is. If you feel like he's someone you can vibe with then keep going out with him and eventually you'll stop thinking about Outlaw or Luke… whatever the hell you call him." She laughed when I rolled my eyes. "But if you go and all you end up doing is comparing to Luke, then drop him and move on."

"Wow… finally you gave some advice that I can make a move on," she joked and I sucked my teeth. She had it twisted. I always gave good advice; she was just too much of goody-goody to see it that way.

"Well, have fun texting back and forth with your man. I have to get myself together because as for me and Cree—" I cocked my head to the side and put my finger in the air to show how much I meant business. "—I'm about to lay something on him that'll have him speaking in languages that no one can understand. I always had a thing for a thug and I don't mind being a ride or die."

Janelle laughed as I walked back down the hall towards my room so I could get myself together. I wanted to speak to her about my job with Zeke and the new condo but I had time. It wouldn't be ready until the end of next week so that could wait until after I took care of a more pressing issue.

Cree came to pick me up an hour late. No call, no text, no nothing. As usual, he'd found a way to mess up the vibe because I went from wanting to give him ass to wanting to kick his.

"Nigga, I shouldn't even go nowhere with you!" I snapped as soon as I opened the door and saw him standing in front of it.

I heard movement like papers rattling from behind me and knew it was Janelle snatching up her stuff so that she could run and hide down the hall. The heavy footsteps that followed about a couple seconds later told me that I was right. She hated confrontations whereas I was always more than ready for one.

"What the hell is your problem now, Mel? Damn, I'm here, ain't I?"

He put his hands in the air like he was frustrated. So typical of Cree to act like I was the one pissing him off when he was the one coming up here an entire hour later than he was supposed to, without even thinking to give me a single reason for it.

"You are my muthafuckin' problem! You do realize that you're a whole entire hour late, right? And not only did you show up late but you haven't given me a single reason as to why. Do you think I just wake up like this, Cree?" I pointed to myself in all my finest. "No... to be this sexy so I can go somewhere, I have to put makeup on, do my hair... this shit takes time!"

Cree sucked his teeth and waved his hand at me.

"You do all that shit for you, Mel, not for me. You know I don't give a damn about that damn war paint you drew all over your damn face."

"And you know I'm not about to step out the house lookin' any kinda way!"

Huffing, I put my hands on my hips and stared at him, waiting for my apology to come. I didn't care what reason he had, there was nothing to excuse him for showing up an hour late for a date that he asked for. But instead of acting anything like he was supposed to, Cree simply crinkled his brows deeper in frustration and shrugged.

"Look, you gon' get cha ass in the car or not?"

Nigga, whet?!

"NOT!" I yelled and slammed the door in his face.

Cree had me fucked up in every sense of the word. Knowing what I now knew about him, I could see why he had that attitude. He was probably used to women kissing his ass just because of who he was and what he did. Well, all of that shit didn't matter one bit to me when it came to disrespect.

Mind set on 'ignore a nigga' mode, I turned around and began strutting in my stilettos back towards my room to snatch everything I had on off so I could enjoy the rest of my night in peace, laying up under my sister and watching chick flicks all night. Sure, I had my mind set on doing something else earlier but that was no longer the plan, thanks to Cree. And I was just fine with that. Then there was a knock at the door.

"Mel! Open up this damn door with yo' spoiled ass! It's fuckin' cold out here!"

"You should've thought 'bout that when you started talkin' reckless!" I spat back through the door, whirling around on my heels and crossing my arms in front of my chest as I stared at the door like Cree could see me through it.

"Mel... shit, I said I was sorry!"

"No, you didn't!"

"Well, damn, I didn't say I wasn't!"

Rolling my eyes, I couldn't help but bite back a laugh. I really and truly did not know what I would ever do with Cree. At the same time, I wasn't sure what I would do without him. If I could only get him to act like I wanted him to, I'd be fine. Or would I? Did I want him to act like any other man I met? Maybe the parts of him that frustrated me was actually what I loved the most.

"What, Cree?" I snapped as soon as I pulled open the door. The frown on his face was still there but he sighed and his shoulders dropped. He reached out and grabbed my hand, tugging me forward slightly. I lost my balance and stumbled forward, nearly plummeting into him.

"I'm late because I was gettin' you somethin'. Didn't want to call or text because I know your mouth and attitude. You would've lost yo' damn mind if I said I was runnin' late. Would've snapped on a nigga and all, taken all yo' shit out and probably been sittin' on the couch with ya sister, tellin' her all about how a nigga wasn't shit."

Damn. Maybe he knew me better than I thought he did.

"What is it that you have for me, Cree?" I asked, but before I could really even finish my question, he already had his hand out. Inside of it was a black box, small like a ring box. My heart almost burst in my chest and I told myself to calm down and not go crazy. There was no way there was a ring inside because it was much too soon.

And it wasn't a ring. When he opened it, he revealed the most beautiful pair of yellow diamond earrings. Earrings that just happened to match the yellow and black dress that I was wearing. I jumped up and right into his arms, covering him with kisses.

"Damn, Mel... that mean you like it, huh?" he asked, laughing. Cree's laugh wasn't something you heard often, but when you did it was something you couldn't ignore. His laugh was deep, dark and robust... a perfect complement to his personality and style. It was just like him, unique and like none other.

In the car, I pulled off my earrings and tossed them in my purse so I could put on the ones he bought for me. As I was admiring them in the mirror, I felt his eyes on me. I looked at him and saw that he had a smile on his face. Another Cree rarity that I was privileged enough to see. He affectionately tucked a lock of my hair behind my ear and started the car. Once we were in motion, he placed my hand in his lap. He didn't say anything but it was all in his actions. He wanted to feel my touch. I was beginning to learn that when dealing with a man who didn't say much, his feelings lay in the things he did which required no words. What he said often rubbed me the wrong way but his actions were usually on point.

"So… I read something," I started slowly, trying to figure out the best way to tell him about the folder of information I'd read on him. "About your brothers… and some things that you all have been accused of doing."

Cree didn't look in my direction or even act like he knew what I was trying to say. So I continued on.

"Some illegal things… things you may or may not be doing," I added when he cut his eyes at me. "But things that take a huge amount of skills, intelligence and courage. Things that turn me on."

"Yeah?"

A smirk crossed his face as we drove on, the city lights making a kaleidoscope of colors on his face. He was so sexy in the night light, even more so to me than he had before. I was hot and ready without him doing a single thing to get me that way. There wasn't anything better than finding out that the man you've been feeling is a boss. Like a real boss, running things and getting money in a way that even had New York's finest perplexed on how to get their hands on him.

"Yeah," I replied, smiling at him.

He brought one hand up and ran it coolly over his mouth as if forcing himself not to smile. Even still, the smirk remained. He bit his bottom lip and then pushed out his lips, further sparking the flame inside of me.

"I don't know what you're talkin' about," he said in a rush way but still with a smile to let me know his ass was very much full of shit. "But if I was involved in some crazy shit, would you be the type of woman to ride with a nigga?"

He asked the question and then turned towards me, his eyes locking with mine. I could see that it wasn't just a simple inquiry but that he really and truly was asking. He wanted to know if I could be with someone like him, knowing what it was he was involved with. Whether I could take the heat. The answer? Yes, I could, without a shadow of a doubt. I was born to be down and when it came to Cree, he already had my heart and my loyalty.

"I would be down for life. As long as you stay true to me, I will to you. Ten toes down fa'sho," I added cutely, doing some motions with my fingers as if I was throwing up gang signs. Cree laughed heartily, his deep baritone sending shivers down my spine.

"That's what's up, gangsta."

"*Your* gangsta," I corrected and he smiled. "So… now when do I get to hear details?" I baited him with a grin. I couldn't help it. I just had to know everything about what they did and how they did it. Just thinking about it had my on edge. I was too hype knowing that I knew a real crime family of New York. To be honest, I was low-key power tripping.

"Details?" he queried and shot me a look.

"Yes! Details," I mused.

Cree shook his head and shrugged, giving me a quick glance before placing his eyes back on the road.

"Once again… I don't know what you're talkin' about."

Rolling my eyes, I crossed my arms and scoffed as I looked out the window. What was the use being down if he still wouldn't let me know shit?

"In due time, little grasshopper," he joked with a smile and then reached out to pinch me on the nose. I swatted him away with a grunt.

"Stop, nigga, you messin' up my makeup!" I ran my hand over my nose to fix whatever he might have possibly smudged thinking he was being cute.

"Fuck all that ugly ass shit you got on yo' face. You don't need that clown shit anyways!"

Shaking my head, I didn't even say a thing about him talking shit about the makeup that took me hours to apply. I just looked out the window and tried to remind myself of the revelation I'd had earlier and tried to focus on Cree's actions instead of his words.

But for real, all I could think was that his rude ass was full of shit.

Will You Be Mine.

Sidney

"Oh God, Tank! Shit… please, yes!"

Rolling around in the bed, I grabbed the biggest pillow I had and pushed it on top of my head, hoping to God that I could drown out Faviola's screams and moans of pleasure. I don't care what the hell Tank had in his pants, that nigga wasn't worth all that shit. No dick was worth all that shit. Faviola was putting on, stroking that nigga's ego but she needed to either whisper that shit in his ear or shut the hell up.

"Damn, baby! You murderin' this pussy! Murder that fuckin' shit. Kill that pussy baby. HELL YESSSS!"

"HELL NO!" I yelled, jumping straight out of bed. Snatching my door open, I walked right down the hall to Faviola's door and banged hard as hell on that shit.

"FAVIOLA, SHUT THAT SHIT UP!" I screamed, now officially mad as hell. "AIN'T SHIT THAT NIGGA GOT THAT MAKE A BITCH DO ALL THAT! ACTIN' LIKE YOU AIN'T NEVER HAD DICK BEFORE! BITCH, I'M TRYING TO FUCKIN' SLEEP!"

Mood fucked up, I walked back to my room and slammed the door behind me knowing damn well I was too wide awake now to go back to sleep. Still, I lay down in the bed and pulled the covers over my body, closing my eyes while praying that sleep would come.

"Oomph! Yes... oomph. Shit!"

"Fuck this shit," I grumbled as I sat up and kicked the covers off. Faviola was trying to be quiet but it wasn't doing any good. Reaching out, I grabbed my phone off the table next to me to see what time it was. Four o'clock in the fuckin' morning. This was some bullshit.

Sighing, I looked at my call log and saw that I had more than a few missed calls from Yolo. I wasn't surprised. He had pissed me off earlier after taking a call from LaTrese in private like he had something to say to that bitch that he couldn't say in front of me. By the time he'd finished his conversation with her, I was gone. I knew he would call and it was the reason I put his number on do not disturb. Yolo never stayed mad at me for long. Knowing it was stupid and I was dead wrong for what I was about to do, I sucked in a breath and pressed the call button. He picked up on the first ring.

"Sid?"

The sound of his voice made my heart flutter. I know that's some feminine shit to say but it did. That was the Yolo effect.

"You called me?" I asked, trying to keep my voice calm so he couldn't sense how much I missed him. How much I loved him. How much I wanted him right here with me.

"A few times," was all he said. Holding the phone, we sat in silence for a few seconds with the phone pressed to my ear. He was breathing hard and I started picking up on some noises in the background and decided to question him about it.

"What's tha—are you outside?"

"Yeah, I'm walkin' to the court. Couldn't sleep because I felt bad 'bout that shit that happened earlier. You know I can't sleep unless I got shit right with you." He exhaled and I closed my eyes, knowing he was telling the truth.

Yolo and I have fought a lot of times. And when I say a lot, I mean that we've probably fought more than we've not fought. But each time, he was always the first to apologize. There were days when we were younger that he'd almost fell asleep outside my window, begging and pleading with me to forgive him before he'd agree to go home. At some point through the night, I always did and then would open the window to let him in so he could sleep on the floor by my bed. Years later and ain't a damn thing changed.

"Come play with me?" he asked, his tone almost pleading for me to agree. It tugged on my heart, making me weak instantly.

"Okay," I agreed and cursed myself mentally.

"I'll see you there."

He hung up the phone and I dropped my head in my hands before getting up and getting ready to go. Yes, your girl was on this bullshit again. But don't be judging me like your ass ain't never been in love with a nigga who has broke your heart. Shit… I can't even believe I was doing this shit with this man again my damn self.

"Where's the ball?" I asked Yolo as soon as I walked onto the court.

Frowning, I looked around as I stepped closer to him, wondering how the hell we would play with no ball. When Yolo didn't say anything right away, I stopped and looked at him, noting that he had a crazy look on his face as he stared at me with them light ass eyes.

"What's wrong?" I asked him, feeling slightly uneasy. He was looking at me crazy and it had my emotions in an uproar. But most of all, I was concerned that something was wrong.

"There is no ball," he said finally, shrugging. "I didn't come out here to shoot hoops. I was walking out here because I wanted to be somewhere that reminded me of you."

Yeah, sounds good, nigga.

"Yolo, why you got me out here?" I exasperated, shaking my head as I pulled my skully down lower over my forehead. It was cold as hell outside and I wasn't here for this bullshit.

"I got you out here because I want to talk to you! I don't wanna do this back and forth shit no more. We did it when we was younger and then you made it clear you ain't wanna have shit to do with my ass no more. Now we together and... I just don't wanna do it. We either doing this or we not. You either gon' be my girl or you not. I don't wanna just fuck around and that's it."

He spoke his words with so much passion that it almost made my jaw drop. I looked at him, realizing that he couldn't even look me in the face. That's when I saw it. His eyes were red-rimmed and puffy. He'd been crying? Hell naw, not Yolo. He wasn't one to cry over no chick ever. Had he really cried over me?

"Nigga, is you cryin'?" I asked him, smirking because I knew I was ready to clown his ass.

"Hell naw," he said but I noticed the smile coming to his lips. His eyes flickered up to mine and once he saw the way I was looking at him, he started to laugh and then crossed his arms in front of his body.

"A'ight. I almost shed a few thug tears because you wasn't answerin' my calls but I held that shit back. This shit had me stressed than a muthfucka. You usually don't do that shit, Sid," he said, frowning as he shook his head. "I been callin' yo' ass all day! You always answer when I call you. You might yell, cuss a nigga out and then hang up on my ass but you *always* answer. Shit… I just felt like you was finally through with me."

"I could never be through with you, Yolo."

It was the most honest thing I'd ever said in my life.

Looking up at me, Yolo's eyes met mine and he smiled, biting his bottom lip and looking sexy as fuck.

"So that mean you'll be mine then?" he asked as he walked over to me. He came close and pulled me into his arms but I batted at him and backed away.

"Uh uh… so that means I'll be your what? Being yours could mean your sidepiece, your fuck buddy or all kinds of other shit. I need you to clarify this for me, please," I shot back and he laughed, rubbing the top of his head with his hand as he shook his head.

"My girlfriend, Sid. Does this mean you'll be my girlfriend?" He looked at me straight, his face void of any comprehensible emotion but everything was in his eyes. I could see that he'd even stopped breathing as he waited for me to answer and the longer I took to respond, the more his eyes seemed to go dim from fear that I would say no. All this time and this nigga didn't even know how much I'd wanted to hear him say those words to me.

"Yes," I replied, looking away bashfully as I nodded my head.

"Yes, I'll be your girlfriend."

"For real?" he asked, and I looked up in time to see his bright boyish ass smile. I couldn't believe this shit. We were really on some high school shit for real, yo. But I'm not complaining.

"For real," I told him.

Yolo stepped close to me, pushing his lips into mine and giving me a kiss that sent fireworks through my whole body. It was like we were communicating through our tongues as he pushed his into mine and began playing the most sensual of games, probing my mouth like he was trying to paint a picture. At some point, the same urgent need came to both of us and we began tearing at each other's clothes pulling them off like it wasn't cold as hell outside. It didn't matter. I needed to feel him.

"FUCK!" Yolo said as soon as he entered me. He had me up with my legs wrapped around his waist. I had my back against the gate surrounding the basketball court and was holding onto it in order to keep balance and to stop from scratching the shit out of my ass on it. Thank God for the shadows because, even though it was late at night, out here there was always someone watching in the shadows.

"God you feel so good," he told me, breathing hard as he pushed into the place that I'd reserved for him long ago. Yolo and I had vowed many things to each other. He'd vowed to never lie to me and I'd vowed that my pussy would always be his. The same way he kept his promise I'd kept mine.

"Shit, I'm about to cum, Sid," he told me as he continued stroking deep. I knew I should have told him pull out but I couldn't say a single word. I was on the verge of an orgasm so enormous that it had my toes curling up and my pupils flipped to the back of my eyelids. I couldn't say a single word even if God demanded it.

My body began to jerk and I opened my mouth to moan but Yolo caught it in his, kissing me deeply as I came, making the sensation even more powerful. Then I felt his body tense up and I knew his time was near. He pulled away and I opened my eyes, seeing that he was looking directly into mine. The lust there… the love… I saw it all at that moment. Fuck everybody he's been with, it was there clear as muthafuckin' day that this nigga only loved me.

"Shit, Sid!" he cursed and squeezed his eyes closed just as he let go, shooting his seed right up into me. I held him tight, not saying a word until I felt his body relax against mine. I knew I had all kinds of imprints all over my ass from laying against that gate but I didn't give a shit.

Yolo released my legs and I slid down off of him, watching as he took his sweatshirt off and then his shirt before pulling off his undershirt.

"Here," he said, handing the undershirt to me. "Use this to clean up."

"How romantic," I teased him and he punched me playfully on the shoulder.

"No, what's romantic is that you said you would make it real with a nigga. So you my girl for real, huh?" he said, looking at me like he'd been the one chasing me for all these years. He could have gotten me whenever he wanted me for the past ten plus years but now he was standing here acting like he didn't know it.

"I guess so, but why you acting like you didn't know I wanted to be your girlfriend, Yo?" I asked, rolling my eyes as I started straightening up my clothes. Yolo frowned and cocked his head to the side, giving me a look.

"Maybe because you never told me!"

"What?!" I looked at him, curling up my top lip. "The hell I had to tell you that for? I didn't have to tell you this time!"

"Yeah but when we were younger, it was different. You had me feeling like you ain't wanna see a nigga in public. Remember, you was the one who made the rule that we had to hide what we were doing from my brothers because you ain't want them saying you couldn't hang around us anymore," Yolo said before bending down to pick up his undershirt that I'd thrown on the ground.

He grabbed it and rolled it tight, pushing it into his pockets before muttering something about not leaving his DNA sitting around. I wasn't listening to him because what he'd said before took me back through time as I started to remember what he'd said. All this time I thought that it was his idea to sneak around but he was right. I was the first one to suggest it because his brothers had this thing where they wouldn't invite their girlfriend around when they talked shit, smoked and drank with each other. I loved hanging out with them and they let me since they saw me as one of the boys, so I told Yolo not to let them know what was going on.

In fact, what we did in private never became a problem to me until he started doing shit in public with LaTrese. But I never said anything to Yolo about it so I guess he never thought anything different. Damn.

"So we goin' to your place or my spot here?" he asked, smiling all the way up to his eyes as he opened the gate to let me out of the enclosed court.

"My place first so I can pick up some clothes and shit and then we can go to yours."

"Okay," he told me and then pulled me close to him as we walked down the sidewalk. "But I don't wanna see you comin' out the crib holdin' no boxers or shit like that. Get you some lace panties or something sexy so I can rub that fat ass while you walk through. And you don't have to bust out in the heels all the damn time but every now and then you can surprise a nigga. You ain't gotta change yo' style but you can be sweet with it still… you feel me?"

"I feel you," I told him laughing. He grabbed my hand, pushing his fingers between mine and we walked all the way back to my apartment just like that. Like two people totally and fully in love.

Ready to Move On.

Janelle

After a long day at work, I came home still feeling devastated but more angry than anything else. The more I thought about it, the more I felt like finding Luke and kicking his ass. And I didn't really know how to fight all like that but I'd figure it out. From day one, he pursued me. I never wanted him. I never asked him to call me or to follow me around after work. He did all of that on his own! And now... after he had me right where he wanted me, he did just what niggas did and got lost. He played with my emotions, but that was okay, because Carmella always told me the best way to get over one man was to find someone new.

So after undressing and taking a long bubble bath with wine, candles lit and my favorite bath bombs in the water that had me feeling extra relaxed once I got out, I called Chris to see if he wanted to reschedule our date. For tonight.

"Janelle," he greeted me as soon as he picked up the phone. His voice brought an instant smile to my lips. He seemed genuinely happy, and surprised, to hear from me.

"Chris," I replied back, copying him. "How are you?"

"I was okay. Much better now," he said and I had to roll my eyes at that line. "I know... that was corny but it's true. I was sitting here eating leftovers from last Saturday that probably should have been thrown out on Saturday because they tasted disgusting then," he laughed and I did too. "So when I say that I'm better now, I really do mean it. It's good to hear from you."

I felt the familiar fluttering in my stomach begin as I lay across my bed with my feet dangling in the air. I don't know why I felt nervous about asking Chris out on a date. It wasn't like I was doing it first... he'd already asked me and I was simply rescheduling the one I'd cancelled. So why was I so damn nervous?

"Well, I was thinking. Since you are eating food that you probably should throw away and I haven't eaten at all... why don't we go get something to eat together?" I asked him and then I closed my eyes tight, waiting in anxious anticipation for his response.

"You know... that actually sounds much better than what I'm doing now," he replied and I finally let out the breath I'd been holding. "What time do you want to go? I can pick you up."

"I'll meet you there!" I said, much more forcefully than I'd intended. The thought of him picking me up here did not appeal to me because I didn't want Luke to see me going out with him.

But then again... why not? I was single and after how things ended earlier, I really didn't want to see Luke again. Ever. Never in my life have I told someone I loved them and they didn't say it back. It was humiliating to say the least and his feelings were the last thing I should have been thinking about.

"Actually, if you could pick me up, that would be great. I'll send you the address. The time is on you. Just let me know when and I'll be ready," I told him, feeling better about myself already about the moves I was making to rid my life of Luke.

After that, we said a few more words and then hung up so that we could get ready for our first date. I was excited. More excited than I thought I would be. With Chris, things were easier. I didn't have to worry about who saw us while we were together. I didn't have to worry about what my daddy would say or whether or not being with him would cost me my dreams. He fit perfectly into my life just the way I'd always imagined it and he was the one I should have been focused on anyways. Not Luke's punk ass.

About an hour later, I was dressed to impress and ready to go. Carmella was out doing whatever it was that she did but I was grateful for it, because with her gone, I was able to raid her closet for the perfect heels. After pushing them on my feet, I admired myself in the mirror, twisting around and loving the way that my body looked in the knee-length red and silver bandage dress I was wearing. Over the past couple weeks, I'd gained a few pounds and initially I flipped out about it, but I actually loved it. Every pound went to the perfect place, giving me a little more of the ass that I didn't have before and nice rounded hips to go along with my toned thighs.

"Damn, you look great," Chris said as soon as I opened the door. My mouth dropped open when I saw that he'd bought flowers for me. And they were beautiful red roses. Smiling, I took them from him and set them on the counter in the kitchen.

"Thank you for the flowers. They are so pretty," I told him, smiling hard. Probably too hard, but whatever.

I turned around to look at him and noticed that his eyes were all over me, taking in my appearance. It was obvious by the look in his eyes that he liked what he saw. There was something different about him. It was like he'd shed the good boy vibe that he had going at work and was more relaxed.

The dress shirt, slacks and tie was gone and replaced with some nice jeans, sneakers and a simple polo shirt. He even had a small gold chain on… nothing too flashy but very nice. He had a diamond earring in his ear and it shocked me. I didn't even know his ear was pierced but I liked it. His whole appearance was much edgier and sexier than what I was used to when it came to him but everything about it was on point.

Walking outside, I locked up and then walked behind him to his car. It was a Mercedes Benz, newer model and very nice. He held the door open for me and I sat down onto the cream leather seats, taking a deep breath and relaxing as he closed the door and walked to his side.

And then, suddenly, I began to panic. I wasn't ready to spend time with another man when my heart and mind still yearned for Luke. Just thinking about sharing space alone with Chris made me feel like I was caught up in the most wicked form of betrayal.

Chill, Janelle. It's just a date! I told myself and took another deep breath just as Chris stepped into the car.

"You good?" he asked, and my stomach jerked inside of me. Those were the same words that Luke said to me all the time.

"Yes," I breathed out, although I still wasn't sure. Tossing him a small smile, I turned and looked out the window as he prepared to drive off.

On the way out of the neighborhood, he took a turn down a street that I didn't normally go down into a neighborhood I'd never seen. That wasn't saying much. I didn't explore at all, I went the same few places every day and nowhere else. As we neared a house, I saw a group of guys standing out front, but what caught my eye was the fact that I immediately noted Luke's car parked out front. I glanced from the car to the person closest to it and there was Luke.

"Oh shoot!" I said, feeling my heart began to beat rapidly in my chest. I began looking around for some place to hide. In my state of panic, I actually thought about diving down onto the floor. Can you believe that shit?

"Are you okay?" Chris asked, interrupting my thoughts and temporarily stalling my panic once I realized how crazy I must look to him.

"Yes… I'm fine. Thanks," I told him and cut my eyes away to the window.

We drove closer to Luke but I was more focused on the fact that he had a woman in front of him. She was standing, facing him with her body pressed up against his and her arms wrapped around his neck. I felt a jolt of jealousy rip through my heart when she lifted up on her tiptoes to kiss him… right on the lips. He dodged her, ducking his head so that her lips grazed his cheek instead and then laughed like something was funny, running his hand around her back and squeezing hard on her ass. The same way he used to do me.

My heart galloped but I sat still like a statute, unrestrained jealousy shooting through my eyes. My glare was so compelling that Luke must have felt it because as we neared them he pivoted, a smile still on his face while he palmed his little ho's ass like it was Playdoh in his hands.

Then we locked eyes. The smile vanished from his lips and he mired, frozen in place by the intensity of our connection. His eyes then swiveled to the driver's side to Chris and he recoiled, as if reacting to a punch, before returning to mine just as we trundled by. His brilliant browns filled with terror and I saw the emotions ripping through him, recognizing them instantly because they mirrored mine.

Jealousy. Hurt. Fear. Panic.

We passed, leaving him in my rearview and I struggled to keep a straight face, pretending that my heart wasn't throbbing in my chest, aching for a man I only wanted to love me back. With Luke behind us, I was determined to not give him the satisfaction of turning in my seat to stare but I couldn't resist a peek in the mirror on my side. I swallowed hard and grimaced when I saw that he was no longer lying on the car with his video vixen ho in his arms. He had staggered to the middle of the street, eyes fixated on where I sat, looking like an orphaned child longing for love but belonging to no one.

"SHIT! Was that Luke Murray?" Chris asked, looking in the rearview mirror as he drove, ping ponging his eyes between the mirror and the road.

"Yes, it was," I told him, tears coming to my eyes.

Clearing my throat, I took a deep breath and tried to blink them away. I wasn't supposed to be this emotional… not over Luke. I had to force myself to get over him but it was hard. Why was it that the heart always wanted to be obsessed with the one person it could not have? The one person who didn't love me was the one I felt like I loved more than anyone ever.

"I mean… I think that was him anyways," I added with a shrug.

"I think so too," Chris said and then turned the corner. I silently said a word of thanks that I could no longer see Luke standing in the streets staring at me with that haunting look in his eyes.

"You've never seen him around here?" Chris asked. "Shit… that's crazy how he was staring at us. Kinda spooky. Like he remembers us."

"I don't get out much to see anyone," was all I said.

My phone started buzzing in my purse and I already knew who it was, but I refused to answer the call. Reaching in, I grabbed it and it was Luke. Just like I thought. My finger hovered over the answer button for a few seconds as I stared at the illumination of his name on my screen. I wanted to talk to him, yearned to hear his voice and hear what he had to say but it was a trap. He only wanted me now that he saw I'd moved on. As soon as he had me, I would be just as unimportant as I was before and I couldn't bear anymore rejection. I hit ignore quickly before turning off the ringer and pushing it back inside my purse.

"Well, this area might not be the best place for you to stay. With them around… it can't be a safe place. Especially not for someone like you."

Looking out the window, I listened to Chris's words, unable to stop them from cycling through my mind. No, it wasn't a safe place for someone like me to be. A lot could happen to a good girl if she happened to cross paths with a man like Luke Murray.

But it was too late. I'd already fallen in love.

No Other Choice.

Teema

"Okay, Kenya, it's time to go!" I said, lifting her up from off the floor. She giggled when I swung her up into my arms before grabbing her diaper bag from the table.

It was another day and I was in a good mood after getting up early enough to spend some quality time playing with my daughter. Being that I'd been working late each night, I was getting in after she had already gone to sleep. I didn't understand it because on the weekends, she stayed up at least until nine o'clock, but I had been getting in each day around eight and her lil' ass was always knocked out.

Closing the door behind us, I hurried to the car and buckled her car seat in so that I could get out of there and get to work on time. The last thing I needed was Danielle to be all up in my face about being late once again. The past few days, I'd managed to stay out of her way and I wanted to keep that trend going strong.

I dropped Kenya off and was barely able to give her a kiss on the cheek before giving Ms. Williams my last few dollars, running back out to my car and racing to work. I made it there with only two minutes left to spare and swiped my badge quickly to make sure that it showed I'd arrived on time. Breathing heavily, I told myself that the good thing about not having money for lunch today was that maybe I could finally lose some weight as I walked to the locker room to lock up my things.

I was about to walk out when I saw that the sole of my shoe had come undone so I groaned heavily and unlocked my locker so I could get my superglue. Once it dried enough to allow me to walk, I stood up, repeated my mantra again and headed to the door. But as soon as I walked out, I ran right into Danielle.

"Watch where you're goin'!" she snapped, stumbling back a few steps before she regained her balance. I muttered out an apology and tried to hurry on by, hoping that she would just let me go. But of course she didn't.

"Stop!" she called out and I dropped my head, closing my eyes for a second to ask God why He was allowing her to do this to me right now. Didn't He know I needed a break?

"Yes, Danielle?" I asked before turning around to look at her. She was in full 'bitch' stance, her favorite position, with her hands on her hips and a stank ass look on her face which meant she was about to be trouble.

"You're late again! And I told you what was going to happen if you were late again, didn't I?"

Blinking, I looked at her, trying to find the correct words to say to defend myself without saying anything to worsen her attitude.

"I'm not late. I clocked in two minutes before my shift starts," I explained but she only shook her head, a malicious smirk filled with evil intent spreading across her face.

"I don't care what time you clock in. I'm concerned with the time that you begin working. And according to my watch, you are ten minutes late!"

"But I—"

"Listen," she began, taking a single step forward. "I don't give a shit about your excuses. I told you what was going to happen and that's the end of it. So give me your badge, I'm writing you up," she ordered with her nose curled up like I smelled.

"My badge? Why do you need my badge?" I asked, brows bunched together in confusion. I'd been written up a few times before by Danielle but never have I had to give up my badge.

"Because this makes your fifth write-up which means that you're being suspended for three days without pay."

"WHAT?!" I shouted, much louder than I'd intended but I couldn't believe this! I was already living paycheck to paycheck so even though three days without work may have seemed like something small to some, it was everything to me.

"Danielle, I can't be suspended for three days because I need my money. If you want me to stay late or come early tomorrow, I can do that! I'll skip lunch to make up the time but please, don't take my hours from me! I need every penny I make so that I can take care of my child!"

I hated begging this bitch for shit, but at the moment, she was my only hope. The kicker was that she was enjoying every minute of my misery, staring back at me with a gloating grin stretched across her ugly ass face. Danielle was a pretty girl on the outside but her attitude was so bad that it overshadowed her beauty. Right then, she looked just like the devil to me.

"Don't do this to me," I pled, tears coming to my eyes. I couldn't stand the fact that I was about to cry in front of this woman who had terrorized me for so much of my life.

"I didn't do this to you, Teema. *You* did. *You* made the choice to not get here on time this morning. So give me your badge." She held out her hand, pushing it right up into my face, so close that her pinky finger grazed my nose.

"Please—"

"Your badge!"

Dropping my head, I pulled my badge out of my pocket and handed it to her just as Cyndy walked over.

"What's going on, Teema?" Cyndy asked, looking from me to the satisfied expression on Danielle's face and then back to me again.

"What's going on is that Teema is late *once* again after I told her what the consequences would be. So now, she's being suspended," Danielle informed Cyndy as she pushed my badge into her pocket. "Do I need to get security to escort you from the building?"

"Danielle, now you're takin' this shit too far. You know you ain't gotta do no shit like that. She can walk out on her own!" Cyndy spoke up for me.

"Cyn, don't," I said and grabbed her arm to signal her to stop.

Smirking, Danielle whirled around on her heels and started whistling a tune as she walked away. Rage set in as I watched her, hating my situation, hating myself, but most of all hating her for everything that she'd ever done to me. Things I never deserved.

"Let's go, Tee," Cyndy said sadly. "Get your purse and I'll walk you out."

Nodding my head, I took one last look at Danielle who had positioned herself a few feet away from us so she could watch and make sure I left the building. She was so happy knowing that she had the power to ruin me. It was like high school all over again.

"Hurry up, I don't have all day," she said, snapping her fingers.

"Bitch," I mumbled under my breath as I turned around.

"What?!" Danielle piped up; I heard her shoes clicking on the linoleum floor. "I heard that. Who said it?"

Eyes wide, I turned around, knowing that I'd made a huge mistake. My mouth moved but no sound came out.

"Who said it?!" she repeated and I licked my lips, ready to apologize.

"I'm sorr—"

"I said it," Cyndy spoke up, pushing me lightly on the arm as she cut me off. "It was me."

Danielle narrowed her eyes at Cyndy, her upper lip curled into a sneer. Then she shot her attention to me, the wheels turning round and round in her evil little head.

"No... I don't think it was you, Cyndy," she said finally. "It was Teema. So Teema, you're fired." Sucking her teeth, Cyndy jumped in front of Danielle and pointed right into her face.

"You can't—"

"And Cyndy, you're fired too for trying to cover for her! Give me your badge and both of y'all get out!" Danielle shouted.

I looked around at the other people in the hall, many of them watching the interaction between the three of us. I recognized a couple CNAs that I worked with standing around, shaking their heads in disgust at what Danielle was doing. It was no secret what she did to me. Everyone knew it, but Cyndy was the only one to ever stand up for me when she saw it.

"I should beat yo' muthafuckin' a—"

"Cyndy, no," I said, reaching out to grab her arm and pull her back. "She's the type of bitch who will try to press charges just because she got her ass whooped. It ain't worth it."

Cyndy held her glare on Danielle for a few seconds longer before snatching her badge from where it hung on the edge of her shirt. She reared her arms back and threw it down the hall behind where Danielle stood.

"Go fetch, bitch!" Cyndy snapped before whirling around and running into the locker room. I followed behind her, grabbing my things. On the outside, I was calm because I needed to make sure that Cyndy didn't get herself locked up. But inside, I was frustrated and devastated. I went from being suspended for three days to having no job at all, but I couldn't blame anyone but myself.

"I'm so sorry about that, Cyn," I said, as soon as we were out of the building and walking to our cars. "I should have kept my mouth closed."

"No, you shouldn't have!" Cyndy corrected me. "It was about time that you said something to that bitch and you should've said a lot more! I don't give a fuck about that job because I'm going to be good. I'm just pissed because I know you needed that money but that miserable ass bitch just can't stand to see you happy living your own damn life."

Wringing my hands together, I felt a burning sensation in my chest as I turned to say something to Cyndy that I hated I'd even have to say.

"I—I might take a little longer to pay you your money back than I thought. I'm sorry but…" Pausing, I blinked away tears of frustration and anger. Every day I was trying to prove to myself that I wasn't stupid for refusing to take money from Kane and instead wanting to do things myself but now look. I was right back in the position I never wanted to be in, depending on someone else to help me. Only this time, I was broke as hell while doing it instead of living lavishly spending up Kane's money.

"Don't even worry about that money, Teema. I'm not gonna take it when I know how much you really needed it. Keep it," she said. I had the best friend anyone could have.

Hugging her tight, I got into my car and sighed when I saw that my gaslight was on. But I'd pushed my car plenty of times and knew from experience that I had enough to make it to pick up Kenya and get home.

With Kenya in the car, my mood only got worse. Not because I wasn't happy to see her but because seeing her only reminded me about how much I felt like I was failing her. I parked in my space wearing a big frown on my face when I saw the apartment manager nailing a notice on my door. The only time I ever saw him was when he was delivering bad news so I already feared the worst. Jumping out the car,

I grabbed Kenya and then ran over to see what he was up to.

"Ms. Teema, how are you doing today, ma'am?"

"I'll be doing better when I know why you're here, Alfred," I replied back curtly.

Sighing, he ran his hands through his bleach blond hair and then pointed to the papers he'd placed on the door.

"I'm sorry to do this because I know you work so hard, Teema, but it's coming from corporate so I have no choice." My throat began to burn. "This is an eviction notice. You haven't paid rent for over three months."

What?!

"Normally, they serve you with these after you're late for two months but I tried to give you an extra month—"

"But there has to be a mistake somewhere…" I licked my lips, eyes darting everywhere around me. "…My rent has been paid. My mama pays it a few days late because she gets her check on the first and—"

Saddened, Alfred shook his head. "No, Teema, she hasn't paid anything. I haven't seen your mama bring a check in there since the summer."

"The summer?! Are you sure because I've been asking her and—"

"I'm positive," Alfred said with a quick nod. "I've called you and left messages for you to give me a call so we could work something out but no one called me back. The order was filed and I even stopped by a few times before we closed this week and told your mom so she could let you know to make plans because you'll have to have your things out soon."

Frowning, I listened to him, realizing that I'd been taken for a fool. All this time she knew she wasn't paying a damn thing and was covering for her own ass, telling me that the office was calling only because she was paying late. Alfred had tried to give me the message this week and she'd even lied then. She saw my struggle up close every day. How could she do this to me?

"When do we have to leave?" I asked softly. Just when I thought I was at the lowest point in my life, I was now seeing there was a basement.

With a heavy exhale, Alfred shook his head softly and said, "You have one day. The sheriff will be out on Friday in the morning to ensure that you're out by then."

I was devastated.

After unlocking my door, I walked into my apartment feeling completely numb. There wasn't a trace of my mother in the living room so I figured she might have still been sleeping in the room. Kenya reached up and pulled hard at my earring, snatching it out and I barely felt a thing. I placed her down on the floor where she sat happily, sticking the large hoop in her mouth and I moved slowly towards the bedroom. When I pushed the door open, I found her sleeping soundly in the bed, *my* bed, like she didn't have a care in the world. Like she wasn't responsible for my daughter having no place to call home.

"GET UP!" I screamed, snatching the covers right off her. She was lying in the bed with her boney ass pointed up in the air, not wearing a single stitch of clothing. Once the cool air hit her, she jumped straight in the air, grabbing the sheet and pulling it on her body.

"Teema! Girl, what do you think you're doing?!" she yelled, bunching her eyebrows together. "Somethin' wrong with the baby?"

She cut her eyes at a Benadryl bottle on the dresser and I squinted at it, my mind putting two and two together. Was this why my baby was knocked out all the time? She was drugging her to sleep? God help me, I was going to kill this woman!

"YOU NEED TO GET DA FUCK OUT!" I screamed, and she jumped to her feet with her hand raised like she was going to slap me.

I beat her to it.

Reaching back, I reared forward with all my might and slammed my hand down so hard against her face that it stung my skin. Later on, I knew I would regret putting my hands on her in front of my daughter but I could only hope that she would never remember this.

"What you do that for?!" she shrieked, holding onto her cheek with both hands.

I opened my mouth, prepared to curse her out but then I looked down and saw her grinding her teeth together. I knew what that meant all too well after enduring years of living with an addict. She looked pitiful and now that I could get a good look at her, I knew for sure that she was using again. I didn't know how I missed it before—I was probably too busy to see it but I couldn't miss it now. Instead of using her check to pay for the place we laid our head, she had been smoking it all up.

Shaking my head, I didn't say another word to her because I was done. She was pathetic and selfish just like she'd always been. Caring about nobody or nothing but herself. Going into Kenya's room, I packed up a suitcase full of her things so that I could make sure she was okay and then I grabbed her and left, not taking anything else with me. There was nothing left in that apartment that I ever again wanted to see.

After explaining to Ms. Williams what happened, she gave me back the money that I'd given to her when I dropped Kenya off that morning, so I used that to put gas in my car and hopped on the interstate. I had no plans, was just driving, but somehow I ended up in Brooklyn, right in front of the house Kane stayed in when he wasn't at his condo. It was pouring down raining, so I quickly grabbed Kenya up and covered our heads with my jacket as I jogged to his front door.

As soon as I knocked on the door, I heard movement from inside but it still took a minute before I heard steps coming towards the door. I should have felt relieved, but I hadn't seen Kane in a year and I didn't know what to expect from him once he saw me at the door. We had a complex history.

I heard the locks in the door shifting and I swallowed hard, gulping down my pride. Tears came to my eyes but it wasn't because I was sad or felt sorry for myself. I was pissed that I had to actually stand here and ask this nigga to do something for me.

Kane opened the door and as soon as I looked at him and noted the surprise in his eyes, I lost my train of thought. Kenya cooed in my arms and reached her hand out to him as if she recognized her father immediately. But he didn't even look at her, purposefully keeping his eyes on me. I saw his jaw clench tight and I had to force myself to just say what I needed to say so I could be gone.

"Kane, you know I hate to ask you for shit," I started and the tears got worse, totally clouding my vision, but I tried to keep them at bay. "But I just lost my job and I was evicted from my apartment. I spent the last of my money to get over here. I'm not asking you if we can move in, I just need to stay the night and a little money to last until I can figure out what I'm going to do."

He was as still as a statue, not moving a muscle. I swear it didn't even look like he blinked. Kenya started squiggling in my arms and I held her tight to protect her from the cold. It was pouring down raining, but the temperature was low so it felt like icicles when it hit my bare skin.

"Kane?"

Shivering, I looked around us, feeling out of place even if it was my old hood. Kenya cooed loudly and then reached out again, this time with both hands aimed at her father but he still didn't even bend his head towards her. It was pissing me off seeing her so desperate for attention that he was refusing to give.

"No."

"What?" I blurted, looking up at him with surprise.

"I said no. You can't come in here." He lifted something to his face and it was the first time I noticed he had a cell phone in his hand. "Cree, you almost here?"

"Right around the corner, bruh," Cree said through the speaker. Kane hung up the phone and then grabbed a fistful of cash out of his pocket and handed it to me. In my anger, I wanted to refuse it but that would have just been stupid. I needed it, and from the looks of it, it was more money than I would have made in months.

"I saw you when you pulled up so I called Cree. He just left from over here so he's close," Kane explained, his voice completely void of any emotion.

I couldn't even say anything, only look at him. The tears in my eyes were gone because I was so in awe of the asshole he'd become since the first day I laid eyes on him. How could this even be the same man I once loved? He was so far removed from the person he'd been. I couldn't even recognize him.

Cree pulled up just as the rain began to subside and jumped out the car. He ran towards me with his hands out and scooped Kenya right up into his arms before grabbing me around the shoulders into a half hug and kissing me on my forehead.

"Been a long time, Teema," he said, giving me a look. "You didn't have to block me; you know I ain't got no beef with you or my niece."

Shrugging, I didn't say a single word. I wasn't in a position to argue with anyone. I glanced at Kane with pure hatred in my eyes as I began to walk away. What parent disowned a child who they knew was theirs? He was worse than my mother. At least she had an addiction that made her stupid as hell. What was Kane's excuse?

"You can ride with me. I'll drop you off and come back to get your car," he told me rather than asking.

When Cree opened the door to help me place my things in the car, I saw that he had someone sitting in the passenger seat. I recognized her immediately as the girl from the club who pushed me down. The bitch responsible for the big ass knot I'd been sporting on my head. She turned to look at me and her eyes widened in surprise. She opened her mouth to say something but I shook my head.

"Don't."

She caught my drift, pursed her lips and turned around to look out the window. I didn't need any more trouble and I had bigger things to worry about than what went down between her and I at the club. Cree got in the car while I was strapping Kenya down in her seat and drove off once she was in securely. I didn't even turn to look at Kane as we drove away.

Love.

Outlaw

I had the radio on low, sitting in the dark, smoking a blunt. It was raining outside and that further mellowed my mood. I could have sat there forever but Kane was making too much damn noise and it was fuckin' up the vibe I had going. On top of that, I was hungry as shit.

Sighing, I sat up and ran my hand down over my face, thinking once again about Janelle. I kept calling her but she wasn't answering so I just stopped. She'd blocked me once and it was obvious that she'd done it again. She was moving on but I was stuck on her. I'd tried calling up some chicks I kept in touch with when I wanted to get my dick wet but I didn't even feel like fuckin' around with them no more. The one woman I wanted was the one I couldn't get.

"What's all that fuckin' noise, nigga?" I asked Kane, walking into his living room.

Cree, Yolo and Tank had left as soon as the rain started coming down hard but Kane said I was too drunk to drive and made me lay down to sleep it off. I couldn't sleep so I smoked and laid on the bed, the image of Janelle and her new nigga running over and over again in my mind.

Kane looked up at me with an expression that I wasn't used to seeing on him. His forehead was wrinkled up in a deep frown, his eyes were wide and clouded over and he was holding onto the glass in his hand so hard that his knuckles were white.

"Damn, bruh. You good, nigga?" I asked, lifting one brow, even though the answer was obvious. "Who were you talkin' to outside?"

"Teema," was all he said and then pressed his lips firmly together.

"Teema?" I echoed. "She was here? Shit... why you ain't tell me?"

He gave me a perplexed look and then I remembered he didn't know I still had contact with her. Or at least I did until her phone got turned off and I started spending all my time with Janelle.

"Why was she here? She wanted something?"

Kane nodded his head. "She said she lost her job and got kicked out her place. Wanted to stay here for a while until she got her shit together."

"Okay then, where the hell she at?!" One look at Kane and I already had an idea what was going on.

"She's with Cree. She had her kid with her."

"You didn't let her stay?! The fuck, Kane! Her kid is your *fuckin'* daughter!"

Grabbing my phone, I shot off a text to Cree before turning back to Kane. I really didn't even want to get into this with Kane because we'd had this same argument plenty times before. The first one was way back when Teema first had Kenya and took a paternity test proving that she was his child. Right then, I stopped riding for Kane and was Team Teema. Kane was my blood and I stood by him when it came to everything except this. I took the thought of kids very seriously and that's why I wasn't trying to have none.

"I can't let her stay here with her kid! Listen, man, I know you don't understand this shit and you don't approve of the way I go about this shit but I don't know no other way for me. I'm not like Tank—that nigga can have a million fuckin' kids and still do the shit we do then sleep like a baby at night. I can't do that shit! I always said that the minute I started having babies would be the same moment I gave up the game because I know with the shit I'm doin', I'mma end up either dead or in jail. I don't want no kid of mine to deal with that."

I was listening to what he was saying, but at the same time, I wasn't hearing him, if you know what I mean. The shit made no sense at all to me and it never would.

"But she's here now, Kane. Fuck your plan because it didn't work so you need a new plan. You got a daughter and whether you want her or not, pretending that she don't exist makes you…well, it makes you a bitch," I said with a shrug. I had tried to think of something nicer to say but shiiiidd, it is what it is.

Kane glared at me and I knew he hated what I was saying but I didn't give a shit. He never held back when he was getting on my ass and now it was my turn to spit him some truth.

"You wrong as hell for what you doin', bruh, and I can't condone that shit. Yolo, Cree and Tank may not say it but I will. Sending money is all good but Teema ain't never been the type to want you for your money and I'm sure Kenya won't grow up to be that type either. She's a Murray… she got *our* blood in her. You always say you're all about family… well, you need to prove that shit. You my big brother and all but you doin' some stupid shit."

Kane sat down on the couch and slumped over, hanging his head down low. This was the first time I'd ever seen him acting like this. When Teema first moved away, he got ghost for a while, wouldn't answer his phone or let us in the house. We gave him his space and a couple weeks later, he popped up like everything was fine. But it was obvious now that he was struggling with his situation more than I'd thought.

"You right, man," he said, and I smirked hard, satisfied that I was getting my moment to shine on his ass.

"I don't mean to be all hard on you but—"

"Yes, your ass do," Kane shot back and I shrugged.

"True. But if you so concerned with your daughter dealing with having a father who is either dead or locked up for life, then that only means we gotta be smarter about how we move. That don't mean you disown her. You need to straighten that shit out and be a man," I finished and then dropped down in the chair across from Kane.

"Shit… that weed got me feelin' wise and shit," I muttered more to myself than him.

"Speaking of being wise and making smart moves, what are you planning to do about your situation with ole girl?" he asked me and I tensed up. Now it was his turn to the tables back on me.

"She moved on so ain't shit I gotta do. You was out there! We all saw her riding off into the sunset with another nigga."

Kane nodded his head. "Yeah I saw her. And I also saw you standin' in the middle of the street lookin' like a lovesick puppy. What was that about?"

Leaning back in the chair, I crossed my arms in front of my chest but didn't say shit. Kane gazed at me with scrutiny and then let out a low laugh, swallowing down the rest of the liquid from his glass before sitting it down.

"She's not moving on because you ain't gon' let her," he assessed on his own. "Figure out what you wanna do and just make that shit work, the same way you just told me. If you can let her go and be good with that, then let her go. But if you want her in your life, you might have to move some shit around and make some changes to fit her in. I trust your judgment so I just ask that you be responsible 'bout your shit and make wise decisions."

"I thought that's what I was doin' though. I left her alone because… you said that—"

"I didn't think you was serious about her, bruh," Kane pressed out in the midst of a heavy sigh. "I thought you was just doin' your normal thing… fuckin' with her head. Figured you'd leave her pissed off with a bone to pick that could get us all locked up."

Cupping my chin in my hands, I frowned and shook my head. I didn't have it in me to just fuck with her head… she was the one fuckin' with mine. The impossible had now been made possible and my need for Janelle to be in my life had finally outgrown my pride. I was learning that everything in this world worth anything at all lay inside of a woman. My woman.

"If it's causing more harm to you to let her go than to keep her. Fix that shit."

"I can do that," I replied and nodded my head slowly as I thought it all through. "I'm going to do that."

I sighed and stood up, feeling heaviness in my chest. I didn't want to think about what I should do about my situation because to do that meant I had to think about her. I had to think about the time I was missing out on. All the passing moments that I could have been spending with Janelle but I wasn't. Mainly because I'd fucked up and refused her right when she needed me most. After telling me she loved me, the single thing she needed from me right then was to hear that I loved her back. Or to at least *feel* that I did even if I didn't have the courage to say it. But I'd given her the opposite and left her cold and alone. Pretty much the same way I was feeling now.

Walking back into Kane's extra room, I closed the door and just lay on the bed. I didn't even know how to begin to try to make things work with a woman because I'd never done that shit before. Never had to. I'd never even *liked* a woman enough to even consider changing anything about how I lived my life to accommodate her. Why? All the broads I'd dealt with in the past were only temporary. Small distractions to hold my attention until the next one came along.

But Janelle was so much more than that to me. She came out of nowhere, a primary observer of me at my lowest point. The first time I laid eyes on her, I wanted to hate her because I knew she was part of the system put in place to destroy me. But even then, I couldn't. I was caught up by something in her and that day at the pharmacy, I knew then that we'd been brought together by fate.

Squeezing my eyes closed, I pushed down hard on my eyelids and forced out a breath. I couldn't stop myself from wondering what Janelle was doing now. Where did they go? Were they alone? Glancing at my keys, I contemplated going to her apartment and waiting for her to come home but decided against it. Thinking back on Kane's advice, I knew he was right. I couldn't move too hastily. I had to think this shit through, because once I got her back, I didn't want to give her any reason to go. Her being with me was no longer just a want but it was a need. I couldn't get shit done with her so heavily on my mind. But it wasn't even like I was trying to rid my thoughts of her, because I only found comfort thinking back on how alive I felt when I was with Janelle.

Fuck it. I had to see her.

Grabbing my keys, I got myself together and left. I didn't know where she'd gone but I was going to be waiting for her to return. Parallel parking in front of her apartment, I got out and sat on the hood of my whip and rolled one up to smoke while I waited. After a torturous hour of thinking every passing car was her only to be subsequently let down, Cree pulled up with Janelle's sister in the car.

"Wassup?" I greeted her when she jumped out and ran by me to go into the apartment. She waved and I turned to my brother.

"Over here waitin' on ole girl?" Cree asked, and I nodded. "I feel ya. I'd be doin' the same shit."

Carmella walked out a few minutes later with an overnight bag in her hands. I stopped her right before she passed by me to walk to

Cree's car.

"Aye, I need a favor from you," I told her. She smirked a little and turned around to fully face me, both of her brows raised. I could tell from the expression on her face she already knew what the business was.

"I fucked up with Janelle—"

"I heard."

"Damn, you ain't gotta be like that with a nigga." She looked at me squarely, not saying a thing.

"All I wanna do is make it right," I said, cutting to the chase. She stared at me, not speaking but analyzing, and I could see a resemblance of Janelle in her, which almost made me smile. It triggered a memory of one of the many times she'd looked at me in the same way and I felt a burning sensation in my chest. I was miserable without her.

"If you want to make things right, don't do it this way. She's on a date with someone from her job and if he drives up and she sees you here, she'll go crazy. The most important thing to Janelle right now is her career; and she loves you but you don't want to force her to choose. It won't end well. Just wait for what feels like the best moment and make a move then."

My stubbornness got the best of me and I shook my head. I wasn't willing to chance it by wasting anymore time.

"I won't force her but I won't let her go."

She sighed and stepped closer. Raising my head, I narrowed my eyes at her, seconds away from telling her to fuck off with all her negative energy. Didn't need that shit in my life right now.

"You don't have to let her go but just trust me. I know my sister. This isn't the time. You have to trust me… I'm on your side."

Squeezing my eyes closed, I dropped my head and exhaled a stubborn breath. It wasn't what I wanted to hear but I had to listen. She was Janelle's sister and knew her better than even I did. I placed my trust in her words, certain that what she'd advised was what I should do. But when Carmella turned around to leave, all of a sudden I was hit with a shred of fear.

"Aye… You sure about this shit, right?" I yelled out, needing to hear some confirmation one last time.

"I'm positive. Now go… I know my sister," she said and then hopped inside of Cree's ride.

Once they drove off, I smoked the rest of my blunt and then left to go home. Not to my place in Brooklyn but to my condo. I knew if I stayed in Brooklyn, nothing was going to stop me from knocking on her door if I knew she was there.

Do the Right Thing.

Carmella

*I*t felt like one of the best days of my life.

After going out with Cree, we stopped at a nice, local spot that I'd never been to before to get a late night snack. It was an ice cream shop that made the best ice cream I'd ever had in my life, with all kinds of ingredients you could stack on top of it. Now I wasn't no small, toothpick kinda chick who didn't know how to eat. I was sexy as hell and my body came about from a lot of hard work, but I still knew how to eat more than my fair share of junk whenever I got the chance. So while Cree kept it simple with one scoop of vanilla ice cream, I made sure to dump Oreos, gummies, M & M's, Snickers, chocolate fudge and whatever else I could find on mine. But you know Cree had to try to steal my joy even when it came to that.

"All that fuckin' sugar. Make sure you brush all that shit off your teeth tonight," he grunted, as I took huge bites of my ice cream, looking at me with his face twisted up like he had caught a whiff of a big pile of shit.

"I know how to take care of my damn teeth, Cree! Don't be telling me what to do!"

I cut my eyes at him before we walked out the front door of the small store. Ole judgmental ass always had something to say.

"Them cavities you got in the back say otherwise," he mumbled back at me and my cheeks stung from embarrassment when I heard someone snickering from behind me in the store. Was this really the kind of nigga I wanted to spend my time with?

Pushing past him, I deliberately knocked into him on my way out the door and stomped right over to the trashcan where I dumped the rest of my ice cream. That shit hurt me to my heart because I had my heart set on eating every bit of it but Cree had pissed me off to the max.

"Stop trippin'. Damn!" he said, walking up behind me. He grabbed my arm and pulled me hard, twisting me around so that I was looking right at him. As soon as I met his eyes, my attitude began to decrease drastically but I tried not to let it show.

"I'm not tryin' to piss you off, ma," he said, the southern accent that he hid very well popping up. "I know I don't say shit the right way sometimes. But just pay attention to why I'm sayin' this shit instead of how I'm sayin' it. I care 'bout you so I can't help sayin' something when I feel like you fuckin' up."

I rolled my eyes. "Fuckin' up, Cree? You got on me about some damn ice cream when it was your idea to come here to begin with. Then you wanna point out some cavities that I got when I was like thirteen years old! That's rude as hell! You act like you was criticizing me for something important instead of because of my damn teeth!"

Cree flinched and frowned down at me, seriously looking like he wanted to snatch me up and shake hard until my brain began to rattle. What was his deal?

"Teeth are fuckin' serious, Mel!"

Cocking my head back, I looked at him like he'd lost his damn mind. I felt like I was in the twilight zone. What was it with this nigga and teeth that had him about to start a whole damn fight? Scoffing, I rolled my eyes and turned around to walk to his car, mind made up to not say a single word to him until he took me back to Janelle's. This was some bullshit.

In the car, I checked my phone and saw that I had a text from Sasha's brother, Zeke, asking me if I could meet up with him in a couple days. That brought a smile to my face instantly. I was ready to figure out what he had in store for me to do. For him to be working in Manhattan he had to be making some serious cash and I couldn't wait to be part of it. I texted him right back, telling him that I would be wherever he needed me whenever he wanted me there. When I placed my phone down, I noticed that the car had stopped at a red light and that Cree was staring right at me, his eyes clear and soft like he wanted to tell me something.

"What?" I snapped, raising my hands up while I gave him a wide-eyed look. "You got a staring problem?"

Sighing, Cree licked his lips and closed his eyes before running his hand over his face like he was distressed or something. Figure that shit… he was the one aggravating me all the time but he wanted to act like I was stressing him out.

"Yo, you gotta do something about that fuckin' mouth."

He spoke with more annoyance than I would have liked. And I was about to say something about it but he lifted his hand up, silencing me right before I was about to tear into his ass.

"Maybe the reason we go through so much shit is because we started fuckin' before you really got to know me and before I really got to know you," he said in a softer tone. He looked up at me, his eyes so sincere, honest and pure that it cooled the storm that he started inside of me.

"Maybe," was all I said, still locked in his gaze. This was a long ass red light but I wasn't complaining. Cree continued to stare at me and I saw that he had something on his mind that he was thinking through. Then he rubbed his hand over the light stubble on his chin and looked away from me. Contemplating.

"I'm going to do something I normally don't do. Don't ever do. But I'm goin' to do it with you," he said. I wanted to ask why but he turned to the road and hit the gas, turning in a direction opposite from the way we would have normally took to get to Brooklyn.

About fifteen minutes later, Cree was pulling up to a hi-rise apartment building in a prime New York location. Just from looking at it from the outside, you could tell that no regular ole people lived here. He pulled into the parking garage and I'll be lying if I said I saw a car in there worth less than $80,000.

"Who are we coming here to see?" I asked, feeling excited all of a sudden at the idea of making a connection with someone important and paid. With any luck, I could flip the situation and get myself another good job opportunity to go along with whatever Zeke had in store for me.

Cree didn't answer me but I wasn't surprised at all. We parked, and I jumped out the car without even waiting for him to walk over and open my door. Not like he was anyways, this was Cree that I was out with.

"Hello, Mr. Murray. Here you go," the doorman greeted Cree, handing him a bunch of papers that looked like mail. I eyed it before Cree folded it up and stuffed it all in his pocket. Frowning, I waved at the doorman who was staring at me with a goofy ass grin on his pale white face and followed behind Cree towards the elevator.

Once we stepped inside, he hit the button for one of the highest floors and I pressed my lips together to force myself not to ask any questions. From the look on Cree's face, I could tell he wouldn't answer them anyways. For whatever reason, he was trying to act like he wanted to keep everything all top secret, like he was taking me to meet the president or someone of greater importance.

And then it hit me. Was he taking me to meet his mama? As soon as the thought hit me, my neck snapped and I stared at Cree, my eyes wide, lips parted as I felt the blood draining from my face. I was *not* dressed to meet anyone's mama! And after the run-in I had with his grandmother, I was good on meeting anyone else in his crazy ass family.

"What?" Cree quipped, seeing me staring at him like I'd seen a ghost. "You got a staring problem?"

You see why this nigga was always pissing me off?

The doors to the elevator opened and Cree walked off, saying nothing at all. I followed behind him slowly as I scrutinized my surroundings. Even the hallway of this place was laid to perfection, decorated with only the finest things. There were only five doors on the entire floor. Cree walked by three of them until he finally came to one and pulled out a key from his pocket, unlocking it before pushing the door open. Frowning, I crossed my arms in front of my chest and walked in curiously and cautiously, hoping I wouldn't see some woman with a stank ass attitude on the other side.

But when I walked inside, that wasn't what I saw at all. The sight was absolutely breathtaking. It was very nice and even that is an understatement. It took me only seconds to realize that this was where Cree lived because I could see his love for music everywhere. On the walls was a very large mural painted with music notes, instruments and some of the world's greatest entertainers: Bob Marley, B.B. King, Michael Jackson, Prince, Lauryn Hill and Jay Z, showing off his wide range of taste. The furniture was very modern and neat, nothing was out of place. You could tell he was a stickler for keeping everything clean and in order. We could never live together because I was a full slob and Janelle was always nagging me about it.

Everything was perfect and screamed out 'Cree'. His style was eclectic and creative. I loved it. Cree walked to the kitchen to do something but I wasn't paying him any attention as I started to walk around slowly, admiring everything in his place. He had photos on the wall of him and his brothers, his parents and his grandmother. I saw some pics of them as children and laughed when I saw that even at a young age Cree always had headphones around his neck or on his ears.

"Who is this?" I asked, pointing at a picture of Cree and a man. It was one of the largest pictures he had in there so I knew he had to be someone important.

"That's my brother, Tone. He was killed about a year ago," he explained further when he saw the confused look on my face.

"Oh," I said, glancing back at the photo. "Damn, he looks a lot like Outlaw."

"Naw, Outlaw looks a lot like him," Cree corrected with a laugh. "Being the youngest, Outlaw was always biting somebody's style. You should see our cousin who lives over in Harlem. You'll swear him and Outlaw are twins... both got gold grills, crazy as hell and flashy as shit. Only difference is Gunplay is a whole lot crazier... like that nigga mental for real."

"You got a cousin named Gunplay? What kinda name is that?" I smirked as I crinkled up my brows. This family was insane.

"If you ever meet him, you'll know why we call him that," Cree answered with a smile and I shrugged. I didn't want no parts of any crazy man who was worse than Outlaw and named Gunplay.

"I can't believe this is your place..." I whispered as I continued to walk around, staring at everything.

And that's when I saw it.

On the wall was a large frame with a diploma inside from New York University's College of Dentistry with Cree's name on it. He had a doctorate level degree making him a Doctor of Medicine in Dentistry. I probably stared at that piece of paper with my mouth wide open for thirty minutes, trying to wrap my mind around it. A big gust of wind could have blown my ass down. And that still doesn't really explain how shocked I was.

"You..." was all I could get out as I turned to Cree and pointed at the frame on the wall. He was smiling from ear-to-ear, nodding as he walked over to me. He had two glasses in his hands and when he handed me one, I put it right to my lips and took a large gulp.

"So now you see why a nigga flips out about teeth," he joked, and I couldn't help laughing at him. This did explain a lot and I was happy for it because I didn't want to tell him, but I was convinced his ass was certified crazy when he flipped out on me about cavities.

Sitting on the couch in his living room, we drank and talked most of the night, which was something I didn't know I would enjoy as much as I did. I'd never heard Cree talk so much but I loved it. It was nice seeing him so excited and happy as he talked about his family, his brothers, his parents and crazy stuff they did during the summers. By the time he was done, I felt like I knew them all even though I'd only met one.

"So tell me about your first love," I asked with a teasing smile. His eyes bent down and a shadow passed over his face, making me instantly regret bringing up what seemed to be an unhappy memory.

"I'm sorry...I—I didn't mean to bring up anything you didn't want to talk about. I just wanted to know more about your past that's all," I apologized quickly, placing my hand on his arm. Just that small touch of my fingers pressed against his skin did something to me. Or maybe it was the alcohol.

"You're good," was all he said.

Looking away, I dropped the subject, but my mind was still swirling with thoughts, wondering what had happened with the first girl he'd fallen for to make him react like that. Clearing my throat, I tried to think up a follow-up question, but before I could, there was a loud knock at the door. Cree's brows furrowed, letting me know that he hadn't been expecting company.

"Hold on," he told me as he walked over to the door. He glanced through the peephole and cursed before unlocking the door. I watched as he placed his body in the opening, blocking whoever it was from seeing inside. Now I was suspicious. If it was a chick at the door, I was going to crazy up in this bitch, I swear. This would be the second time someone popped up at some house he'd taken me to and interrupted us.

"Nigga, what the hell you doin'?" a voice said from the other side of the door. Before Cree could get a word out, whoever it was forcefully pushed the door open, knocking Cree clear out the way.

"What you tryin' to hide up in this bitch?"

I swallowed a giggle when I saw Outlaw stomp right in after knocking Cree out the way, his eyes searching the room to see what his brother was hiding. When his eyes landed on me, he grinned and cut a sneaky side-eye in Cree's direction. I had to cover my mouth to not bust out laughing at his ass. He was looking at Cree like he'd caught him red-handed with his hand in the cookie jar.

Standing in a thought-provoking position with one arm folded over his chest and the elbow of the other resting on top of it with his hand under his chin, Outlaw looked from Cree to me like he understood something from the first time. I had to roll my eyes. As usual, he was acting overly dramatic.

"Isn't this the chick you said you couldn't deal with because she had too much damn mouth?" Outlaw asked, poking out his lips as if he was trying to remember correctly. "So now she wifey now?"

"Man—"

Cree pushed Outlaw on the shoulder, trying to guide him back towards the door, but Outlaw only started to laugh, pushing past Cree to come over to me. Extending his arm, he held out his fist to give me dap. Smirking, I crinkled my brows and reached out slowly, bumping his fist.

"My bad for interruptin' y'all, sis-in-law," he said, and I cracked up when I saw the expression on Cree's face. "I was only comin' over to ask bruh 'bout advice on somethin'. I been blowin' up the nigga's phone but he been ignorin' my ass. Now I know why."

"Luke, get da fuck out, man," Cree groaned crossing his arms in front of the chest.

Raising his hands up in surrender, Outlaw turned around. "My bad, man. These walls thin as hell. I heard noise over here and figured you was home. I ain't know you had company!"

Frowning, I worked his statement out in my mind. "Wait… you live next door?"

"Yeah," Outlaw answered, looking at me like it was something I should've known. "We all live on this same—"

Before he could finish, the door popped open again and in walked a man I recognized instantly as one of Cree's brothers. Which one? I had no idea.

"Man, I thought I heard y'all over here. I got a dilemma that I need help with," he said, stumbling inside, rubbing the top of his head as if he'd had a long ass day. Then his eyes fell on me sitting at the couch. "Oh shiiiiiiit!"

He looked from me to Cree as Outlaw stood next to me, crossing his arms in front of his chest, cheesing hard like he was about to watch the greatest show on Earth.

"Cree, that you, bruh? Damn!" Cree didn't say a word, but his brother didn't wait for a response either. Walking over to me, he did exactly what Outlaw had, reaching out to dap me up.

"My name is Tank… pleased to meet you, sis. Welcome to the fam," he said and I blushed, bumped his fist and sat back in my seat watching them.

"Man, I'm happy as hell that my nigga done found the one, man. Luke, you ever thought that shit was gonna happen?"

"Hell naw," Outlaw chimed in, shaking his head. "Yo, for real, Cree… I was thinkin' maybe your ass was gay. You'on never be gettin' no pussy and I ain't never seen you with no bitch. Well, besides her—." He pointed at me and I had to bite my tongue to not say something about being called a bitch. "But I thought she was just some experimental shit. Like one last try before you went full gay. I mean… if you was gay, that would be cool too. You still would be my bruh and all. We just wouldn't be able to share the same blunt no more because you ain't puttin' yo' lips on the same type of shit I'm puttin' mine on, na' mean?"

"Luke, shut yo' stupid ass up!" Cree snapped, as Outlaw and Tank started cracking up laughing at Cree's expense. "Fuck outta here wit' dat bullshit!"

"Man, you can't blame me for thinkin' that shit!"

"Naw, Luke, you stupid for that one. Cree be pullin' panties, nigga," Tank said, still laughing as he came to Cree's defense.

"You ever seen it?" Outlaw queried with a raised brow to Tank, lips twisted up, looking at him suspiciously. Tank thought for a minute and then shook his head.

"Naw, can't say that I have."

Cree held his frown, so furious at his brothers that you could almost see steam coming from his head.

"Just because I don't publicize my shit don't mean I ain't doin' it!" Cree argued back with his arms crossed in front of his chest. None of them were looking at me as they spoke; it was almost like they had forgotten I was even in the room. I found it hilarious.

"Yeah but what nigga gettin' pussy and don't talk to none of his boys about it?" Outlaw asked doubtfully. "We blood, nigga, and you ain't really said shit! I was convinced yo' ass was still a virgin."

Outlaw paused for a beat, he and Tank looking at Cree thoughtfully. And then finally, Outlaw turned to me, a question lingering in his eyes.

"I wouldn't normally ask a chick this shit but you fam now. So answer me this, did he fuck you like he was a virgin?"

"LUKE, GET DA FUCK OUT!"

Outlaw laughed and raised his hands once again as he moved to the door with Tank right behind him.

"My bad, I ain't mean no harm, bruh."

Outlaw did nothing to hide the guileful look in his eyes as Cree glared right into his face, watching him leave. Then, just as he got to the door, Outlaw stopped and turned around to look at me, all of the humor completely gone from his face. He moved to let Tank pass as I waited for him to speak.

"Aye… I don't want to put you in no uncomfortable position but I been tryin' to call Janelle and…" He paused and tore his eyes away, pressing his lips together for a second. An internal battle ensued before he sorrowfully surrendered with a slight shake of his head.

"Never mind."

"Hey!" I called out to him and he stopped, turning around to look at me with a hopeful look in his eyes. "Janelle's birthday is on Saturday. I just wanted to let you know."

Nodding his head, Outlaw shot me somewhat of a smile and I marveled at the expression on his face. I hadn't said much, but it seemed like it was enough to give him a ray of hope that hadn't been there before.

He walked out without saying another word and Cree closed the door behind him, locking it. I didn't know what Janelle was planning to do about her love life, but if she really wanted Outlaw, it was obvious that he was hers for the taking. His pride was on another level, which apparently ran through the Murray family, but he was head over heels for my sister. That much, I knew.

"Sorry about that," Cree apologized as he walked in. "That's why I ain't really want you meetin' them niggas yet. It's not 'bout you, it's 'bout them. I guess I wanted to keep you to myself first before you saw how fucked up we all are."

Giggling, I shook my head and wrapped my arms around Cree, sliding into his lap as soon as he sat down. He grabbed me, pulling me close to him and I heard him take a deep breath with his nose pressed into my neck.

"You smell so fuckin' good," he told me and I smiled deeply. Then I thought back to something Outlaw had said. My mind was telling me not to ask about it from how he'd responded earlier but I couldn't help myself. I just had to know.

"So they've never seen you with a woman before... like a serious relationship?" I asked him and he shook his head.

"Nope."

"So... when I asked you about your first love and you acted like you didn't want to talk about it... was it because whatever happened was so bad that you didn't want to tell anyone, not even your brothers?" I inquired further, trying to choose my words carefully so I wouldn't offend him.

Cree sighed and pulled his arms away from my body. I started to move from his lap but he grabbed me around my waist, stopping me from moving.

"No, don't go," he said and I stayed put.

"The reason I didn't really wanna talk about it is because..." He paused and a deep frown crossed his face. For some reason, my heart started beating so fast. Like it was going to explode.

"...Because the first woman who I can say I'm really feeling—like *really* feeling to the point that I feel it's love—is you."

The words were out and he licked his lips, staring at me as I ran the words over backwards and forward in my mind.

"I love you too," I told him, knowing for certain that I meant it. Cree drove me absolutely crazy 100% of the time but, he also had the opposite effect: the ability to make me feel like the happiest and most content woman in the world. And from the look on his face after I confessed my love, I wasn't the only one feeling happy and content.

Next thing I knew, Cree's hand was under my dress and he was using his thumb to massage my clit, staring right into my eyes the entire time and watching my reaction. I moaned and I felt his dick get rock hard under my ass. I began to grind against it as he nudged my legs open wider and went deeper. Flipping me on my back, I laid down on the couch as he continued to massage me with expertise. He leaned up and kissed me deeply and I moaned against his lips, feeling like I was going to explode. I wrapped my thick thighs around his body and lifted my hips, urging him not to stop. But he knew better and understood what I really wanted.

Unbuttoning his jeans, he pulled himself out of his pants, not breaking our kiss. I waited in anticipation for his next move but I felt him pull back a little, pausing.

"I gotta get a condom right quick," he said and I shook my head.

"I'm on the pill. You're good."

Squinting at me a little, he still didn't move and an awkward, bug-eyed expression crossed his face.

"But… Ok, so when the last time you had a checkup?" he blurted out. Cocking my head to the side, I probed his eyes with mine, realizing exactly what he was asking me.

"Nigga! What da fuck you tryin' to say?! I get checked up *regularly* and my shit is disease free. But fuck all that, get the fuck up off me! This will be the second time tonight that you tried me like I'm a dirty bitch!"

Rearing back, I pushed him hard but he took it like it was nothing, pinning me down with his body.

"Shit... calm down, Mel! That's not what the fuck I meant and I'm not sayin' you dirty because I wouldn't be fuckin' with you if I really thought that," he tried to explain but I wasn't hearing it.

"Well, then what do you mean, Cree?" My lips twisted up as I waited for him to reply. It didn't matter what came out his mouth next, he was about to get the hell up off me and drive me right back to my sister's house. I was not staying with his ass.

"Look, I'm sorry. I'm always sayin' the wrong shit at the wrong time... but this my first go round with a woman. And then of all women on the fuckin' planet, I fall for a fuckin' spoiled ass princess who is used to niggas fallin' all over her, sayin' and doin' all the right things. I got heavy competition and I get that shit... I know another nigga can probably do things the way you're used to and I need to get up on my game. But can't no other nigga out there feel for you how I do. They can't love you as much as I do. So just remember that and work with me sometimes, Mel. I'm a work in progress."

Okay, scratch all that shit I was just saying. I wasn't going no damn where any time soon. I couldn't even get a single word out to reply to Cree but I didn't need to because he understood how I was feeling and now I understood him as well.

Without warning, he lifted up and pushed right into me with one quick thrust. I moaned loudly and my head dropped back as I rocked my hips to match his tempo. I was so used to him fucking me that he had to put a hand on my hips to slow me down. He didn't want to be rough this time. It was clear that he wanted to make love.

And that's exactly what he did. I don't know how long we lay there, enjoying the feel of each other's bodies, but I wasn't worried about the time. Cree explored every piece of me, placing soft kisses all over my body, marking his territory with his lips, discovering hot spots I wasn't even aware that I had. He rolled me onto my stomach and started at the base of my neck, running his tongue down my spine. I shivered, a bit ticklish from the sensation. Then he got to the crack of my ass and I sucked in a breath of anticipation, wondering what it was he had planned to do next.

Without a single second of hesitancy, Cree pulled my cheeks together and licked straight on through, pushing his head and shoulders between my thighs as he went from back to front, lifting me up and tickling my clit from behind. Pushing my feet until I was on my knees, he lay down beneath me, face to my mound, and began to make love to me with his mouth. He grabbed my thighs and pulled them down, shoving me into his face. I couldn't help myself. I started winding my hips slowly at first and then faster, riding his face with no shame. I came almost instantly.

By the time Cree was done with me, I was in a half-daze, nearly asleep but still moaning for more. This must be what it meant to be drunk in love because I was all the way gone. My head was heavy, my legs were wobbly and my strength was gone but alcohol didn't have a damn thing to do with it.

"I gotta get you in the bed," I heard Cree say, and the next thing I knew he was plucking me up from the couch into his arms. Leaning my head against his chest, I must've fallen asleep to the sound of his beating heart because the last thing I remembered was feeling absolutely comfortable and complete in his arms.

Daddy Approved.

Janelle

"That was a pretty good movie," I said to Chris as we walked out of the movie theater. "I thought I would be tired of Madea by now but Tyler Perry did his thing."

After having a few days of perfect weather, it was now cold again. But this time I was fully prepared for the frigid New York weather, because after seeing me nearly freezing to death on my way to work that morning, Chris brought me a nice coat. Initially, I refused it. I didn't like taking handouts from anyone, and on top of that, I could afford my own things. I just hadn't gotten around to getting one because... who thinks about getting a coat until the moment they are outside somewhere freezing their ass off? But Chris insisted and I eventually took it after making him promise that he'd let me treat him to dinner and a movie. He agreed then but as soon as the bill came, he paid it each time.

"It was and I didn't really think I would like it at first," he revealed with a smile as we walked down the sidewalk, not even heading to the car. We were just enjoying the night.

"Really? Why not?"

"I'm more of an action type of guy when it comes to movies. Don't get me wrong... I love to laugh but I can't say I don't get excited about seeing someone blow up some shit," he told me, and I gave him a cock-eyed look.

"Oh so you're obsessed with the dangerous life, huh?"

He winked at me. "More than you even know."

Reaching down, he grabbed my hand and threaded his fingers through mine, making my stomach flutter. I tried to keep my cool, clearing my throat as we walked on. The cold air was refreshing against my skin that was now warm thanks to Chris's touch.

"So if that's true, what made you want to be a prosecuting attorney? Shouldn't you be on the other side helping the people blowing shit up be free?" I asked, teasing him a little. He looked down at me and pressed his lips together in a small smile before exhaling heavily, creating a fog of cold air in front of his lips.

"You would think that, I guess. But growing up with a mother like mine, there is no way I would have peace in life with her knowing I'm helping some of New York's finest criminals go free," he laughed after speaking, but I didn't join in because I recognized and understood the hidden meaning beneath his words.

Like me, at some level Chris felt obligated to live up to the expectation imposed upon him by his mother. Even though he was still doing something he loved, some of the joy of doing it was taken out of it because, at some level, he still probably felt pressured to perform at the level expected of him.

"But it's okay though," he continued, his tone lighter as he spoke on. "I always find ways to still do the things that I want to do. And, interesting enough, my day job helps me with that in ways I'd never thought."

Cocking my head to the side, I wondered what he meant by that statement and then decided to just let it go. We talked about work all the time and I didn't want to get caught up in a discussion about it now. We continued to walk in silence, enjoying the look of the city at night. It was truly the city that never sleeps. The sidewalks were just as crowded at night as it was during the day, people running around, hustling to get to their destinations like they had something important to do.

My phone began to ring and I reached in my pocket, pulling it out to see who it was. It was my father. Pausing, I looked at the screen wondering if I should answer and then decided to go ahead. He usually didn't call me this late at night.

"Give me a minute. It's my dad," I told Chris before answering the call. "Hi, daddy."

"Good evening, Jani... are—are you out?" he asked, probably picking up on all the sounds around me.

"Yes..." I said with a smile and then cut my eyes to Chris. "I'm on a date."

Shocked, Chris's eyes shot down to mine and he smiled, squeezing my hand a little.

"With Mr. Harvaty?" he asked, and I confirmed it with a simple 'yes'. "Let me speak to him."

"Huh?" I asked, my jaw dropping. Stopping in the middle of the sidewalk, I pulled my hand from Chris's and pushed my finger on my ear to block out the noise around me so I could make sure I was hearing my father correctly.

"I said let me speak to him. Pass him the phone," he said emphatically.

Pulling the phone from my ear, I turned to Chris who was looking right at me with a frown on his face. His eyes searched mine and I knew he was trying to figure out why I had the stricken and stunned look on my face.

"Everything okay?"

"Yes…" I started and then held out my phone to him. "He wants to speak to you."

Chuckling a little, Chris grabbed the phone with ease and placed it to his ear.

"Hello sir! How is your evening?" he greeted my dad, as I listened intently to every word he spoke. I stared at him hard, hoping to decipher how the conversation was going from every expression that shifted through his face.

"Yes, she is incredible. The pleasure is definitely all mine," Chris said, darting his eyes at my face and I felt myself blush. Then he began to speak on, the conversation obviously getting more serious with my father doing most of the talking.

"Yes sir… I definitely will. Yes, sir…"

I was dying a thousand deaths wondering what the hell they were talking about. You don't understand… the only guy I was dating who had met my father was my ex-boyfriend. And the reason he met my father was not because I'd introduced them. It was because he introduced himself after stopping by my dorm unannounced. One of my sisters, I was still unsure of which one, had told him that my ex was possessive and they were worried about my safety. After my father intervened, it was curtains for that relationship. He had my stuff packed up by the end of the day and threatened to move me back home if I didn't end things immediately and cut off all contact.

"I most certainly will… it would be a pleasure, I'm definitely honored for the invitation. You have a good night too, sir," Chris finished before handing the phone back to me.

On the verge of a panic attack, I pulled the phone back up to my ear.

"Hello daddy?"

"Well, that was a good conversation," he said, and I exhaled my relief. "And I guess I'll be seeing you soon. Have you heard from Carmella? I've been trying to reach her."

"Not since she left out this morning."

"This morning? She's there?" he asked and I frowned.

"Yes… she didn't tell you?"

My father didn't answer and I cursed myself on the inside. Obviously, she hadn't and there must have been a good reason why Carmella didn't want him to know.

"Just tell her to call me when you see her, please. It's extremely urgent," he said and I agreed. We spoke for a few seconds more before hanging up. Then I sent a quick text to Carmella to warn her in case he called her before I could tell her what I'd done.

"So... I guess your dad likes me," Chris said, just as I tucked my phone back in my pocket. "Because he just invited me to come down to Atlanta for Christmas."

"WHAT?!" I nearly screamed, drawing attention from a few people around us. "He did?"

The smile dropped instantly from Chris's face and he fell right into a slew of apologies. "I'm sorry... I wouldn't have agreed if I knew that you didn't want that. I was just—shit, I should have asked you first. I'm so sorry!"

"No!" I said, holding up my hand to stop him. Closing my eyes, I took a deep breath and slowed the conversation down.

"No, that's not it. I would love for you to come. I'm just shocked. That's definitely not something my dad has ever done and... it caught me off guard. But I'd love for you to come."

Biting his bottom lip, Chris smiled and then wrapped his arm around my shoulder, pulling me closer into him. We walked like that all the way back towards where his car was parked, chatting, laughing and talking about any and everything. I was having the time of my life with Chris and my feelings for him were growing steadily, especially now that I knew I had my father's approval. That was big for me.

It wasn't until later that night when I was lying alone in my bed that I realized, for the first time since I'd started really dating Chris, I hadn't thought about Luke a single time while we were together.

I'm Sorry.

Teema

Cree had his girl at his place so Kenya and I were staying at Outlaw's to give them some privacy. I had to admit that Cree's spot was much more comfortable than Outlaw's, definitely cleaner, but the last thing I wanted was to be in there while he was putting the moves on his Coke Queen. It didn't seem like Cree knew that she used, or he didn't know just how often she did it, but I picked up on it and I didn't like it one bit. I didn't trust her, but I couldn't say anything about it because I'd just come back into the picture and was in no position to be telling that nigga about his relationship with whatever woman he was already with.

"Aye, you cookin' a nigga breakfast or somethin'? I'm starvin'," Outlaw said, walking out from his room fully dressed, complete with shoes on his feet.

His signature 'sexy thug' swag he'd exchanged and was rocking a look that gave me pause, wearing gray slacks, a gray button up shirt and a red polo vest to match the red Giuseppe loafers on his feet. His gold chain hung low on his neck and both of his ears were adorned with diamond studs, on his wrist was a gold watch to complete his look. Had I been any other woman, I would have been lying at his feet, ready and willing to make him my next baby daddy. I was fully convinced that no one on Earth could have sported that attire quite like he did.

"Oatmeal."

"The fuck? Who you expect to eat that sloppy shit?"

"Um, Kenya," I replied pointedly. "The one I cooked breakfast for. I didn't even know you came in last night but there is enough on the stove for you, if you want it."

With his face twisted up as if that was the most disgusting thought that had ever occurred to anyone, Outlaw walked over to the stove and peered down into the pot, holding the lid like it was diseased. Grunting with repulsion, he dropped it back down and shook his head, his wild mane of hair shaking with the motion. I stared at the disorderly haloed strands atop his head and shook mine as well.

"What you gon' do wit' all that damn hair?"

He shrugged.

"I can't fuck with the chick who used to braid it up no more," was all he said, but from the look on his face, I knew there was more to the story.

"Why not?"

"She be wantin' me to pay her with dick."

"Well, offer her cash instead like normal people do." I posed with a twirl of my eyes, but he only gawked at me like I'd said the most ridiculous thing in the world.

"And you really think a few dollars gon' stop her from wantin' a nigga? I ain't even tryin' to go down that road with her ass because I already know how it ends."

Scoffing, I bent down and pushed a spoonful of food into Kenya's open mouth, realizing that there was no point in even arguing with a man whose ego was as big as his. It wasn't without reason because the entire hood threw themselves at Outlaw's feet, male and female. Men regarded him in awe and women with thirst, everyone wanting to be one of the ones to get his attention even if it were for only a minute. And it had been that way for as long as I could remember.

"Why you messed with all my shit?"

Looking up, I saw him standing in the living room, hands out, staring at the room around him, which was clean in contrast to how it had been when I first came in. Clothes had been everywhere, placed miscellaneously around as if tossed from wherever he'd stood when he pulled them off, jewelry lay in bundles on his tables and his shoe collection, which I was sure was the subject of many envious stares, circumferenced the room, enclosing us in his materialistic splendor. I couldn't even think around all that mess.

"What do you mean? I cleaned up! Obviously, you don't bring too many women here. Not any worth shit anyways," I added with a grunt.

With a devilish smirk, he came over and put his elbows on the kitchen table, looking at me like he was about to spill the details on a quietly kept secret.

"Naw, but that is all about to change."

"Oh?" I quipped. "Who is the lucky girl?"

He blushed. He *actually* blushed from just thinking of her and I was caught totally off guard. Not Outlaw, the selfish playboy with no conscience, the one who had no issues with running up in a woman right after fucking her friend, sister or even mother if she was fine enough. Naw, it couldn't be so.

"Just a little someone I'm feelin'. You'll meet her and I promise it'll be before our wedding day."

"You asked her to marry you?"

His eyes dimmed but the sparkle was still there as he looked off someplace behind me. I watched him bite the inside of his cheek and then he shook his head.

"Not yet, but I will."

My heart swelled in my chest as many seconds passed, his eyes still planted on something behind me but his mind elsewhere. Someone had his heart and looking at him only reminded me of how it was with Kane when he had mine. I hadn't felt it in a long time but looking at Outlaw had me fiending for someone's love, a man who could just stare at some random place aimlessly, forgetting everything around him because his heart, mind and soul was on me.

"Today's her birthday," he spoke, but I wasn't sure if he was speaking to me or simply walking through the thoughts in his mind.

"What are you going to give her?"

"Me."

His eyes flickered to mine and I saw the honest and pure emotion that lay beneath. Wasn't directed at me but it still warmed my heart. And then he sighed and his expression shifted as he stood up and finessed his beard with one hand. He was letting his facial hair grow in and it looked good on him. Made him look like he was really on his grown man shit.

"And a car. I'mma cop her a ride… Just in case I'm not enough."

Fear flashed through his eyes when he added the latter statement, and I noticed it even though it was gone the next second. This was a new Outlaw, but I was grateful that he felt comfortable enough to be honest and open with me, if no one else. Everyone needed someone to speak to and I would rather he talk to me than them raggedy hos running after him in the street. All they had for him was bad advice and friendly pussy. They didn't care about what was best for him, but I regarded him like a brother and wanted to see him happy.

Looking down, I saw that Kenya was no longer chewing her food but was battling sleep, her pretty eyes drooping with exhaustion from being up since four am that morning. Grabbing her, I stood up to lay her down in the playpen that Cree had bought for her to nap in.

"Let me get her down and I'll do something to your hair. If it's your girl's birthday you can't go to see her looking like that."

"I don't have no time for nothing fancy," he said. "Just hook me up right quick so I can get to Kareem and see what he doin' with the whip."

Running to his room, it took me what felt like forever to sort through his organized clutter and find a brush and comb for his hair. I parted up the right side and quickly made four braids before taming the rest of his mane into a long braid that fell past the middle of his muscular back. I didn't know what side of his family gave him this curly, thick hair that females in the hood paid good money for. Probably the same side that gave Yolo them crazy colored eyes and Cree his light-bright complexion.

"Good?" I asked him and he nodded his head, a distant look on his face that told me he wasn't paying too much attention to what I'd said.

"Don't be nervous. She'll choose you over the car."

He smiled. Like really smiled. Not his evil ass smirk, it was a real smile with perfect white teeth. Wait… *white* teeth.

"You removed your grill!"

He massaged the back of his neck and ducked his head, still smiling as he nodded. He was boyishly cute. Whoever she was, she brought out the best in him and she definitely had my vote.

"Yeah, she wasn't a fan so I let that shit go."

"Damn, you must really love this girl!"

Eyes on mine and expression straight, he didn't say anything, but his response was as clear to me as it would have been had he actually uttered the words.

I do.

God, how I wanted to be loved.

There was a knock at the door, pulling Outlaw out of his trance and he looked at his watch.

"Right on time," I heard him mutter under his breath as he walked over to answer it, leaving me all the way in my feelings.

Since Kenya had been born, I put all my attention and focus on her, refusing to do anything for myself. Little things that I used to do that made me happy, like going to the gym or getting my nails and feet done… even getting my damn eyebrows waxed, I no longer did because I didn't want to take anything from her. But I was seeing now that I had a severe need to get my shit together so I could be ready when the right man came around. I needed to shed these extra pounds and dote on me for a change, make myself feel like somebody who was worthy of love.

As soon as I sent my request up to God that my day would eventually come, preferably sooner rather than later, Outlaw opened the door and the next face I saw belonged to Kane. His eyes went immediately to me as if he'd known all along I would be sitting right where I was, not at all expecting to see the first man I'd ever loved at the very moment that I was praying for another. Something about his stare settled my spitfire of a spirit that usually had me twisting up my neck, rolling my eyes and sucking the skin off my teeth as soon as I laid eyes on him.

"C'mon in, bruh. I'm on my way out," Outlaw said, slapping hands with his other brother in greeting.

Kane regarded him briefly, saying nothing as he returned the quick embrace before turning back to me. Outlaw glanced behind him into my face as if quickly assessing my mind state before he made his exit, apparently assured that I wasn't going to do anything to harm his brother.

The door closed and we stood there, me looking at Kane and him staring at me. His eyes were soft, not combative but not completely void, the way they had been since we became strangers to each other. And then, he released me and turned, placing his attention on his daughter who was sleeping peacefully, unaware that her father was looking at her for the first time. He walked over to her cautiously, like a child creeping through the halls afraid to wake up mama, stopping only when he was standing above her, peering down thoughtfully into the playpen.

Shoving his hands in his pockets, his head dropped, his shoulders slumped and my heart skipped a beat. Then the tears came the second I saw him lean over and grab her up into his arms. Though sleeping, it was almost like she knew it was her father who held her in his arms. Kenya nestled up against him, one of her little arms instinctively winding around his neck as she sucked on her thumb. He rocked her gently, closing his eyes as he kissed her repeatedly on her head as if making up for lost time.

I flicked a tear away and inhaled heavily. This was a moment I'd long ago stopped dreaming about because I was certain it would never come. But everyone had a heart, some just used theirs more than others. I guess it was Kane's turn to realize that letting his guard down wouldn't destroy him.

Sitting totally still, not wanting to do anything to ruin the moment, I watched as he continued to cradle her while thinking to himself. Part of me wondered what his thoughts were, but the biggest part of me was just happy to finally see them together. Even if this didn't last, even if he changed his mind about her tomorrow, at least Kenya would have this moment with her father. He placed her back down carefully, too carefully. The way one does when they've never held a child to know that being *too* careful is an unnatural motion that is sure to stir them awake. And that's exactly what happened. Before

Kane could even back away, Kenya opened up her mouth and let out a high-pitched, tired whine and he jumped, turning around to look at me with wide, frightful and apologetic eyes, waiting for instructions on what to do next. I had to bite down hard on the inside of my cheeks to keep from letting go of a laugh.

"Don't flip, she'll go right back to sleep."

He eyed me doubtfully.

Walking over, I leaned down and ran my hand over her back a few times, and seconds later, there was silence once again. A mother's touch.

"I want y'all to move in with me."

Kane spoke the words like he said everything; with vigor, brass and affirmation, as if there was no alternative. And when I was younger, back when we were together, that type of thing worked on me because he was my man and I was his girl. I trusted him because he said he'd never hurt me and he never had.

Until he did…

And now those days of me mindlessly, carelessly and obediently bending to his command were over. I wanted him to be in Kenya's life, be the father she needed, but there was too much damage between he and I for me to move in without refute.

"I prefer not to," I protested. "I'm glad you're open to being with Kenya so we can work out some kind of agreement, but I can't live with you, Kane. This is about you and her. Not me and you."

"I'm not living apart from my daughter."

"Nigga, you just *met* your daughter!" I snapped with potency, on the brink of delivering the tongue-lashing he was owed after being deliberately absent the full first year of her life. The audacity of him to finally come forward making demands!

He stared back at me, confused. Like, sincerely perplexed as if I were speaking another language.

"I'm not understandin' the shit you sayin', ma. It holds no relevancy with me when it comes to what I just said."

I knew Kane well enough to know that his confusion was genuine. His genetic makeup was lacking when it came to giving him the ability to understand anything from anyone else's point of view.

"What I'm sayin' is that you can't come to me issuing demands when I haven't heard from you in over a year, Kane!"

He said nothing. Didn't even blink.

"I'm the one who has been taking care of her! And I did it all *on my own*." Jabbing myself in the chest, eyes pulled tight as my fury built up, whirling around us in waves. "You weren't there and we aren't together. You lost your right to tell me what to do or to even have an opinion about where I choose to live. When it comes to your daughter, if you want to stand up and be a man, a *real* man—" His jaw clenched. "—then we can talk about that, but I'm *not* moving in with you."

Still silent, Kane didn't respond to my anger and I halfway figured he wouldn't. In all my life, he'd never argued with me about a single thing. Probably never would. I used to think that he didn't because he didn't care enough about me to even put forth effort in a verbal battle of wills. But then I understood eventually that it had nothing to do with emotion and everything to do with respect.

Running his hand over the side of his face, he pulled his eyes from me once my words ran dry and surveyed his surroundings thoughtfully. Then, he walked behind me, down the hall and I followed him with my eyes until he disappeared. When he emerged again, it was with Kenya's diaper bag over his shoulders and the small bag of clothes and personal items that I'd picked up from the store the day before.

"What are you doing? Did you hear what I said, Kane?!"

He nodded his head, glanced into my face. "Yeah."

Frowning, I observed his blank expression as he moved about, grabbing items that belonged to me as well as what belonged to Kenya, either stuffing them into the bag or draping them over his shoulders.

"But I—you're…I told you that I wasn't—Kane, PUT ALL MY SHIT DOWN!"

Finally, I'd said something that merited a real response. Turning, Kane shot his eyes at me, holding his lips tight before pulling them apart to utter a reply, a little more bite to the tone than what he normally used for me.

"Lower your voice before you wake our daughter."

Huh? I couldn't with this nigga. Like really couldn't.

"You know I'm not gon' argue with you 'bout this, Teema. Right now, all you doin' is just fuckin' up your mood."

"But I—"

"I said what I said and I ain't sayin' shit else."

A sentence I'd heard all too often, whether it came from him or one of his brothers. They all had the same stubbornness when it came to things that mattered most to them and it was futile to fight once their mind was set. Kane, unarguably the most stubborn of them all, had just finalized my fate without my consent and without debate, in the same way that he lived his life: without anyone's consent and without debate. But then, as if something occurred to him for the first time, he turned around and lifted his irises to meet mine. He wet his lips and I felt my chest get tight.

"I'm sorry."

All the air left my lungs and I sat down in surrender, eyes stricken wide open and mouth clamped firmly shut.

Anyone watching me right then would be confused, wondering what changed to make the fire in me cool to even less than a flame in only a matter of seconds. But anyone who really knew Kane would have understood. Born as the oldest of six brothers who didn't know what it meant to compromise or not have things their way, Kane was unapologetic to the core. He *never* apologized because he was *never* wrong. His actions were carefully thought out and constructed after heavy consideration and acceptance of the consequences that he could face. Meaning: He didn't apologize for *shit*. I've literally never even heard this nigga say 'my bad' because in his mind, it was *never* his bad.

"But you're still going," he ended with finality, and I nodded my head before turning around to collect the rest of our things that he'd missed.

"Just give me a second to take a shower and get dressed," I muttered with eyes low, a traffic jam of thoughts running through my mind.

"Take all the time you need, love," he said and I was hit with a bout of nostalgia, hearing him use the pet name for me that I hadn't heard in years.

Old feelings rose up inside of me and shook them away stubbornly, reminding myself that it was healthier for me to hang on a little longer to my anger. Forgiving a man too quickly was a disease that plagued the heart of many women and I vowed not to be one of them. If Kane wanted to get through to me and make me into the woman I used to be—and, trust, I'm not saying he did—we had a long way to go.

His Heart.

Sidney

I never slept heavily at Yolo's. I don't know why, because it wasn't like I felt uncomfortable around him. Everything there was to me, he knew about already. Didn't matter if I was laying in the bed snoring, slobbing, and farting all at the same time, I knew for a fact, his ass wouldn't bat an eye. Might leave me in the room by my damn self, but that was about it.

But those facts didn't matter because whenever he made the slightest movement, my eyes jarred open and I startled awake, the first few nights frantic as I tried to remember where I was and whose bed I was in. But now I was used to being with him almost every night. So when I heard a noise and I stirred awake, yawning loudly and obnoxiously like it wasn't a sinful hour of the morning, I was surprised to see him sitting on the edge of the bed, fully dressed and pulling shoes onto his feet.

"Where are you going?" I squinted at the clock next to me. "It's three am."

He nodded. His jaw clenched tight and then he stood up, his eyes everywhere but on mine.

"I have to go handle some shit right quick and then I'll be back," he lended and I sulked, sitting up on the bed with my arms crossed in front of my chest. I was ready to brood quietly and without protest until a single fact came to mind, the most important one I could've recollected at that moment.

"Hell no, Yolo. Not happenin.'"

"What?" he half-battled, not really giving my words much thought as he continued to get himself together.

See, I never called him on his shit in the past and when you didn't do that, niggas got comfortable. Much too comfortable. But the difference between then and now, a difference I'd only seconds before remembered, was that I wasn't just his best friend that he had sex with and claimed to love anymore. I was now his girlfriend, his woman. And with that title came a lot of responsibility but also a hell of a lot of expectations.

"I'm your girlfriend now, Yolo, and I'm not dealin' wit' this kinda shit no more. It's three am and you're gettin' dressed up to leave but don't wanna tell me why. Not happenin' and I'm not doin' it so unless you want to fight with me before you leave and after you come back, you need to start talkin.'"

Standing up, his eyes went to the ceiling and I saw him thinking… *actually* contemplating whether or not whatever he was trying to do was worth the fight.

"I'm going to LeTrese's," he started and it was like a million stabs to my heart all at once. Feeling deflated to the point that I no longer had the gumption to tread on with my attitude, I grimaced as if in pain.

He sighed.

"She called. When we broke up a while back, she started fuckin' with a nigga who used to beat her ass. I got with her and that killed that shit but now he's come back. She was cryin' and shit… said he broke in and put his hands on her because she wouldn't let him in on her own."

Anger burned in my chest when I realized what he was saying. It wasn't that he was leaving me for her, which I'd initially thought, but he was still falling right into her little games. I highly doubted that her ex had returned or that he'd beaten her ass. In fact, I was willing to put money on the fact that once she had successfully drawn Yolo to her place, she would be waiting there with lingerie and open legs, complete with a determined mind, willing to do whatever she had in order to get what was mine. Oh hell no.

Pushing the sheets from my body, I jumped up and started pulling on my clothes. If he felt some type of duty to this chick, for whatever reason, that was all fine and well, but I wasn't stupid and there was no way I was letting him out alone.

"Where you goin'?"

"To some nigga's house," I tested.

"It's too early for those girly mind games, Sid. And don't get caught up by this shit because I ain't gon' do shit with that girl. I just know she ain't got nobody worth shit in her family who can help her keep this nigga from killin' her."

I pressed my lips together and pulled on my sneakers.

"And that's why we are goin' to go over there."

"We?"

"Four hands are better than one and she needs all the help she can get, right? It's like you said," I mused, flipping his words on him.

Yolo seemed less than enthused about me going with him but he didn't argue. There wasn't anything he could say anyways. If everything was like he said it, then he had nothing to worry about.

We got to LaTrese's apartment about thirty minutes and some change later. She stayed in a nice detached two-unit apartment building that looked too nice for me to feel comfortable. LaTrese had a job somewhere, I was sure. But I was also sure that wherever she worked couldn't have helped her afford all this. No, her place wasn't excessively full of luxurious splendor, but it was a far cry from cheap, making me eye Yolo suspiciously, knowing that he had something to do with this. Avoiding my stare, he kept his eyes straight ahead, but I knew he felt my glare because he was remained overly focused on everything ahead of him.

He parked and jumped out and told me to wait for a minute. I almost protested but held my tongue when I saw him pull out his pistol. Running up the steps to her door, he pushed the door open and walked right in. My stomach was in knots and every second seemed like an hour. Lights flipped on through every window and then he was out once again.

Pulling his fitted cap down low, nearly blocking out his eyes, he walked over to my side of the car and opened up my door, appearing calm but I picked up on his anguish right away. I stepped out with his help and he held my hand, nearly pulling me as he walked briskly back inside the apartment.

"I need your help," he said and I swallowed hard while looking around.

The entire inside of the apartment was in complete and utter disarray. There was no doubt in my mind that prior to whatever tornado had ripped through the inside, it was decorated plushly, barring no expense, but now? There was utter chaos. Lamps tossed to the floor, furniture seemingly butchered with a machete, television busted. Even the kitchen was a mess, all of the contents of the refrigerator thrown onto the floor.

We found LaTrese in the bedroom, lying dead center in the bed. I gasped and released Yolo's hand, shooting it to my mouth just as the tears began to trickle down my cheeks. I didn't like LaTrese… hated her even. But no one should've been done like this.

Her face was bloodied and swollen almost beyond recognition, one of her eyes so big and purple that it seemed only seconds away from bursting open. Her nose was crushed and twisted into some awkward, unnatural position. Though she had a red lace bra on, her bottom was completely bare and exposed with blood seeping down from somewhere between her legs. She was breathing but it was labored and jagged, like her lungs were filled with glass, painful even to listen to.

I wiped my cheeks as Yolo went through her drawers, pulling out clothes for her to wear. He needed me to help but I couldn't because I couldn't move. My eyes were pinned on LaTrese, the mere sight of her tore at my heart.

"Did you call 911?"

Yolo shook his head.

"No cops," was all he said.

Walking into the bathroom adjoined to the bedroom, Yolo pulled out a small black bag that he'd obviously known was there and maneuvered about her room with familiarity, grabbing up various tools that he needed. He pulled off his shirt, leaving on only his undershirt and dumped the contents of the black bag on the bed beside LaTrese's body.

My throat got tight as I watched him clean her gently and carefully, making a clicking sound with his teeth as he observed all of her injuries. He spoke to her in hushed whispers, letting her know when something would hurt, warning her to brace herself as he tended to her with careful precision and expertise like the physician that he would soon be.

I knew she needed his help, but I couldn't help the envy rising up in my heart, watching my love tend to another woman with care, in gentle ways that I wanted to be reserved for only me. His every sense was focused on her, totally blocking out my presence like I wasn't even there. He dressed her, and then once he was satisfied that he'd done everything he could, he finally turned in my direction.

"There is a bag in the closet. Grab it and just pack it up with her things for me. I'm going to get her in the car."

I hesitated.

"She needs a hospital, Yolo."

It was true but it stemmed from my jealousy rather than rational thought. I didn't want him to be the one to care for her anymore. Give that job to someone else.

"Not taking her there because they'll ask too many questions."

"Shouldn't they do that so the cops can get the man who did this to her?"

He shook his head.

"He's dead already," was all he said and I knew what it meant. Yolo didn't want the cops involved because he'd already pledged to handle this himself.

He lifted her up into his arms and she let out a horrifying screech, resembling the torturous crooning of a banshee. It chilled me to the bone.

"Shhhh, it's okay," he whispered in her ear before cradling her close to his chest as he made his way out of the room. Leaving me alone with the tables unfairly turned against me, my uncertainty about what I should feel, *how* I should feel, stalling every single creation of thought in my mind.

I packed up LaTrese's bag while biting back tears, snatching and grabbing her things and tossing them angrily and devastatingly inside. It seems heartless, right? Definitely selfish. But see, the thing is you don't know Yolo like I do because if you did, if you *really* knew him, you'd understand. LaTrese had been searching for an open door back into his heart for quite some time now, and even though of no effort of her own, she'd found it.

Yolo had loved her once and one second of watching the way that he tended to her showed me what was obvious: he still did. Maybe it wasn't that he loved her in the way that he loved me but he definitely loved her as someone from his past, a woman he'd almost had a child with and shared many experiences with, many he'd never experienced

ith me. And if I knew anything about any of the Murray boys, I knew
ne thing: when they loved someone, even if only a little bit, they went
ard for them and didn't let up until they were satisfied they'd righted
ny wrongs. So this incident with LaTrese was far from over.

As I placed the last few things I felt like she would need into her
ag, I was just about to walk out of her bathroom when I saw something
nat caught my eye. Leaning down, I grabbed up a prescription bottle
nat must have fallen behind her toilet and held it in my hands. The
bel had been scratched off the bottle but it was filled with pills inside.
nable to stifle my curiosity, I quickly opened it and poured them into
ny hands, scrutinizing the small pink pills.

I heard the front door slam open and hurried footsteps followed.
noving the pills back in the bottle, I pushed it into my pocket and
ormed out with the bag in hand at the same moment that Yolo ran
nto the room.

The urgency in his expression wasn't as much as the agitation
aught in between his furrowed brows as he pierced into me, obviously
oset that I was taking so long to get her things together.

"You get everything?"

Tight-lipped, I nodded my head.

"Then let's go."

Pretending to have the same earnestness to assist his ex that
e seemed to have, I treaded on behind him, eerily feeling that not
verything around us was at all what it seemed.

A Thug's Lady

Carmella

"Welcome back, pretty lady," Zeke said, greeting me as soon as I walked into his office.

I was late but I had a good reason. I had to get myself dolled up for my first day so that I was on point. Now I was walking in with my brows freshly threaded, my bundles styled and flowing down my back like a runway model, my manicure and pedicure done to perfection and a fresh bikini wax to make sure that there was nothing stopping me from letting the photographer get all close and personal if the job called for it. Zeke wanted me to be the face of something and I made it my business to represent well.

"Thought you were backing out," he added, and I cringed, knowing that he was referencing the fact that I was running late.

"Never that, I'm excited about this. I'm just late because—" I stopped speaking when he shook his head dismissively.

"I'm not worried about you being late, Carmella. I just realized this morning that you haven't moved anything into the apartment yet and the company car is still in your assigned garage."

"Oh! No, I'm thankful for everything. I just need to settle a few things before I can move in."

And learn to drive, I added in my mind.

Seeming satisfied with my reply, Zeke nodded his head and then gestured for me to follow behind him.

"Let's get started," he said and I took a deep breath. I was more excited than anything else. Modeling was my thing and I did it with ease, not even with a second thought because it came natural to me to perform once the camera hit me.

As soon as I walked into the room that Zeke was leading me to, I was delighted to see that he had hooked me up with my own glam squad. He introduced me to everyone, the person in charge of my make-up, the one in charge of my apparel, the photographer and even someone whose only task was to get me whatever I needed. In less than an hour, I was dressed and ready to go.

"It's time to make magic happen," Nero, the photographer said. And that's exactly what I did for the next four hours, only pausing to change quickly and to take quick bathroom breaks to snort a few lines and maintain my high. It took the edge off and I performed much better with it than without it.

"We got some good shots," Zeke told me after looking over the film. I was excited to see them, but they didn't offer to show me and I didn't voice a request. Once the editing was done, it would be better seeing the final product anyways.

"Thank you."

After packing up my things, I thanked everyone who assisted me with my look and started to leave. Zeke ran up behind me just as I got to the elevator and grabbed me lightly on the elbow.

"I was thinking… we should go to dinner or something sometime soon. Just to catch up a little and get to know each other better. We are working together and I treat everyone like a family here. I'm not a boss; I'm more like a friend." He licked his lips and dipped his eyes below my neckline, making me feel like he actually wanted to be more than a friend too.

"Maybe," was all I gave him.

Cree may have not been my boyfriend at the moment but you couldn't tell his ass that. When it came to me having dinner with another man, he'd already made it known that he wasn't feeling it. And I really didn't want to spend time with any other man but him. My career was important to me but the difference between my sister and me was that my career wasn't my everything. I wasn't willing to risk being in love for a professional come up.

"Can I walk you out?" he pressed and I nodded my head, not wanting to be too rude.

As soon as I was free, I hopped on a taxi to Cree's house where he was waiting to give me my first lesson on how to drive. I was nervous because I didn't want to mess up his car but I was still excited to be behind the wheel. I'd never driven anything at all but for the first car that I drove to be a Maybach was insane. Not many could say that! So imagine my surprise when I got out of the taxi and saw Cree already outside standing next to an old school black Toyota Camry that looked like something made in the 90s.

"What's this?"

I scrunched up my nose and peered over the bridge of my nose at it. It was dusty and ugly. It would have made some sixteen year old with a brand new license jump for joy, but it did absolutely nothing for me.

"This is your car. The one that you'll be learning how to drive in," he informed me with a coy smile. "Stop lookin' like ya ass too good for it when you ridin' public transpo 'round the city. How you gon' have an attitude when you don't even have a car?"

"Correction, I do have a car now. And where is the Maybach?"

"It's in my garage. I know you ain't think you was playin' bumper cars in my shit."

"Okay and where the hell did you get this? You didn't steal it, did you?"

Cree didn't even open his mouth to reply, just gave me a pointed look.

With an indignant sniff, I rolled my eyes and tied my hair up into a bun. My weave was too expensive to be loose and collecting up whatever was crawling around on them dingy seats. Visibly grimacing, I took a deep breath and stumped over to where Cree was standing with a wide smile, holding the door open wide with his hand out, directing me as if he was standing in front of a Bentley.

"You not cute," I muttered at him when I walked by but it was lie.

He was very cute… actually sexy, standing there in a simple black tee, black jeans, and shoes with his black cap low on his head, nearly blocking out them sexy eyes. The tattoos on his arms glistened in the sunlight, dancing over his nicely toned physique like a spotlight to his sex appeal. And then there was this ugly ass car.

"Okay, start it up but put on yo' damn seatbelt first, Mel."

"You gon' wear yours too?" I cut my eyes at him and he grinned.

"Hell yeah. I always stay strapped... sometimes," he added, when I twisted my lips up at him, silently calling his bluff at the double meanings behind his statement.

Without saying anything else, I reached down to push the button to start the engine. But there wasn't a button anywhere near the steering wheel. Bending my head down, I looked all around the bottom, wondering how the hell I was supposed to crank up this old ass car Cree had found.

"You might need these."

He jingled something in his hand and then tossed it into my lap. Keys. Duh, Carmella. There are no push-to-start capabilities for old ass cars like these. Pursing my lips, I ignored the humored expression on Cree's face and stuck the keys in the ignition.

"Okay, now press the gas lightly. We'll drive around the parking lot for a little bit before you get to go out on the road."

I followed Cree's instructions and everything was going just fine until we were on the way back. Feeling like I'd mastered something in record time, I loosened up a bit and relaxed. Even cut on some music because after a few hours of practice, I felt I was just that good. Cree shot me a doubtful glance, but I ignored it as I shook my shoulders on beat to a Drake song. Then out of nowhere the car in front of me mashed on their brakes. I tensed, froze as my brain rattled through Cree's instructions.

The right is the gas and the left is the brake, right? No the left was the gas and the right... No, that's wrong, Carmella! Your foot is on the gas so obviously the other one is the—

BOOM!

I ran right into the back of the car, a Porsche Panamera. Worth a whole lot more than the garbage I was pushing and a hell of a lot more than I could afford.

"Damn… you busted that shit, bae," Cree stated the obvious with a flat tone like he wasn't talking about an $80,000 car, much too composed.

"Shit!" I jumped out and ran around to the front to observe the damage. The Porsche had only a small scratch but the front bumper of the Toyota was hanging on one side.

"The fuck you were fuckin' lookin' at?! Are you fuckin' blind? Who taught you how to fuckin' drive? There isn't even any traffic on the road!"

I looked up right into the face of a white man, tall and wearing and expensive suit. He stalked over to me with his hands in fists to his side and I mired, my lips parted slightly as he came closer to me. Cree stepped in between us, using the side of his arm to push me fully behind him.

"Who da fuck you think you talkin' to? And back the fuck up!" Cree spat with venom, the dark gruff in his tone causing me to gasp. I clasped my hand to my mouth and paddled my eyes back and forth between Cree and the guy.

"I'm talking to that bitch that just ran into my fuckin' car!" the man roared, not once noticing the murderous glare in Cree's eyes or the tense way he was holding his mouth. But I saw it and my heart began to thump heavily in my chest. I knew something was about to happen, I could see it and feel it.

"I'm sorry, I'm just learning how to—"

Cree stopped me with a light tap right above my hipbone.

"You don't have to apologize for shit."

"Damn right she has to apologize! And she has to pay too. The damage to my fuckin' car is going to cost—"

Bringing his fist up, Cree delivered the first ruthless crack right against the man's jaw, stupefying him instantly. Then there was another and I opened my mouth wide, delivering a silent scream of horror when I saw the blood burst from his nose, spraying hard like a sprinkler, and he dropped to the ground like his feet were attached to weights. Cree reached down and checked the man's pockets as I looked on and then pulled out an object.

"Let's go," he said, stepping over the man's body, not even bothering to take a second glance at him. "Get in the driver's seat. You wanted to try out your skills while sittin' in the lap of luxury… well, baby, you got your chance."

My hands were still to my mouth and it wasn't until that second that I realized how much they were trembling, shaking like dry leaves. I was petrified. Swallowing hard, I grabbed my things out of the Toyota and did just as Cree asked, jumping into the driver's seat of the Porsche.

"Push it," was all he said and I took off, leaving the man still in the middle of the road, in front of the busted Toyota.

With my hands at the 10-2 position like Cree had taught me, I drove through the streets tight-lipped, following his hand motions that told me where to go. We pulled up to a shop in Brooklyn and Cree told me to park right in front of the building while he jumped out to speak to a nice but casually dressed white man with tan skin as if he was Italian or something close, who was standing up front.

"Fuck this shit up, Navi, and then deliver it to this address." Cree handed him a license.

The man laughed and nodded his head, seeming to know without being told exactly what happened. I got the notion that this request had been asked of him plenty of times.

"You got it. I got something new for you around back. I'll have someone pull it up," Navi replied and then disappeared inside of the building.

Stepping out of the Porsche, I caught Cree's eyes on mine as he held his cellphone to his ear, not saying a word. I stood next to him and he kissed me lightly on the cheek before walking a short distance away to complete his call. I looked down at my hands that were still quivering even worse than they were before.

But what was I so afraid of? I'd said I wanted to be a thug's lady and play the part of the ride or die. So how could I be afraid about the life I'd chose?

It's My Birthday.

Janelle

"**W**hat *exactly* did you say to daddy?" Carmella asked me as soon as she stepped through the front door. I was sitting in my favorite chair, enjoying my favorite pastime: reading.

Sighing, I placed the book down on my lap, pushed my glasses further up on my nose and looked at her. And yes, I said glasses. They were huge, thick and I hated them but being that my eyes were acting extra sensitive to my contacts that morning, I had no choice.

"I didn't say anything really. He asked if I'd heard from you and I told him not since you left out that morning. That's when he asked if you were here… I didn't know he had no idea. Why are you hiding the fact that you're back here with me?"

Carmella dropped her purse on the kitchen counter and then came over to where I was, flopping down on the sofa as she came out of the oversized hoody she had on. The clothes she was wearing obviously weren't hers. Under the hoody she was wearing black tights and an 'I Love NYC' t-shirt that she'd probably grabbed from a vendor on the street. She had on the biggest darkest shades I ever saw in my life even though there was barely any sunlight outside. It was freezing cold in the city.

"And where have you been dressed like that? Where are your

clothes?"

She pressed her lips together, forming a straight line and then shook her head.

"I was with Cree… long fuckin' story that ends with me finding out that nigga is crazy. I'm dressed like this because my ass is incognito. I don't wanna get caught up in no Murray family static and catch a charge."

I giggled and cut my eyes at her. So much for being a ride or die.

"Daddy's been pressing me about school so I've been avoiding his calls. I'm failing one of my core classes."

I gasped. Eyes stretched as wide as they could go, I pulled up my knees and wrapped my arms around them as I shook my head sadly at Carmella. Maybe to the average person, a failing grade was nothing, but to me, it was a serious crime.

"I lost my scholarship and I'm low on money because of some stupid decisions I made, thinking that I had everything under control. What I told you was true… I did come here for a job opportunity, but I guess I didn't tell you how important it is that it works out for me," she explained. The corners of her eyes tugged downwards and I saw her lip began to tremble a little. Carmella never cried so just seeing her like this broke my heart.

"Carm, if you needed money, I could've given it to you," I offered but she shook her head.

"I don't want any handouts from anyone. I made the decisions I've made and I want to fix them on my own. I don't want you or daddy helping me. And I don't want him finding out about any of this either because the first thing he'll say is that he was right by telling me I needed to focus more on my studies than my modeling. I just want to prove to everyone that the things I want to do with my life can be done and I can be just as successful as anyone else!"

Clamping my mouth shut, I didn't argue that point with her because if anyone could understand the desire to be successful, it was me.

"On another note," she started with a sniff. "I saw Outlaw the other day when I was at Cree's place. He asked about you."

My ears perked up at the mention of Luke.

"What did he say?"

"I think he wanted me to ask you to call him. He said he's been calling you and I guess you haven't been answering," she said, and I looked at her with one brow lifted in the air.

"Did he ask you that or you're assuming that's what he meant?" I queried back.

Carmella pressed her lips together and looked down, thinking about it before replying.

"Janelle, you didn't see him. It wasn't characteristic of him, but he seemed so desperate that he was going to ask me anyways. He wants you to call him. And you're playing games right now but you love him and he loves you back. Anyone can see it! That man is crazy over you!"

Without saying anything, I thought about what she was saying. Luke wasn't in the room, I hadn't seen in what felt like forever and hadn't talked to him in even longer than, that but the memory of the way he made me feel was so strong that I could feel every single fiber of my being longing for him. When I let my mind marinate on him, it was almost like an uncontrollable obsession.

The night he left after I admitted my love, I had been at the point where I didn't want to be anywhere if he wasn't there with me. Things that seemed so important to me before were beginning not to matter as much. Instead of studying cases late at night to prepare for the next day, I was staying up late and making love to him with no regrets. Being with him was unhealthy. My feelings for him were all consuming and destructive, tearing down the principles that I'd outlined my life by. Chris fit neatly into my life, like a missing puzzle piece that completed the image I'd constructed for myself. Maybe he wasn't the one I desired more than anything or anyone else in the world. But he was the one I *needed*.

"I'm with Chris now," I replied, forcing myself to say it without showing the tumultuous thoughts that were swarming inside my mind. "He's perfect for me and I'm a better person with him. Since Luke's been gone, I'm doing great at work, eating better and I've lost five pounds. Every area of my life is looking up."

Carmella rolled her eyes hard, letting me know that I might as well have been talking to the wall because she wasn't hearing it.

"You're being stupid and I never thought I'd say that. Get over yourself and stop pretending you not lying. Life is too short to be out in these streets acting like you too good for the one you love."

I lifted my brow. "In these streets? What you know about the streets now?"

She nodded her head and pushed her shades back on her face.

"Trust, messin' around with Cree has made me an official gangsta," she explained, and I laughed. "But seriously, I'm telling you the truth."

Maybe she was right.

***

In spite of going to bed, tossing and turning all night because I had Luke on my mind, I woke up on top of the world. Today was my birthday and I wasn't planning on doing a damn thing that I didn't want to do. It was crazy how I didn't even realize it was coming until the day was here. I was so caught up in everything else going on in my life, I forgot all about the most important person in my life: me.

When I finally pulled myself out of the bed, I stepped in the shower to clean up before really starting my day. A note on the kitchen counter told me that Carmella had already left but next to the note was a box and card that read 'Happy Birthday'. Already excited, I tore it open and inside was a bracelet that had an engraving on it with all of my sister's names as well as mine. The card had all of their signatures on it and explained that they all had the same bracelet to match mine. I was such a baby for this type of thing and by the time I finished reading the card, I was boohoo crying. I'd been telling my sisters that we should get matching necklaces or something for the longest, finally dropping the subject a few years back after Vonia suggested matching tats. Them remembering how much this meant to me was really sweet.

As soon as I wiped the tears from my eyes, my phone rang and I answered it when I saw that it was Mixie calling.

"Hell—"

"HAPPY BIRTHDAY TO YOOOOOUUUUU…"

Laughing, I listened as Mixie, Vonia and Carmella all sung to me. By the time they finished, I was crying again.

"Jani, I know it's your birthday and you can cry if you want to but damn!" Vonia teased me after they finished singing. "The way you sound over there got me thinking that you might be cryin' because Mixie can't sing for shit!"

"It's the thought that counts," Mixie said in a flat tone that made me laugh.

"Well, I have to go. I am meeting someone this morning but I wanted to make sure I was on the call," Carmella jumped in.

"Meeting who?" Vonia asked, ignoring the urgency in Carmella's tone. "And daddy told me that you in New York too. So that's why you told me I couldn't come to Cali over Thanksgiving break? I'm still mad about that shit! I got a lil' boo thang out there I met over the internet and he been pressing me about coming out there to visit him."

"So you are going to fly all the way across the country for some dick, Vonia? Why can't he come to you?" Mixie shot in and I gasped, shocked at her language. I shouldn't have been. Mixie didn't talk to me like that because that wasn't how I was, but Vonia was wild, so in order to get through to her, it made sense Mixie would meet her on her level.

"I'm not flying all the way across the country just for some dick, *Maxine*. I just needed to use Carm as an excuse so daddy would let me go. And anyways, he paying for my ticket, first class might I add, so what's the big deal?"

"The big deal is that you need to calm your ass down! Every night this week, you've come in the house later than me. You're still in high school and you need to be—"

"No, you need to be stop actin' like you're mama, Mixie, because you're not. And don't think I haven't heard about what you and that ugly big-headed girl you be hangin' with be up to when you not pretending to be all innocent and shit. You should be happy that what I do distracts daddy from finding about you!"

Frowning, I listened to them go back and forth wondering what in the world Vonia was talking about. Mixie and I spoke regularly but obviously she was hiding something from me.

"Listen… don't y'all live together?" Carmella said, annoyed. "Y'all can take all this catty shit and discuss it on your own time. We called to wish Janelle a happy birthday and that's what we're going to do. This day is about her not you two!"

"Carm, why yo' ass on the phone? Didn't you say you had shit to do?!" Vonia shot back, not missing a single beat. I laughed as she and Carmella started to bicker back and forth just like they always did.

I spent the majority of my day out in the city, doing things that I always wanted to but never did. I went to a pricey place by my job and got my nails and feet done, stopped by a spa to get a facial and massage, treated myself to lunch, caught a movie and then treated myself to dinner, complete with cake for dessert. By the time I got home, I was ready to curl up in front of the TV for the rest of the night.

Halfway into some movie on Lifetime that caught me up; there was a knock at my door. I stood up to answer it, pausing for a second as I looked down at my clothes. I was dressed decently enough, in a crop top and some shorts so I went ahead and answered it. Opening the door, I saw there was a medium-height white man dressed in a nice suit with a black box in his hands standing at my door. Next to him was Chris with a huge smile on his face and a bouquet of flowers.

"Happy Birthday!" he said and I smiled at him, glancing over at the guy standing with him who I still was confused about.

"Thank you!"

Stepping up a little, Chris held out his hand towards the man next to him. "This is Yosef. He needs to walk inside so that he can set up your first gift. He would've came by earlier but I had to wait until he closed down his store for the day... sorry it's so late."

"Oh no, he can go on inside." I stepped to the side and let Yosef walk in. He was a man of few words, only giving me a small smile and nod before he made his way in.

My attention went back to Chris, waiting for him to come inside as well but he was too busy looking me up and down, a longing stare in his eyes. We'd been on a few dates but never had we taken a step into the physical side of things. From how he was eyeing me though, it appeared he was ready for the next step.

Stepping forward, Chris reached in with one hand and grabbed my arm, pulling me into him. Capturing my lips into his kiss, he embraced me deeply in his arms.

Damn, was the only thing in my mind as I kissed him back while wrapping my arms around him. He definitely could kiss, almost better than anyone I'd ever kissed before. But there was still one thing missing. The passion that I had when I first kissed Luke... it wasn't there.

"Shall we go in, Madame?" Chris asked once he pulled away. He lifted his elbow out for me to take it and I giggled before I grabbed it and let him escort me in.

Once I stepped inside, there was another jaw-dropping moment when I saw what Yosef had in the black box. Jewelry. Lots of it… all different kinds, every piece absolutely beautiful. My mouth dropped open for probably the tenth time that day and I placed my hand to my chest.

"Pick one… whichever one you want and it's yours," he said, smiling as he wrapped his arm around my waist. I shook my head profusely.

"No, I can't. This is way too expensive a gift—" I started but Chris hushed me with a stern look.

"It's not. I can afford it and I want you to have something from me to celebrate your first birthday that you're sharing with me. I hope the first of many…"

Nodding my head, I smiled and then took a deep breath before turning back to the countertop where Yosef had spread out all the jewelry. My eyes focused right on a piece that I hadn't noticed initially, and I knew instantly, that I had to have it. It was a necklace that had a golden owl hanging from it. Its eyes were blue sapphires and it had diamonds adorning its wings.

"I think you'd be an owl… You're mysterious, elegant… wise. You do everything that is expected of you, goin' through the motions of your regular ass life… But when I'm here at night, you wake up and become a different person…"

Luke's words came to my mind as soon as I looked at it and I knew I wanted it to be mine.

"This the one you want?" Yosef asked, pointing at the necklace. I bit my lip and blinked away the tears in my eyes while the both of them looked at me, confused by my reaction.

"No..." I whispered. The word tasted salty on my tongue as I said it. Even my own body was aware of the lie and seemed to be passively punishing me for refusing my heart's deepest desire: not just the necklace, but Luke.

"No, I'll take this one," I said, pointing to a beautiful necklace right next to it. It was a gold chain with a 'J' pendant, covered with diamonds, hanging at the end.

Yosef nodded his head and Chris grabbed it, helping me put it on. As Yosef began to pack up his things, I watched him carefully; feeling like my heart was being torn from me when he grabbed the owl necklace. I had to stop myself from saying that I changed my mind when he wrapped it up in soft tissue paper and placed it back in his black box.

"There," Chris said once he'd fastened the necklace on my neck. I looked down at it, feeling like my skin was burning right at the point where the pendant touched my skin. Right then, I knew it wasn't right. It was like a sign. I'd chose the wrong necklace.

I was with the wrong man.

Desperado.

Outlaw

"*D*amn, how long is this goin' to fuckin' take? I gave you all the money in cash. Wash that shit up and give me the keys, I gotta go!"

Kareem apologized and muttered some other shit but I wasn't trying to hear it. Looking down at my watch, I saw that it was almost eight o'clock at night. I'd been at the dealership all damn day trying to get Janelle's birthday gift squared away. She didn't have a car, and even though she never complained about it, I hated the fact that she had to use the train or walk all the damn time. A car was the first thing that came to my mind when I was trying to figure out the perfect gift for her. But, there was no damn way that Outlaw was gonna buy a whip for a chick without icing that shit out, so I had Kareem rushing to make some custom changes just for her.

A few minutes later, Kareem pulled the ride out front, stopping it right in front of me. All I could do was stand there and stare at the shit in awe. It was even better than I'd even thought it would be when I requested it. I'd copped her a creamy white brand new Mercedes Benz S-class, so she was rockin' the big body. The inside had cream interior to match the outside but I'd had them pull out the red woodgrain and replace it with pink colored wood. The steering wheel had a cursive J in the center and so did her seats. Her rims were official as hell too. I didn't want to go too flashy because I knew it wasn't her style but I couldn't resist blinging that shit out with some custom pink rims to match the inside.

"Damn, Kareem, you did this shit. I was gon' beat yo' ass for takin' all damn day but you redeemed yourself, nigga!"

"Preciate not gettin' my ass beat, bruh," Kareem replied, dapping me up before he handed me the keys.

"Yolo, you ready?" I asked and he nodded his head. He was going to follow me out to Janelle's in my car so that I'd have it with me once I dropped her new ride off.

"Yeah," he said with a crazy ass look on his face.

"Nigga, you good?"

"Yeah," he repeated. "This shit with Trese is fuckin' with me."

"Yo, handle that shit. I like Sid," I told him, meaning every single word I said as I jumped inside of Janelle's new ride.

I couldn't stand LaTrese. She was a mutt and I tried to tell Yolo that when he got with her. She looked all good and shit on the outside but that didn't fool me. She was grimy to the ultimate degree. While she was starting something with Yolo, she'd even tried to fuck me. And, only I knew it, but she'd fucked Tone before even getting with Yolo. It was like she was trying to find a way into the fam by all means necessary. I was the only one who knew about her and Tone because he begged me not to say shit when Yolo started bringing her around, looking like he had a bad case of puppy love. He was innocent but LaTrese, on the other hand, knew exactly what she was doing.

We got to Brooklyn after the sun went down which pissed me off a little because I wanted Janelle to be able to see clearly how fly her ride was. But it was alright. She wasn't materialistic at all so she would be hype just off principle. I could have bought her ass a scooter and she still would be happy as hell. Or so I hoped.

Pulling onto Janelle's street, I slowed down wondering if I should park it right out front or a little down the way. I didn't want to risk her seeing it before I knocked on her door so I pulled over and parked on the corner by the coffee shop she loved. Killing the engine, I jumped out and Yolo got out right behind me.

"Since I'm over here, I'mma go holla at Sid," he said and I nodded my head while making my way to Janelle's apartment. Then I stopped suddenly when I saw something ahead of me that was probably the last thing I had been expecting.

"The fuck?" I muttered under my breath making Yolo look up.

"Who the fuck is that, bruh?"

I didn't answer him because my eyes were locked in on the scene in front of me. Janelle was standing outside her door in some little ass shorts. The kind she used to wear for me when I came over. Instantly, I was heated but I stayed completely still. Just watching as my heart raced in my chest.

The guy from Janelle's job was there and my mind couldn't even comprehend how he was still in the picture. Or why Janelle was looking at his silly ass like she wanted to give him some ass or some shit. My thoughts merged and I felt my body go cold as I waited for whatever was going to happen next.

Then he grabbed her and kissed her, kissed my woman, cupping her ass while he did it. She tongued him down right in front of my face and then walked in the house with that nigga, letting him close the door and shit like he owned the place. Right then, I lost my muthafuckin' mind.

"LUKE!" Yolo yelled, grabbing one of my arms just as I took off towards her apartment. My gun was already in my other hand, ready to get shit started.

"Get da fuck off me, Yolo!" I roared. I tried to shake him off, my eyes still locked on the house. If he didn't move up off of me, I was prepared to bam his ass right there in the middle of the street.

"Fuck naw, man! What the hell you gonna do? Kill that nigga and wind up in prison? Nigga, she a lawyer and so is he! Think with yo' fuckin' head, Luke!"

I wasn't trying to hear that shit. My brain couldn't even comprehend his meaning. The only thing I knew… the only thing I could understand was that Janelle, *my* woman, the only one who I still wanted after trying to force myself into believing I couldn't have her, was in her apartment probably about to lay down and fuck another man.

I couldn't believe this shit. I never thought that she would really fall for this corny ass nigga because I knew her. I peeped how she was with me. She let loose, didn't worry about what anyone had to say about it and became the person she truly was inside. I knew that only a nigga like me could bring that out of her and I also knew that once she saw her feelings weren't the same with anyone else, she would come back to me. Or at least start answering a nigga's calls.

But *this* shit? Naw, bruh. It wasn't right.

What was fuckin' me up the most is that I didn't see it coming. I wasn't prepared for it. So I couldn't react rationally. Yolo was urging me to think but I *couldn't* fuckin' think. I was about to set it off like fireworks in this bitch and that's all there was to it.

"Yolo back the fuck off me, dawg. I promise I don't wanna swing on you, bruh!" I warned him while trying to shake him off of me at the same time. He still held on so I bent down low and charged right at his ass, using my body to knock him backwards, hopefully loosening his grip. Yolo fell back right on his ass and I turned around to take off, my eyes focused back on Janelle's spot. Then I heard feet running up behind me and turned around just in time to see Yolo jumping through the air, arms out to tackle me from behind. We both fell to the ground but I went down swinging.

"Shit, they fightin'!" Someone yelled out from somewhere around us. "The Murrays out here fightin', yo!"

"Bruh, I told you to leave me the fuck alone!" I yelled at Yolo, wiping my face as I glared at him. He stood up, fixing his clothes up like anybody gave a shit about what the fuck he was wearing. Pretty ass nigga.

"Luke?! Yolo, what da fuck y'all doin' out here?"

I turned around and saw Tank running down the street towards us, coming from out of the apartment that his baby mama lived in. I took off, trying to dodge him before he had a chance to gang up with Yolo against me.

"Tank, get da crazy ass nigga! He about to run up on ole girl and some nigga she got in her crib!" Yolo yelled out from behind me.

"Oh SHIT!" Tank shouted and tried to grab at me just as I reached him but I was too quick, ducking around him before he had the chance to touch me.

"The hell? Luke?!"

It was Sid. And I guess she was a little smarter than Tank because as soon as she saw the gun in my hand she didn't need any explanation. She ran up and jumped on my back right when I reached the stairs leading up to Janelle's house.

"Get da fuck off me, Sid, 'fore I hurt yo' ass! I know you a bitch but I don't give a fuck!" I grunted, trying to breathe with her arms locked around my neck. She squeezed harder the more I tried to shake her loose. Her ass didn't look it but she was heavy as hell.

"Fuck it," I grumbled when I realized I couldn't shake her off. But I was about to spin her ass just like the nigga did Will Smith on the credits of the *Fresh Prince* if she didn't get her ass up off me.

Tank and Yolo came up breathing hard then grabbed onto my arms, dragging me away from the stairs to Janelle's place. Only then did Sid let go.

"Fuck!" I gritted when Tank snatched my gun from my hand.

"Calm the fuck down, Luke! You can't do this shit here," he told me. "Let's go home and let that shit be! You can't lose your freedom or your life over this shit. It ain't worth it."

What he was saying probably would make sense to me tomorrow, but right now, in this moment, I had no fucks left to give.

"JANELLE!" I yelled out, still bumping with both Tank and Yolo as they tried to pull me away. "JANELLE!"

"Damn, that nigga got it bad," Sidney said.

Her ass was right. I was about to make a damn fool of myself if Janelle walked out this bitch hand in hand with this nigga, claiming she was done with my ass for good but I didn't care. Right then, I wasn't thinking about myself, my life, her job or anything that would happen after this night, but I knew I wasn't leaving until I got a chance to look her in her eyes and hear her tell me she was through with my ass for good.

"JANELLE!" I shouted even louder than before, hearing my voice echo all down the block.

"Who is Janelle?" some chick asked and a bunch of people started grumbling, mumbling about how they didn't know.

"Well, we 'bout to find out!"

"Shit…" Yolo said, releasing my arm. Walking over to Sidney, he stood next to her before popping a squat on the steps leading up to her place.

"Tank, let that nigga go. Ain't no use. He ain't goin' nowhere."

Sighing, Tank let go of my arm at the same time that Janelle's door opened.

"Luke?" she asked, squinting into my face. Her mouth dropped and she turned into her place before stepping out and shutting the door behind her.

"What are you doin' here?" When she looked out and saw my

brothers and the crowd that had gathered in the street, she gasped and her eyes went wide before she dropped her head back to me. Crossing my arms in front of me, I walked up the stairs slowly, not stopping until I was right in front of her, towering over her as I glared down at her from above.

"You got that nigga in there. Tell him to bring his ass out here… or I'm comin' in," I instructed coolly.

"But I—"

"Speak up, girl! We can't hear!" some ghetto ass broad yelled from out by the street.

"All y'all get the fuck outta here!" Tank shouted back.

When no one moved, he raised his arm in the air and cocked my gun, making the crowd scatter. I heard him and Yolo making sure everyone left but I had my eyes locked on Janelle's face. She had her head down and she had her hand to her chest, clutching the end of the gold necklace around her neck.

Before she could say anything, the door opened and a short white man scurried out with his head down, walking away fast like he wanted to make sure everyone knew he had no parts in what was going on. He didn't stop until he jumped inside of a car parked across the street and then drove away. The door popped open again and this time, a dead man walking came out.

"Everything alright out here?" he asked, looking at Janelle. And then his eyes met mine.

"Oh shit!"

Snarling, I curled up my lips and locked my glare on him, ready to beat his ass right where he stood.

"That's right, nigga, you know who I am. It's the muthafuckin' Outlaw in the flesh. What you gon' do wit' it?"

"LUKE, STOP!" Janelle yelled, pushing herself in between the two of us. She put her hands out and pressed the palms against my chest, trying to make me back away.

"You protectin' this nigga now?"

I squinted hard at her, watching her use herself as a shield. Was she taking sides against me? Impossible. It couldn't be.

"Janelle, how do you know him?!"

My throat tightened up and I clamped my mouth shut, waiting for her to answer his question. She hesitated and I felt my jaw lock in place. The back of my eyes began to burn and I tasted something unfamiliar in the back of my tongue.

"Open up yo' fuckin' mouth and tell him how you know me!" My tone was angry but the anger was fueled by my panic and fear. "For once in your life, be real about yo' shit!"

This was it. If she denied me to my face just so that she could be with another nigga, it had to be the end. I wouldn't be able to take that shit. It would hurt me but I would have to let her go because it would mean that she wasn't the woman I thought she was. The Janelle I knew did the right thing to protect the ones she loved even when it hurt. She was selfless and always put others before herself.

Even still, as I looked down at her waiting for her to admit that

I was the nigga she'd been with, the one she said she loved, I could see the struggle in her eyes. My mind was racing, fragments of sentences that held no weight to anyone but me, running through my mind. I closed my eyes and took a breath to try to control the stampede in my chest. What would be my next step if she refused me now? Did I have it in me to leave? No... there was no way. Would I beg?

Fuck no, I wasn't beggin' her for shit. I shouldn't have to, right? She promised herself to me when she gave me her love. And yeah, I fucked up because Tank had my mind on some other shit, but this wasn't the way to pay me back.

I silently pled with her, my eyes locked on hers funneling words to her that I couldn't even open my mouth to say. I felt like all the wind was being suctioned from my body, leaving me just a shell, my existence relying totally on whatever words fell from her lips.

Her expression shifted. But not in the way I wanted it to. She looked at me with apologetic eyes, already asking forgiveness for words she hadn't even said. She was going to crush me but still I found a little bit of hope in knowing that she still cared enough to at least warn me first. I closed my eyes and let out a staggered breath, realizing in that moment just how terrified I was over the idea of losing Janelle forever.

Decisions.

Janelle

"I—I..."

My throat went dry and I stopped speaking, swallowing hard in a futile attempt to provide myself with some relief. I found none.

With Luke's eyes no longer looking at me, I should have been able to find the courage to do what I needed to do but I couldn't because I could see how badly I was hurting him. Destroying him. He didn't even look like the same man I was used to seeing: the childish, jokester with no filter who didn't give a damn how anyone felt about what he had to say. He was broken, his shoulders slumped and his head down, seemingly shaving inches off of his height, making him appear as a good but faulty replica of the magnificent man he truly was.

Had Chris not been here, my decision would be easy. In fact, I'd already made it before I'd even opened my door and saw Luke standing there, his eyes on fire, his hair a bushy mane partially pulled into a lopsided ponytail. Blazingly sexy and irresistible even in his distress. I'd already decided that I was going to sit down and figure out how to end this thing I had going with Chris so that I could decide how to get the man I wanted and still live the life I've always dreamed of.

And then this happened.

I knew Luke was hurting inside but he'd forced my hand and I didn't react well under pressure. He'd placed me in a situation where I was panicking and I couldn't think. The only thing running through my mind was that if I told the truth right now about me and Luke, Chris would be obligated to reveal what he knew to Pelmington and that would destroy my career. My degree would be useless. My *life*, everything I worked for, would be useless. All I ever wanted was to make my daddy proud and choosing him right now would ruin that.

And so I prayed that, at some point, Luke would forgive me.

"I—I don't know him."

I heard him, felt him, take in a sharp breath and flinch. He couldn't even look at me.

"You need to go."

Just saying the words crushed me and it was taking everything in me to maintain my composure.

Behind Luke, I saw Sidney's eyes on me, glowering like she wanted to beat my ass right there in front of everyone and I could understand why, but there was nothing I could do about it right now.

"You heard her," Chris said and then echoed my request. "You need to leave. You already have enough trouble on your head right now being that we're investigating you for the armed car robbery."

My breath caught up in my throat and Luke's head snapped up. His piercing stare fell on Chris first before he turned and caught me up in his glare. I knew what he was thinking without him even saying a word. It wasn't enough that I had betrayed him by denying his relevance to my life, now he was aware that I was part of an investigation that could land him in prison for life and I hadn't said a word about it.

I thought I would crumble under the weight of his gaze but then he shook his head and the edges of his eyes tilted downward in sadness and grief.

I pulled my hand away from my neck where I was holding on to my necklace and exposed the charm at the end: the owl sitting comfortably between my breasts. After deciding I couldn't let it go, I convinced Chris to let me pay Yosef for it and settled on him getting me a pair of earrings instead. I saw Luke's eyes lock onto it and I hoped that he understood the sign I was giving him… understood that I still thought of him and that I wanted him. I loved him still but he needed to leave so we could deal with this later.

"Leave," I said once more and he glanced up, dread filling his eyes.

He turned his body and focused on me, like he didn't see anything else around us. And when I saw his eyes cloud over, I realized it was because he really *didn't* see anyone else but me. He moved his lips but nothing came out. He shook his head with agitation, as if trying to rid himself of a thought. He was tortured, fighting a battle… a war that he'd waged in his own mind.

"This isn't you, baby. I know it's not you," he started, pleading with me as his eyes probed mine, searching for the truth. "I can feel it and I know this isn't you. So why are you doin' this? Is it…is it the job?"

"Janelle, come inside. If he doesn't want to leave, I'll call the cops. We don't have to stay out here and—"

"Is it the job?" Luke repeated, probing further. Searching deeper. He grabbed my hand and my knees weakened.

"Fuck that job, baby. You know I got you. You don't need Pelmington for shit and I put that on God. You wanna be a lawyer? You can do that shit, bae. I'll buy you yo' own shit tomorrow. You can practice under your own damn name... I already found the building and everything. See? I been thinkin' bout this shit, baby. You can have both... I'm not gon' ruin yo' life, ma. I don't want to destroy your dreams, just don't rob me of mine. Please, just don't—"

"She. Doesn't. Want. You," Chris started again. "She told you to leave and now you need to go. Janelle, just come inside. I won't tell Pelmington a thing but you have to come in now."

A thinly veiled threat. I didn't catch it at first but Luke did and he cut his eyes to Chris, giving him a glare so severe there wasn't a shred of doubt in my mind that he would have killed him, had I not been there. I trembled and, mistaking the movement for me pulling away, Luke clutched my hand tighter, jerking me slightly towards him.

"You gon' leave me over a nigga who threatenin' you? That's what you want? You want a nigga to control you and tell you what to do? Like your ex? Like your father? I never wanted you to be anything but who you are, baby. You bein' yourself has always been enough for me. I've never wanted to change you. Please, just..."

He looked away, let out a forced chuckle and then pulled his lips into his mouth and shook his head incredulously.

"Yes... I will beg," he whispered, speaking only to himself, so low that I could barely hear. Then he turned to me.

"Nell, please just listen to me... I fucked up because I was doing exactly what I tell you not to do. I was letting what my brothers thought fuck with me, making me think that I wasn't right for you and that we couldn't make it work. But I don't give a fuck about none of that shit and no one else but you. I'm not gon' force you to be with me but I need you to know how much this shit is fuckin' with my head right now."

The tears finally came. Pulling my hand from his, I pressed the bottom edge of my hands hard against my closed eyes, trying to stop them from flowing but they still wouldn't stop. Luke reached up and grabbed my hands from my eyes and I only cried harder. The desperation in his tone broke me down in a way nothing else ever had.

"Janelle?! What's wrong with her?"

It was Carmella. The sound of heels clicking against the pavement followed her voice before I felt her wrap her arms around my body.

"What did you do?!" she asked, her attention focused on Luke. His eyes stayed on me and he shook his head slowly.

"I would never hurt her," he said calmly. "Never."

Chris made a scoffing noise. "Just the simple fact that she even had a relationship with you could get her arrested. For all we know, you two have been together the entire time and she helped you in your last case, feeding you our evidence and convincing the witness to leave."

"She wouldn't do that!" Carmella shouted at Chris as she held me in her arms. I rubbed my tears away and noticed that while everyone was focused on Chris and Carmella, Luke's eyes were still pinned on me.

"I'm not sayin' she did, I'm just telling you what it looks like. Being with him put her career as an attorney in jeopardy and could cost her her freedom. It's not smart. I'm just saying."

"Okay but who is going to tell on her?" Carmella shot back at him. "You?"

Silence as we waited for him to respond. Luke's full attention was still on me like he hadn't even heard a word Chris was saying or wasn't the least bit concerned.

"As an assistant district attorney, I've sworn to uphold the law. Not disclosing what I know could cost me my license to practice as well. I care for Janelle deeply but I've worked too hard to risk it all for someone I've only known for a couple months. The same should go for Janelle."

He was right. His words made absolute perfect sense to me and even to Luke because I could see it in his eyes when I nodded my head. He froze, almost as if from shock, not because of Chris' words but because of my agreement of them. But it was true. I've loved before and I'll love again. But a bad professional decision, definitely one like this, would follow me forever.

"I'll go."

My words startled Carmella and she narrowed her eyes at my face.

"I'm sorry, Outlaw," Carmella whispered. He said nothing but I could hear his breathing with difficult staggered breaths. Turning to walk away, I kept my eyes low, letting Carmella guide me away.

"C'mon, bruh," one of Luke's brothers said to him. "It's fucked up, man. But you gotta let it be."

"Naw, fuck that. Janelle!" Luke called as soon as I stepped over threshold, walking into my apartment. The urgency in his tone stopped me right in place, my heart and soul shredded to the point that I could barely think.

"Janelle, look at me! Just look at me, please!"

Carmella clutched my hand in hers, tight enough to probably crush bone. I may have felt it had I been left with any feeling in my body besides my despair. I saw the tears in her eyes before I pulled away to look at Luke. He was standing in the same spot as before with both of his brothers behind him, looking on.

"I—need you, man," he started, biting his bottom lip before pressing his palms to the side of his head and growling in frustration and anguish.

"Janelle… please. Can't you see how much I love you? Seriously… Look. At. Me."

And I did.

I didn't just see him, I looked into him and his soul connected with mine. It was a unity so great that I knew then that nothing was going to separate us. Nothing. Our hearts intertwined into each other's and our love combined into one magnificent force. Together, we were unbreakable, unstoppable even. I didn't know how I was going to make this life I'd paved for myself work with Luke by my side but I was no longer willing to live it without him. I knew exactly what I needed to do.

So I let go of Carmella's hand. And I took his.

"Janelle! What are you doing?! You know this could ruin your career!" Chris yelled but I didn't hear him. All of my senses were honed into Luke and there was nothing else.

"I love you."

They were the sweetest words I'd ever heard him say and I knew I never wanted to go another second without feeling the way that he made me feel right then. He wrapped his arms around my waist and turned around, leading me away. I fell right into step beside him.

"You took out your grill for me," I mused, smiling hard. He glanced in my direction, eyes sparkling in the moonlight.

"I'd do anything for you."

And I believed he would.

"Janelle, I'm trying to warn you that—"

"Warn her about what, muthafucka?" one of Luke's brothers thundered behind us, cutting right into the middle of Chris' last threat. "You open up yo' fat fuckin' mouth and I'll be sittin' on ya mama's porch with an AK full of them hot balls, country ass nigga. Play wit' it if you want to."

"She prolly got dick suckin' lips just like you do, gay ass muthafucka," the other one added. "I'll test that shit out before she go. It'll be a shame to let them shits go to waste."

"Damn, Yolo, that's fucked up. But the nigga do look sweet."

"Don't speak ill of the dead," Luke said, his voice dangerously calm.

At the time, I dismissed his words as an empty threat but there was nothing empty about them. After that night, I never saw Chris again.

We were walking down the sidewalk when I stumbled mid-step,

almost fell and would have if Luke hadn't held my hand tight and helped me regain my balance. A bad feeling fell on me, like a dark cloud. It wasn't because of what his brothers were saying and it wasn't because of Chris or my career. It was something much greater, something devastating. I could feel it like an impending storm. Something bad was about to happen.

"You good?" Luke asked me and I shook my head. "What—"

Before he could finish his sentence, a black town car turned onto the street and my eyes honed in on it as if my name were called, although I didn't know why. It stopped right in front of where Luke and I stood, hand in hand. My lips parted and I sucked in a breath, my eyes unable to move away from it. The windows were tinted so dark that I had no idea who was inside. Until the door opened.

"Daddy?"

Stepping out of the car was my father, dressed in a custom-made suit that fit his 6'4, muscular frame perfectly. His mahogany brown face was pulled tightly into a frown, making him appear nothing like the gentle man I'd known my whole life. The one who had taught me everything I knew, been there during my best moments and at my worst. The one who would never in life accept the man who now had ownership of my heart.

I moved towards him, releasing Luke's hand. I didn't have to see his body tense up because I felt it.

"Nell—" Luke began, his voice wavering slightly from his fear and disbelief.

I shook my head, not even looking in his direction. My father's eyes stared right through me and I felt like time had back-tracked, turning me from a grown woman back into a small child. I ran to him and hugged him tight.

"Janelle, I really need to see your sister." His eyes were tight with emotion and I knew something was wrong. He had something in his hand, a piece of paper that he was holding so tight in his fist that it was nearly crumpled.

"Daddy, what are you doing here?" Carmella asked. I didn't even have to turn around to know that she was walking forward because with each step that she took, my father's eyes narrowed more and more in anger. I never saw him this furious in my life. He was seething, boiling on the inside.

"How could you do this, Carmella?" he bellowed, waving the paper in the air.

I put my hand to my chest and fell back a few paces. Luke stepped up and stood next to me with his head high. His stance said it all. He'd battled for me once already and he was prepared to fight the war with my father if it came to it. His heart was on the line and he wasn't backing down.

"Do what, daddy? Are you talking about my scholarship? It's okay, I have a job now and—"

"This isn't about no damn scholarship! The fuck is this?!" He held up a piece of paper, an advertisement of some sort with Carmella's image on it. I squinted, trying hard to read the words. I couldn't make anything out other than porn. Wait... *porn*?!

"What?" Carmella looked just as perplexed as I did. She snatched the paper from his hands and looked at it, her eyes growing wider and wider with each passing second.

"Oh… my… God." Stricken, she looked up at my father as she gripped the paper in both of her hands. "I—I didn't know! I was just—"

"Get in the car, Carmella! I'm taking you home now. Let's go!"

My lips parted as I looked back and forth between the two of them. I was on edge, wondering what was about to happen in this brutal standoff. Had it been me, I would have folded like a paper plane. I wasn't as strong as she was and I would not defy my father. It wasn't in me to do it. At least, I didn't think it was.

"I'm not going," Carmella said, finally. Her bottom lip was trembling but she was firm in her statement, shaking her head as tears fell from her eyes.

"Carmella, I didn't come here to—"

She shook her head again. This time with more determination.

"I'm **not** going," she repeated as I looked on, my mouth open wide. "I'm a grown ass woman, and to be honest, you can't tell me what to do."

My father pressed his lips together and an impasse ensued as they both stared at each other, both stubborn and unbending, refusing to give even a little. They were more alike than either of them knew or cared to admit. Finally, my father's eyes left Carmella and he looked to me. His expression was gentler and more compassionate but also pleading. He was requesting my help without using words. But if he knew my sister like I knew he did, there was no point in even attempting to sway Carmella.

But then there was a shift and his attention was no longer on me. His eyes were on the man by my side. I sucked in a breath and my blood went cold when I saw his eyes flash with recognition and shock. Did he know Luke? But of course he did.

"I know you," he said, his finger pointing right at Luke as he staggered forward slowly, as if his feet were heavy. "Luke Murray. You were just on trial here. Janelle, didn't you—"

Luke stayed quiet and so did I, although I was much less composed than he was. My insides were churning and my mind was racing. All I wanted to do was get away.

"Not my daughter," he said, shaking his head defiantly. "No… not mine. Janelle, get over here!"

With his lips folded into a sneer, my father stepped forward and reached out to grab me but Luke stepped in front of him, blocking his way.

"She's your daughter but she's going to my wife," he told him, speaking with an even tone that didn't ask for permission or even indicate that he felt he needed any. "So I respectfully ask you, sir, to back away."

"Who are you to get in the middle of this?! I'm talking to my daughter and this does not concern you!"

My father reached out once again and Luke blocked his way again. I placed my hands to my mouth as my tears began to fall. My heart was literally being ripped into two. Noting that Luke was not going to let him get by, my father stood back and crossed his arms in front of his chest. Then, he looked right into Luke's face, his eyes boring through his and I could've sworn I saw a hint of a smirk on his face. Then his attention fell on me.

"Janelle," he started with an even tone, beckoning me to use reason. "You've worked your whole life towards being the woman you are. I've always had your back, but this, I can't condone. I can't condone this from either of you. As your father, I'm telling you to get in the car right now and I'm taking you back to Atlanta so we can correct all of these mistakes." He looked pointedly at Luke when he said that. "If you don't want to come back with me, that's fine. But I'll have to wash my hands of both of you."

His words stole the air from my lungs. Wash his hands of me? How could a father do that to his daughter? The daughter that he brought into the world and had been with for her entire life. He'd told me he would always love me and would always be there for me. How could he threaten to take that all back now?

Turning around, my eyes landed on Chris who was still exactly where I'd left him, with Luke's brothers standing at the base of the stairs watching everything unfolding before us. My father and him were the same. They both resorted to threats in order to control me. But the difference was, whereas Chris had no stronghold on me, my father did and he'd perfected it over twenty-three years. But was the power he had over me stronger than love?

"Don't go with him, Janelle," Luke whispered into my ear. He tugged my hand, beckoning me to look into his eyes. "Don't let other people decide your life for you. I don't want you to be anything other than what you want to be. I want to make you better not make you into what I want you to be. Don't do this."

"But…" he continued, licking his lips and then flinched a little as if the mere thought of his next words hurt him. "… if you do leave, just know I'm not going to stop. When you get to Atlanta, I'll already be there waiting for you. I'm not letting you go."

"Janelle!" my father shouted once again and I recoiled, the brass in his voice stung my ears. "*Think!* All your life I've told you to think. Did you really work this hard and this long to destroy it all for him?"

"No. I didn't," I replied and I felt Luke's panic inside of me. It was like we shared one body and our emotions were linked. I could almost hear his thoughts, coming from his mind to mine.

My father shot a gloating look at Luke who simply stood silently by my side. I couldn't even bring myself to look at him because I knew it would kill me. Clicking his teeth, my father… my daddy, stepped forward and grabbed my hand. I held it tight as tears came to my eyes.

My heart was breaking because I knew I had to leave him. There was no other way. My mind had already decided what I was going to. The decision was made and all that was left was for me to act. But it was so hard. There was nothing in life harder than leaving the one you love.

"Then get in the car. It's time to go," my father said, visibly more relaxed now that he knew that he'd at least won over one of his daughters. The one he'd taken for granted that he'd never lose. But he was wrong. One thing about me is that I should never be underestimated. Never taken for granted.

"No."

"Wha—what did you say?" The pain in his voice was evident but

I was sure of my decision.

"I said no," I repeated with vigor and certainty. "I'm not going with you."

Luke let out a heavy exhale and it renewed my strength.

"Janelle, you're making a mistake." It was his last plea but it wasn't enough. Not nearly enough.

"No, I'm not, daddy. But I love you," I told him, but he shook his head stubbornly and pressed his lips together, refusing to say it back.

The man I'd sacrificed everything for my whole life in order to make him proud couldn't even tell me he loved me because I couldn't be controlled. For once, I was choosing me and he couldn't deal with it. But Luke would never have done that. He wouldn't have made me choose between two things I loved. He would have found a way to make it work out so that I could be happy. He wouldn't want me to miserable just so I could be with him.

So I let go of my daddy's hand. And I took his.

A Glimpse of Part 3:

Janelle

"You might feel a little pinch."

I closed my eyes, sucked in a sharp breath and tried to think about rainbows or unicorns… anything that could settle my mind. And then, just as I was able to conjure up an image of the perfect rainbow, complete with a leprechaun at the end of it holding a pot of gold, there was a pinch, no a stab, right through my flesh.

"OWWWWW!"

"Punk."

Cutting my eyes at Luke, I frowned, pushing my lips out in disapproval at the teasing grin on his face.

"I'm not a punk! That hurt."

He only smiled. He was doing that more and more often and I loved seeing it.

"Done," the woman above me said, pulling away her instrument of torture. "See, that was it!"

Pursing my lips, I looked down at the small piercing on my navel. The pain had just begun to subside and I could fully appreciate her work. It was cute. The owl belly ring that Luke had picked out for me sat nicely at the top, pressed snuggly against my flat stomach.

"It's beautiful," I whispered.

Luke bent down and kissed it gently, erupting a series of butterflies in my stomach. I squeezed my thighs closed and tried to ignore the aching in my middle. We'd been at it all night and I was sore but my body was still begging for more torture.

"We really came in here for tats but she punked out," Luke informed the woman who was now sitting at my side and I felt my cheeks go hot when she gave me a side eye, accompanied by a mocking smirk. Yeah, I knew what she was thinking. She had a full sleeve of tattoos, piercings all down her ears from top to bottom, in her nose, her lips and God only knew where else. But I was not the type of person who welcomed this type of torture.

"There is still time, baby," Luke whispered, leaning close to my ear.

I shuddered when he flicked his tongue out and licked my earlobe. It had been this way since I left my apartment with him the night before. He craved me with no shame and no care of whoever was around. I wasn't used to the public displays of affection but I enjoyed it all too much to push him away.

"No, I don't think I can right now... you can still get whatever you wanted but I'll wait."

He shook his head.

"No, I won't get that one until you're ready for yours."

Handing the woman a few bills to cover the payment and tip, he grabbed my hand into his and we walked out of the storefront together, as a couple. For the first time ever, I was his and he was mine but it was no longer a secret that we cherished together while holed up inside of my small apartment. It was now something we were willing to share with the world, without fear and without wondering if they approved of our love. There was no better feeling than being free.

"You passed the car," I informed him when I noticed that we were walking much farther than we had to come into the store.

"No, I didn't. That's not what we're getting in right now."

Smirking, I cut my eyes in his direction and saw him biting back a smile while trying to keep his attention straight ahead. Unable to resist my probing stare any longer, he turned slightly and glanced at me for only a second. Still, I saw the twinkling in his eyes. He was hiding something and I knew it was a surprise. I sighed and didn't press further. I'd enjoy the wait.

We stepped into a building right in the middle of the Manhattan. A tall skyscraper filled with offices that housed several top-level companies. I instantly felt out of place in my jeans, Converses, and hoody, surrounded by what looked like executives all in suits. Luke, on the other hand was completely at ease. He'd switched up his style and though different, it was so sexy to me. The gold grill was gone and he had swapped the jeans for slacks, the Giuseppe sneakers for Giuseppe loafers and had on a button down with the sleeves pulled up, showing off his sculpted tattooed arms. The jewelry remained—he wasn't willing to make those kind of changes. He was on his grown man and I was loving every bit of it. And every bit of him.

I wasn't loving the extra attention he was getting. Luke always drew the focus of women in the hood but now? It didn't matter if it was a Black chick from Brooklyn or a White one who was the chair of a Fortune 500 company, he had them all salivating over him. It didn't matter if all they could get was a simple glance in their direction, they were panting for it. And God forbid if he actually waved...

But he was mine. *All* mine.

"Hello, Mr. Murray. Wow, you look..."

A young white woman with blond hair and a slender build walked up to us and lost her words, actually and completely lost them, as she looked at Luke.

"Thank you," was all he said with a small smile. Her eyes fluttered and she stammered her next sentence, struggling to regain her composure.

"Y—you just look different... in a very good way. I mean..." She paused and her eyes came to mine. I gave her a warm smile to relax her. I wasn't a jealous person and I knew the effect seeing Luke had on her because he had the same effect over me.

"Is it ready?"

"Y—yes, it is, Mr. Murray. Everything is exactly as you requested it. Bob will escort you there. And you'll need these." She handed him a folder of papers. "It's just a little something I put together to make sure everything is perfectly set up for you. Enjoy!"

Without a smile, Luke nodded his head and turned around to look at another man who was walking towards us, pale and balding with a bright smile.

"Mr. Murray! It's so nice to see you!" He reached out to shake

Luke's hand and then turned to me. "And who do we have here?"

He reached his hand out to me as well but Luke didn't loosen his grip, instead he laced his fingers between mine, deepening our embrace. Bob's eyes connected with Luke's and he understood, tucking his hand back into his pocket. Caught of guard, I didn't know what to do but Luke stepped in.

"This is Janelle." And then he added with a tiny smile, almost childish in nature, "And I would let her shake your hand but I'm not ready to let go of it yet."

My heart skipped a beat and I blushed. Bob's eyes ping-ponged between the both of us as he smiled brightly. I didn't know the type of relationship he and Luke had but it was obvious he was surprised and delighted to see him act this way over me.

"Well, in that case, it's *very* nice to meet you, Janelle. I'm Bob, a long-time business partner of Mr. Murray's. Both of you can follow me."

Bob led us through the building and to the elevators. All throughout our walk, people greeted Luke, addressing him with the upmost respect, to which he always replied with a subtle nod of his head. It was as if the boss was in the building. We were the only black spots in a sea of white ones dressed in custom made suits and pricey shoes but everyone from the lowest to the highest knew Mr. Murray had walked through the door and made sure to make contact with him.

I was intrigued. I was beginning to see the type of hold Luke had on people, whether male or female. I was so used to the man he was with me, that I'd forgot that his named meant something; not just in the hood but throughout the city. He made shit happen and people respected that. Whether they agreed with how he did it or not, the fact was they still wanted to remain in his good graces.

We were led into an elevator and went up to the highest floor. The entire time my stomach was bubbling with excitement. I could barely contain it. Bob was in front of us and we stood side-by-side, hand-in-hand behind him. Luke pulled me close to him so that I was standing in front and he wrapped his arms around my stomach. I felt him breathe in deeply and then lean down to kiss me on my ear before whispering softly.

"You smell so good."

I melted like hot butter.

When we stepped off of the elevator, all I heard was the loud sound of propellers. The wind whipped around us viciously but Luke held me tight, wrapping his arms around me to block out the cold. And then I saw it. A helicopter. With my eyes wide, I turned to Luke and jabbed him in his stomach as Bob trotted away towards it with his head ducked down.

"Ow, shit, Nell! Yo' boney ass elbows hurt!"

"Where are you taking me?" I asked, giggling as he rubbed the place I'd hit him. I could no longer restrain my excitement or hold my peace. I needed answers now.

"I'm taking you away. This helicopter is going to take us to a jet. The jet is going to take us somewhere else. And we will be at that somewhere for a however long it takes for you to get your plans straight."

I was confused.

"What plans?"

Looking away, Luke licked his lips and let out a low chuckle. I watched as he pushed his tongue through the inside of his cheek a bit before he began to speak. I was so on edge and he was killing me.

"Nell, when it comes to you, I'm not believing in doing no small time shit. You had grand dreams when I met you and I want them to be even grander now that you're with me. So I'm takin' you away and yes, it's a vacation and yes, I will enjoy your body." His lust-filled eyes fell below my neckline and I felt my skin prickle as he looked me up and down. "But I want you to make me a list of anything and everything you want with your career and I'm gonna make it happen for you."

I squinted up at him, a smirk tickling the edge of my lips.

"Anything?"

He looked straight at me with a deadpan expression, no smile, no laugh hidden behind his eyes, nothing.

"Anything. I don't care if you say you wanna be the fuckin' President of the United States… whatever you write down, I'm going to make it happen by any means necessary. I won't let you have any regrets because you chose me."

He spoke with absolute confidence and certainty but there was a hint of dangerousness there. 'By any means necessary' he said and I knew that was exactly what he meant. Whatever he had to do and whoever he had to get rid of for me to get what I wanted, he had no issues doing it. Luke was a dangerous man and I knew there was a side of him that would scare me, a side I probably never wanted to see but right then and there, I decided to put a blind eye to it. To not think of it. There was a lot of forgiveness in the heart of a woman when it came to her man and we were no different.

"I have no regrets," I told him and kissed him gently on his cheek. The embrace relaxed him and he sighed.

"And that's how I want it to stay."

He grabbed me and pulled me towards the helicopter, both of us ducking down as we neared it.

"Can you at least tell me where we are going?" I yelled over the blaring sound of the propeller. Luke glanced at me, smiling so sexily that I momentarily forgot my question.

"I'mma take you to the moon, baby," he joked and I rolled my eyes and laughed. But to be honest, I already felt like he had me there.

TO BE CONTINUED!

...The wait won't be long!

NOTE FROM PORSCHA STERLING

Thank you for reading!

I love these couples but I'm curious to know what you think so please leave a review. In the review, tell me which Murray brother you like the most - that is one question that is always running through my mind. As for me, I can't really decide! But I do have to say I love the men they are becoming! It's hard for me to resist a thug with a heart but if you read my work, you already know!

Up next is Gunplay & LeTavia 2 - as you NOW know, Gunplay is Outlaw's cousin… HA! I'll also be finishing up Didn't They Tell You I Was a Savage 2 before coming back to this part 3. Make sure to read those!

Check out my website to get an overview of the characters mentioned in this installment of the series. I pulled some visuals so you'll know what they kind of look like to me when I'm writing about them. Hope you like what you see! Visit www.porschasterling.com to check them out!

I love to interact with my readers because I APPRECIATE ALL OF YOU! Hit me up!

Please make sure to leave a review! I love reading them!

I would love it if you reach out to me on Facebook, Instagram or Twitter!

Also, join my Facebook group! If you haven't already, text PORSCHA to 25827 to join my text list. Text ROYALTY to 42828 to join our email list and read excerpts and learn about giveaways.

Peace, love & blessings to everyone. I love allllll of you!

Porscha Sterling

MAKE SURE TO LEAVE A REVIEW!

Text PORSCHA to 25827
to keep up with Porscha's latest releases!

To find out more about her, visit www.porschasterling.com

Join our mailing list to get a notification when Leo Sullivan Presents has another release! Text **LEOSULLIVAN** to **22828** to join!

To submit a manuscript for our review, email us at <u>leosullivanpresents@gmail.com</u>

Get LiT!

Download the LiT app today and enjoy exclusive content, free books, and more!

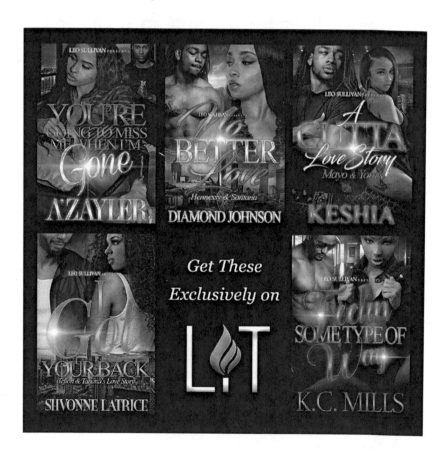

CPSIA information can be obtained
at www.ICGtesting.com
Printed in the USA
LVOW12s1544030317

526084LV00002B/452/P